M. T. Vasudevan Nair

KAALAM

Translated from the Malayalam by

GITA KRISHNANKUTTY

Orient BlackSwan

M. T. VASUDEVAN NAIR: KAALAM

ORIENT BLACKSWAN PRIVATE LIMITED

Registered Office
3-6-752 Himayatnagar, Hyderabad 500 029 (Telangana), INDIA
E-mail: centraloffice@orientblackswan.com
Other Offices

Bangalore, Bhopal, Bhubaneshwar, Chennai, Ernakulam, Guwahati, Hyderabad, Jaipur, Kolkata, Lucknow, Mumbai, New Delhi, Noida, Patna

First Published 1998
Reissued 2010
Reprinted 2011, 2012, 2014

ISBN: 978 81 250 1377 8

Printed in India at
Glorious Printers,
Delhi

Published by
Orient Blackswan Private Limited
1/24 Asaf Ali Road,
New Delhi 110 002
e-mail: delhi@orientblackswan.com

KAALAM

Born in 1933 in the small village of Koodallur, Kerala, Madath Thekkepat Vasudevan Nair is the best known among his generation of storywriters in Malayalam. With a publishing career spanning a little more than fifty years, he is renowned as a chronicler of life in the matriarchal joint family of Kerala, a milieu he describes with intimacy in novels such as *Nalukettu* (1959) and *Kaalam* (1969). He won the State and Kendriya Sahitya Akademi awards respectively for these two novels. He is also among Kerala's most popular script writers and directors of mainstream cinema. He has won four National Awards for his screenplays. The very first film he wrote, produced and directed, *Nirmaalyam* (The Floral Offering) won the President's Gold Medal in 1973 and *Kadavu* (The Ferry) won the Japanese Grand Prix. He was also awarded the Jnanpith in 1996.

Apart from short fiction in which he has excelled, Nair has published novels and novellas, travelogues, literary criticism, books of children and a sizeable number of miscellaneous notes, reviews and memoirs. Nair's stories have been translated into major languages in India and abroad. He was associated with the editorship of *Matrubhumi* periodical publications for well over four decades. The Government of India honoured him with the Padmabhushan in 2005.

Gita Krishnankutty has a doctorate in English from Mysore University. She has a number of translations from Malayalam to English to her credit, including *Cast Me Out If You Will*, a collection of short stories and memoirs by Lalithambika Anterjanam (Stree, 1998), several short stories by M.T. Vasudevan Nair and his novel, *Nalukettu* (Oxford University Press, 2008). She is the author of *A Life of Healing: a biography of P. S. Varier* (Viking Penguin, 2001). She won the Sahitya Akademi Award for her translation of N. P. Mohammed's *The Eye of God* (Macmillan, 1997), the Crossword Award for M. Mukundan's *On the Banks of the Mayyazhi* (East West Press, 1999) and for Anand's *Govardhan's Travels* (Penguin, 2006). She lives in Chennai.

Translator's Preface

Born in 1934 in the village of Kudallur in the Palakkad district of Kerala, M. T. Vasudevan Nair (known affectionately as M.T. to his friends and readers) grew up against a backdrop of lush paddy fields, with coconut and areca nut palms dipping and swaying in the winds, heavy with the fragrance of mango and jackfruit, in the vicinity of the river he loved, the Bharatha Puzha, which is believed to have nurtured some of Kerala's finest writers and poets on its banks. Kudallur provides the setting for much of his work. Its changing seasons, the rhythms of its agricultural cycle and the dreams and hopes of its people have never ceased to offer him rich material.

The youngest of four boys, M. T. longed passionately from the time he was very young to be a writer. He recalls repeatedly in many articles and interviews a childhood incident that left a deep impression on him. While he was still a schoolboy, he was sent one day to a neighbouring village to fetch a handwritten copy of Changampuzha's well known poem, *Ramanan*. It was lent on condition that it would be returned the next day. The boy brought it home and watched with astonishment while his brothers and sister-in-law sat up all night copying it out. "All this passion and hard work to copy out a poem?" he mused.

He began to read Malayalam poetry himself—the works of the great triad Vallathol, Kumaranasan and Ulloor; he also read Balamani Amma, G. Sankara Kurup, Changampuzha, Idassery, Vylopilli. He was fascinated to discover that the words they used were familiar to him, only the arrangements were new and magical. Mesmerised by the verses he read and learnt by heart, he took to wandering over the hillsides, chanting them aloud.

He went on to devour all the short stories that he could lay his hands on, stories by Basheer, Thakazhi, Lalithambika Anterjanam, S. K. Pottekkat, Karoor Neelakanta Pillai, Keshavadev. These writers became his heroes—he would cut out their pictures from magazines and paste them on the walls of his room. His desire to join their ranks grew rapidly.

M. T. began to write at the age of fourteen. He sent the stories he wrote to all the magazines that he could find the addresses of, his only problem being to somehow get hold of the three quarters of an anna that he needed to despatch them by post. In 1953, he won a prize for a short story competition organised by the weekly *Mathrubhumi* for his story "Circus Animals" (Valarthumrigangal). He never looked back after that.

M. T. has always said that the short story is his favourite literary form. He has eighteen short story collections to his credit. "In a short story you can almost achieve perfection. Structurally, it is closer to a poem. You go on chiselling it, removing unwanted portions till you finally get the exact form."[1] He continues to experiment with this form and some of his finest short stories, "Sherlock" and "Stone Inscriptions," for example, have appeared in this decade. If a tendency to sentimentalize mars some of his earlier work, his later prose is very finely honed, elegantly crafted and disciplined. Ayyappa Paniker points out that there are few writers whose style and craft have changed so much and so effectively within a lifetime.[2]

However, M. T. has not confined himself to short stories. He has written eight novels, all of which have been widely read and appreciated in Kerala, a play, and several successful screenplays. He was one of the first writers in Malayalam to invest fiction with a dimension that moved beyond the description of character and event and gave greater importance to thought and emotion, that examined the human mind and analyzed its secret desires and longings. His protagonists, both in the novels and the short stories, are generally outsiders, isolated from family and society, victims of circumstance, introspective and often full of self-loathing.

And when I woke, the marrow
Out of my bones ran out
that you were the friend I
                    dreamt for
But not the dream I woke for
And so I put this down for
Doubt for doubt.

—Ezra Pound

Kaalam (1969) is his sixth novel. It describes the life of the protagonist Sethu from the age of fifteen to thirty, the inexorable movement from a dream-filled, ambitious youth, confident that it can reach out and possess the whole world, to a maturity where material and social success go hand in hand with an overwhelming sense of disillusion and a tragic consciousness of failure. Although the novel is not strictly autobiographical, M. T. confesses, "Sethu of *Kaalam* is a lot like me. I share with Sethu his emotional experiences and the situations he has been through."[3] Many of the characters in the novel were a part of the life of his village as well.

Written in lyrical prose, the novel captures the changing moods and seasons of the landscape of M.T.'s childhood. The river, a mute witness to every crisis in Sethu's life, mirrors his journey from adolescence to an adulthood empty of hope and love. At the end of the novel, it lies as parched and dry as his own heart. Marked by his experiences, the river is transformed from the rippling surface over which the ferry boat had carried Sethu to his new life as a college student into a stretch of dry sand, "dreaming of floods," which he must cross in order to return to the meaningless existence he has carved out for himself in the city as Sethu Mudalali. M. T.'s sensitive portrayal of Sethu, of his capacity to analyze himself and his ability to realize what is happening to him at every instant, the fine portraits of the multitude of other characters and the evocative images of the Kudallur landscape give the novel its emotional intensity and a remarkable richness of texture.

The disintegrating matrilinear tarawad system of the Nairs of Kerala, its conflicts and problems, its petty rivalries and burning jealousies, which were part of the background that M.T. grew up against, furnished him with an inexhaustible fund of material. The sambandham system of marriage followed by the Nairs, in which men entered into contractual relationships with their wives and visited them in their houses, was still in force when M.T. was a child. To an outsider, it may not be immediately clear that the men in Sethu's household are visiting husbands who do not form strong or lasting bonds with their wives and children. His father, for example, is deeply attached to his own sisters and their children—an attachment that Sethu's mother detests both for its own sake and also because she believes that it influences him to give his sisters' children the greater part of his earnings. Sethu's own relationship with his father is ambivalent and unsatisfactory, he is haunted by the feeling that his father does not appreciate him and is reluctant to help him. His father's house, Pushpoth, where his paternal aunts live, and where he can go only as an honoured guest, symbolizes a happiness and security that he cannot attain at home, that he covets deeply and contrasts resentfully to his own dilapidated house with its chipped floor, its worm-eaten wooden pillars and its total absence of comfort.

Sethu's aunt, Cheriamma, has two visiting husbands. The first terminates his relationship with her when he stops visiting her regularly; the second moves into her household after taking his share of his own tarawad property and is obviously regarded as something of a parasite. Madhava Ammama, Sethu's uncle, moves briefly to Vadakkethu when he marries Devu, only to return to his sisters when things start to go badly there. However, Sethu's brother Parameswaran brings his wife home, but both move out when his mother quarrels with her daughter-in-law. They are representative of the new generation, Sethu's generation, which finally breaks away from the joint family system.

The real protagonist of the novel is kaalam itself, the ceaseless flow of time that shapes Sethu's life, alienating him from everyone and everything he loves and carrying him from one mistake to the next. The word "kaalam" holds within it a deep consciousness of the present, the past, and the future and an implicit awareness of the unrelenting passage of time. The title of the novel has been left untranslated because "time," the nearest English equivalent of "kaalam," suggests neither its complex connotations nor its infinite span.

The novel has forty-one chapters which are divided into seven sections. The first five sections deal with Sethu's life as a college student, his hopes and aspirations. In the sixth section, he searches for a job and finds one with great difficulty, only to lose it. The seventh and final section unfolds the stages of Sethu's transformation into Sethu Mudalali. Except for the third and fourth sections, where the perspective shifts from Sethu to his uncle Madhava Ammama, the rest of the novel revolves steadily around Sethu. Moving backward and forward in the time span allotted to each section, the novel sometimes concentrates on short periods marked by great intensity of feeling and sometimes condenses long periods into a single chapter. In the last part of the novel, for instance, the events of nine years flash rapidly through Sethu's mind when he returns to his house after a very long absence.

In *Naalukettu* (1958) and in *Asuravithu* (1960), M.T.'s other long novels of the earlier period, the protagonists avenge themselves on their families and on society for the sufferings they have endured, but Sethu of *Kaalam* misses fulfilment in every aspect of life—with the three women he loves and betrays, in all his personal relationships with the members of his family or with friends and colleagues, in his career which forces him into a pattern of action he detests. He is bitterly conscious of each successive failure but is never able to extricate himself from its unhappy consequences. In spite of all this, perhaps because of his tendency for relentless self-analysis, he emerges in the final instance as a person who somehow manages to keep his dreams alive even when he knows for certain that he cannot achieve them. It seems possible then to hope that the poem trapped in the morning sunlight shimmering on the parched river, struggling to find words, as Sethu leaves home for the last time, may still take shape.

1. "Vanajam Ravindran in Conversation with M.T. Vasudevan Nair," in *Wordsmiths*, ed. Meenakshi Sarma, Katha (1996), 205.
2. M. M. Basheer ed. *Kathayum Porulum*, Current Books (1996), 146.
3. "Vanajam Ravindran in Conversation with M.T. Vasudevan Nair," in *Wordsmiths*, ed. Meenakshi Sarma, Katha (1996), 207.

Kinship Terms

Achan	:	father
Amma	:	mother
Ammama(n)	:	mother's brother
Cheriachan	:	father's younger brother or mother's younger sister's husband
Cheriamma	:	mother's younger sister
Edathi	:	elder sister
Ettan	:	elder brother
Muthassi	:	grandmother
Oppu	:	elder sister

Part One

Night.
    Grasshoppers, asleep in the newly sprouted shoots of karuka grass at the edge of the rain-drenched field, wake up startled at the sound of footsteps. They brush against my calves as I walk and rustle softly, evoking a memory that my troubled heart cannot define. When had I last heard this familiar, happy sound?

Scent of wet earth and the grey dark. It suddenly occurs to me that darkness and the night have a scent. The paths picked out by the men who came to spray the fields are full of pools of stagnant water which still reflect an overcast sky, even though the rain has stopped.

The flaming torch ahead lights our way.

I can hear the old cheruman gasping as he walks behind me carrying my tin trunk and mattress. The murmur of the river grows clearer as we leave the fields behind and climb onto the rough country road.

We stop and listen to the river ripple beneath the ferry boat, which is anchored to a stake on the shore. A river of darkness, with an endless stretch of half-light above. Do I hear train wheels roar over the trembling steel railroad bridge on the farther shore?

The ferryman, a sleep-dazed shadow, emerges from his hut. He knows the train timings by heart.

Is this the four thirty train? I dare not ask. For I am no longer an ignorant little boy. I am sixteen years old and on my way to college in a city fifty-three miles away, where a sultan once built a fortress. I am a young man now; I grew up in the space of a night.

(A night that has stayed undimmed in my memory all these years, as vivid as the sight and smell of fresh blood.)

The ferryman hangs his smoky, soot encrusted lantern over the boat and begins to bale out water with a palm spathe. I hear a pigeon coo inside my heart, a solitary temple pigeon that had descended on the tiled roof at dusk.

The river, the ferry boat.

The river I have crossed so many times to go to the eye doctor's house, the temple, the cucumber fields. And the ferry boat that still waits for me, after all these years.

Will the cheruman hold the tin trunk steady on the boat's seat? I don't want it to slip and fall when the boat moves. But I dare not say, "Chathappa, hold the trunk carefully, don't let it fall."

I place my hands firmly on the plank behind me and balance myself so that my clean, starched mundu, folded and tucked above my knees, does not get wet. The huts on the deserted shore begin to take shape in the morning light.

Cold water seeps into our footprints as we walk over the wet sand. I wish we could walk faster. Do I hear the steel bridge clatter? Embers fall from the torch and burn out on the moist sand. The worn railroad track flashes silver in the soft darkness.

I feel more frightened than happy.

Ammaman strides ahead, swinging his huge hands, his mundu folded and tucked above his knees, a towel wound around his head. He turns and calls.

"Hurry up, boy."

His voice is unnecessarily loud. They always talk too loudly, the grown-ups—Amma, Cheriamma, Ammama, that rare visitor, Parameswara Ettan—so that I never recall their faces, only their loud voices.

Careful now, there are sharp fragments of stone scattered over the sleepers on the railroad track.

Suddenly, I forget the four thirty train, the red signal lights, the city I had been trying so hard to imagine yesterday. I know it is foolish to feel sad, for I am not really going away. No, this uneasiness in my heart is not sorrow. And my eyes smart only because . . . yes, because the sweat makes the oil from my hair dribble into them.

The memory of the infinitely soft rustle of the grasshoppers moving through the field suddenly comes to mind. They sound exactly like press studs snapping open on a blue blouse.

Why had I not remembered earlier? As I walk faster over the sleepers, I accuse myself with all the fervour of a sixteen-year-old—why, why, had I not remembered earlier?

1

Sethu washed his face once more, sprinkled the last handful of water from the copper pot on his face and neck, came back to the eastern verandah and sat down with his back against the pillar.

Outside, the afternoon sun blazed. It was unbearably hot. An occasional breeze that strayed through the areca palms seemed laden with flames. If only the floor had been swept and mopped with a wet cloth, he could have lain on it. But it was dirty, cracked, and full of dust.

It was not yet time to go to the post office. Perhaps there would be a letter from Achan today. Parameswara Ettan had promised to send thirty rupees a month. If Achan sent the rest, he could go to college. Ettan had refused to write and ask Achan. Amma had written. Achan's reply had been full of complaints: he was ill, the work on the estate was not as lucrative as it used to be. Sethu had read the letter out to Amma and then gone through it again. No, it said nothing about him, Sethu. He had enclosed a letter of his own along with Amma's reply. That was nine days ago. Letters from the Anamalais usually took only two days to come.

If you watched from the hillside, you could see the mail train crossing the bridge. Sethu always made sure the red mailbox was on the train before he left for the post office. Even so, he often arrived there earlier than the local runner with corn-infested feet who brought the mail from Kuttippuram.

He would sleep till four. It was pleasant to lie with his head against the railings, where Amma slept during the summer.

He could not bear to look out. Flames seemed to hang over the fields. The sand beyond was white hot and he dared not keep his eyes on it for more than a minute.

They had hoped it would rain for Vishu, but it had not rained even for the talappoli festival at the Srirankara temple, later in the year. Cheriamma said she had never seen such a hot summer all her life. She said so every year, and always predicted that people would be scorched to death. Nobody ever died though.

"Sethu, have you seen Padmu?"

That was Cheriamma, from the verandah above.

"No."

"Wretched girl, she'll fall into a tank or a well one day. Children should be obedient. Wait till I get my hands on her."

Cheriamma would begin now to describe all the ways in which she would punish Padmu. He said,

"She must be playing next door."

Cheriamma slapped Padmu for the most trivial reasons and hit her with anything that came to hand. Whenever she quarrelled with Amma, she usually took it out on Padmu. Not that Amma cared. Padmu would sob until she was out of breath and then Amma would tell Sethu to take her away. "If she dies, there'll be no one except me to haul her body away."

Hours later, Cheriamma would give Padmu an oil bath and smear her forehead with vibhuti. She would take her on her lap, caress her and cry.

Cheriamma would pace up and down the verandah, her shabby undergarment visible beneath an inadequate little towel wrapped around her waist. She never wore a rowka in summer, preferring to leave her breasts uncovered. She would not go in even if there were visitors. Sethu often thought to himself angrily, wretched woman, why did she have to stay on the verandah half-clothed?

Even Madhava Ammama did not dare say anything to her. After all, he was younger than Amma or Cheriamma, so they did not have to listen to him.

Cheriamma said, "I left a fan here this morning. Where is it?"

Sethu did not answer. She had not asked him directly. All she needed when she began to talk was someone in her vicinity.

"There's not a soul to help me. Only plenty of people to torture me."

Cheriamma wiped her discoloured lips and spat into the courtyard. She was ready for a fight. "I had to ask a hundred people before Chathappan's son finally brought me a spathe to make the fan. Now everyone wants it!"

Sethu maintained an angry silence. Amma complained, to no one in particular, "I'm not allowed a little rest even in the afternoon."

Cheriamma shook out the last of the snuff from the bottle tucked in at her waist, inhaled it, wiped her nose and laughed contemptuously into the sunlight.

"Can't open my mouth, can I? Everything I say is wrong. Kalyani is the abandoned one, she has no one to speak for her. Tell me, boy, did I say anything wrong? All I said was that I left a fan here and that I can't find it now."

Sethu turned away, unwilling to play the role of a witness. When would he escape from all this?

Amma would not give in. Sethu went down the steps and walked up to the fence. Devu called out from the illam compound, "Sethu, is Madhavettan there?"

"No."

"Tell him that Kunhathol wants to see him when he comes back."

It was Madhava Ammama who looked after the affairs of the illam, now that Kunjan Namboodiri had died. He had the areca nuts plucked and sold and collected the paddy from Govindan, the tenant-farmer. Kunhathol had great faith in Madhava Ammama. She knew he would not cheat her. And he seemed happy with whatever she gave him now and then.

Cheriamma complained that Madhava Ammamma never gave her even a quarter anna for snuff, in spite of what he made from the banana garden and his earnings as the manager of the illam.

Amma always defended him, "He's a man, after all, he needs money for his own expenses."

Sethu listened. Was the quarrel over? No. Amma had moved into the verandah, ready for battle.

What if he picked up a fallen palm spathe from Kunhathol's compound, made a fan with it and threw it into the verandah? No, it would not stop them. Both women loved to quarrel. Amma always won—after all, it was she who ran the household. Which meant that Padmu would surely be beaten today.

When Cheriamma's husband was alive, she had squabbled with him all the time. He used to sit like an ascetic, wearing a small mundu that barely covered him decently and stroke his beard and listen to her. He was Cheriamma's second husband. The first one was Kandulikkaran Krishnan Nair. He had had a sambandham relationship with her for two years.

Amma often accused Cheriamma. "A woman should stand in her man's shadow."

"And are all the noble ones who lived in their man's shadow prospering now? Don't provoke me." Cheriamma would retort. What she implied was that my father gave everything he earned to his nephews and nieces.

Actually, Cheriamma's husband, Krishnan Nair, had not been rich in those days. He used to take over the tenancy of an empty plot of land once the paddy had been harvested, and sow sesame seeds in it. Or bid for pieces of land near the river that had not been entrusted to tenant farmers and grow cucumbers in them. Amma had thought well of him, he was considered to be the sort who cared about his family. And she had had proof of this when Parameswara Ettan was a child. He had fallen ill once and nearly died. Vaidyan Kudumundukkaran could do nothing for him. Everyone thought he would die. Krishnan Nair had crossed the river at the dead of night and brought a washerwoman from five miles away. She was old and blind, could hardly walk and seldom went anywhere. But Krishnan Nair had persuaded her to come home. They arrived at daybreak and as soon as the old woman placed some herbal medicine on the child's forehead and chest and began to chant mantrams, Ettan had opened his eyes.

We lost touch with Krishnan Nair when he stopped visiting Cheriamma. All we knew was that he had left the village. After Cheriachan surrendered his property to his nephew and came to live with us, we once heard that Krishnan Nair was in business in Pazhani and that he had sent his sister five hundred rupees.

A pujari who had gone from our village to the temple at Pazhani for Thaipooyam told us that Krishnan Nair had done well for himself and made money, that he had a wife and children.

Krishnan Nair came to the village five years ago, a few days before Parameswara Ettan's wedding. Achan was at home. Madhava Ammama and Ettan had gone to Kunnamkulam to buy clothes.

A man in a blue shirt and a gold bordered veshti opened the gate. Krishnan Nair.

He had white stone earrings in his ears, gold chains on his neck and left wrist, huge rings on his fingers. An image of Krishna playing the flute was tattooed on his arm. Amma grew very agitated. There was a small commotion to serve him tea and snacks.

Achan and Krishnan Nair had much to tell each other. Amma came to the front door from time to time to join the conversation.

"Is Appu Nair at home?"

"He was here a while ago." Only Sethu had observed Cheriachan go to Vadakkethu.

When he was leaving, Krishnan Nair asked Amma, "Where's Kalyani Amma?"

Sethu thought Cheriamma would stay inside, nursing Padmu. But she had come, with Padmu on her hip, pulling her grey hair back over her left ear. Sethu saw her make an effort to smile.

"Are you all right?" Krishnan Nair bared his gold teeth in a smile, his hand on the door.

Cheriamma made a sound of assent. Her smile, as faded as a flower that had been used for the Onam decorations and then swept into the rubbish heap, stayed fixed on her face.

"I'm going back tomorrow. I thought I'd come and see all of you before I left."

Sethu saw Krishnan Nair place something in Padmu's hand. A five rupee note. As he said goodbye to Achan, he asked Sethu, "Which class are you in?"

"Sixth." Sethu never forgot the fragrance of the new, uncreased five rupee note which Krishnan Nair gave him.

Amma waited on the verandah, fumbling in her betel leaf box, until Krishnan Nair left. Then she said, "However rich he's become, he's not forgotten the past. He has a good heart."

We saw Cheriachan dragging his stout frame through the fence, gasping for breath, his eyes on the ground.

Amma said, "It's all a matter of destiny, don't you see? She's younger than me, but what's the use? Her foolishness brought about her misfortune. She could have lived like a queen. A queen."

Cheriamma stood on the inner side of the door, like a forgotten creature, running her hands through her hair. She did not say a word, or look at Amma.

Achan scolded Amma, "There he is. Keep quiet."

"Sethu". That was Cheriamma.

The verandah was quiet. Amma seemed to have lost the battle. Cheriamma came up and whispered, "Are you going to the post office?"

"Maybe."

"Get me snuff for half an anna. I don't have any money." Sethu hoped Amma had not heard. It would start another quarrel. Amma hated women using snuff; it made her furious.

Where would he find a half anna? He said nothing to Cheriamma. She stretched out on the verandah, leaned her head on her elbows and spat into the yard.

He saw two people coming across the field towards the house. Who could it be, at this time of day? Parameswara Ettan? His heart sank as he made out one of them. Haridas! God, no!

His first thought was of Cheriamma, lying in full view without a rowka, her breasts uncovered and her undergarment showing.

"Cheriamma, someone's coming."

"Who?"

"A boy who was at school with me, and someone else."

"That's nice."

He dared not ask her to go in. Swallowing his embarrassment, he waited while Haridas came up the steps. When he realized that his own mundu was worn and dirty, he could not even manage a smile.

"It was difficult to find your house, Sethu."

"You could have dropped me a card."

"This is Chandrettan. We came to Gopi Menon's house and thought we would drop in on you since you were in the neighbourhood."

There were no chairs downstairs. Where would they sit?

Haridas's white poplin shirt was wet with perspiration. Haridas placed his hand on Sethu's shoulder and said, his eyes full of laughter, "Didn't I say I would give you a surprise one of these days?"

"Come, let's go upstairs."

Cheriamma raised her head, then lay down again.

They went upstairs. The easy chair which was usually on the verandah had been folded and put away. He invited them into the room, "Do sit down." They sat on the wooden ledge of the window in the dingy room. Dust and rubbish had been swept into a heap and left on the verandah. Sethu felt disgusted.

He would show Amma, if she boasted again, "It's not easy, keeping a mansion like this clean." Mansion indeed!

He thought of Haridas's pretty, tiled house. Potted plants on ledges beyond the iron gate, a jasmine bower in the courtyard. Chairs arranged around a circular table in the front room and a crocheted tablecloth with the designs picked out in colours. Haridas had introduced him to his mother. She wore a starched mundu of pristine white with a black border. Haridas's eldest sister had served them tea and sliced mangoes in a white porcelain plate.

He had dropped in at Haridas's on his way back from a debating competition. He had not won a prize that day. But the sweetness of Haridas's welcome still lingered in his mind.

He excused himself and ran down. It was shameful—he had pretended that his father was an important official who sent home huge sums of money every month, that his house had a big nalukettu, a four-pillared inner courtyard, that he even had a room of his own.

Cheriamma was no longer in the verandah. Good. He stepped inside. Where was Amma? He asked Padmu, who came in trailing a coconut shell tied to a string. "Where is Valiamma?"

"Don't know."

He made a face at her.

"Cheriamma, where's Amma?"

"Look in the kitchen."

"She's not there. Cheriamma, I have to give my friends tea."

"Your mother runs the house, child. I only eat what I am given. And I don't complain if I get nothing. Who am I, after all? If I had just the interest now on the petty cash I used to have, I could have bought my own soap and clothes."

"Please, Cheriamma, can you make me some tea?"

"With what? Your mother locks up the tea and sugar."

It was futile talking to her. He went out in search of Amma. God! Don't let Haridas hear.

Amma was at the Vadakkethu fence, talking to Ammayi.

"Amma, I have visitors, my classmate Haridas and his brother. Please make some tea quickly."

Amma said, "There's no milk."

"Amme!" He was on the verge of tears.

"What can I do if there's no milk?"

He ran next door and spoke to Sumitra. She went to fetch the goat she had let out to graze. He rushed back to the kitchen.

"Amma, what shall we give them to eat?"

"Your head. Get out, boy. You're lucky you don't have to starve. And you think I'll make little snacks for you whenever you want?"

Why did Amma have to talk so loud? He ran up the stairs. Haridas and his brother were at the door.

"Hari, you're not leaving?"

"Yes, we must."

He said with an effort, "Stay and have a cup of tea."

Haridas's brother answered, "We have a couple of places to go to."

He could not bring himself to insist. They hesitated for a moment in the courtyard. Padmu was playing on the verandah.

"Where is your mother, Sethu?"

"In the kitchen, I think. I'll call her."

Chandrettan came to his rescue. "Let's go. Tell your mother we had to leave."

He walked with Haridas across the fields and along the road. It was the first time he had come out without a shirt on.

Chandrettan walked ahead of them.

Haridas asked, "What do you do with yourself during the vacation? I saw TKP the other day."

Sethu tried to smile. "Which college will you go to?"

"Let me wait for the results."

"Oh come on, of course you'll pass. I can't go to college even if I pass. We don't have the money."

They stopped by the canal. Sethu said, "So long, Das. I'll write."

"You must. I'll tell TKP I saw you."

Sethu walked back. The field was white hot beneath his feet.

When he reached back home, he felt furious with the whole world. He wanted to pull down the old thatched house with its chipped beams. A great tarawad indeed! He imagined Haridas describing his visit to Sethu's house to his friends.

"Sethu." Amma called out. "Padmu, tell Sethu I want him."

He did not move.

A little later, Amma came up with two brass tumblers of tea. "Here you are."

He hid his hurt and resentment and said, "They've gone."

Amma left a glass of tea beside him and went down. He poured it on the ground.

How would he ever face Haridas again?

They had become friends the year Haridas repeated his tenth standard. Haridas had curly hair, a mischievous smile and was always late for class. He took snuff, scoffed at the teachers and was often sent out of the class. Once, when he sat down next to Sethu, he had noticed a collection of Changampuzha's poems amongst Haridas's books and asked to borrow it. That was how they got to know each other.

They soon became friends, the most intelligent boy in the class and the naughtiest one. They went together everywhere. To the temple festival at Kallathoor. To meet Colonel Lakshmi, who had fought with Subash Chandra Bose. Haridas had brought the news that she was expected at a meeting nearby. Haridas was a year or two older than Sethu. If you looked hard, you could see the faintest shadow of a moustache on his lips.

Haridas recited poetry beautifully. So did Parukutty.

Parukutty, with the big, black pottu on her forehead, always came to school with a crowd of girls. She was the leader and the prettiest among them.

Haridas once showed him a letter. "Want to know who wrote it?"

"Who?"

"TKP."

"Who's TKP?"

The letter, which ran into four pages, was signed T. K. Parukutty.

Haridas began to come to school early. Sethu lived four miles away from school and found it hard to come early. However, at Haridas's insistence, he would gulp down his kanji and rush to school by nine. Class Ten B was one of the new classrooms upstairs. He would wait outside until he saw Parukutty come out of the girls' common room. Pretending she was going to the toilet, she would walk into the classroom and talk to Haridas, while Sethu kept watch on the verandah to make sure no one saw them.

Parukutty pronounced the consonant "sh" as if it were a "s." This was most noticeable when she recited poetry. But none of the boys laughed at her, because she was Parukutty.

One day, when Haridas had not come, Sethu heard someone call him as he went past the girls' common room.

It was Parukutty. He felt inexplicably happy.

"May I borrow your Physics notes?" she asked.

It was not a surprising request, for he was the brightest in class and always had the highest marks, although he was the youngest. That night, he copied the notes into a new notebook by the light of an oil lamp and covered the book with a sheet from an ancient calendar advertising Vinolia soap, that had hung on his wall for ages. He gave it to Parukutty with a great sense of achievement the next day.

He wondered whether to tell Haridas about it on Monday, but did not. He treasured this secret between him and Parukutty, a secret that Haridas did not share.

Sometimes, he looked at Parukutty timidly in class. She was so pretty and when she walked, her long skirt trailed on the ground.

One day Haridas said to him, "Parukutty is ill." She had typhoid. Haridas told him later that Parukutty would not come back to school. She did come once though, to collect her certificates. Sethu saw her from a distance. She had cut her hair, the long, swinging plait in which she used to weave red flowers, and cropped it short like a boy's. His heart ached. He turned away before she saw him.

He said to Haridas that day, "Parukutty had borrowed my Physics notes. Can you get them back for me?"

"She gave them to me long ago. I forgot."

Had her hair grown again? He had not dared to ask Haridas today.

"Who threw this tea out?" Amma asked.

He did not answer. He went upstairs and put on his shirt.

He heard her shout, "Why throw it away? Who are you angry with? I know you wanted me to produce tea and snacks. But it's sixty rupees your old man sends me to feed all of you. Ah, I'd like to know what you would have done without me."

She would start now, about her efficiency, her superiority, the respect that the women of the neighbourhood had for her. He hurried away before she could begin.

2

"Sethu, have you forgotten what I asked you for yesterday?"

"What?"

"I wanted snuff for half an anna."

Sethu did not answer. He was trying to figure out how to get hold of two annas for himself. And here was Cheriamma reminding him again.

Cheriamma sighed, "People don't care for you if you don't have anything of your own."

He had heard that Cheriamma had lived a comfortable life until Cheriachan gave up his rights to the family property and came here. But ever since Sethu could remember, Cheriachan had had financial problems. He would listen silently to whatever Amma and Cheriamma said.

He died one summer, a summer exactly like this one. Sethu had been in the eighth class at the time. The examinations were over and he was at home. It had been the first time he saw death.

Before that, Cheriamma had lost two babies as soon as they were born. But he had been at school on both occasions. On one occasion, he had heard Cheriamma moan in pain when he woke up in the morning. Her baby was due and Sethu was sent to fetch Chummukkutti Amma, the midwife. Amma and Paru Ammayi from Vadakkethu kept scolding Cheriamma because she would not lie down and insisted on pacing up and down the hall. "Go and lie down, wretched girl," said Amma, "I've had babies as well."

Ammayi from Vadakkethu gave Sethu his kanji that morning. When he went to fetch his school bag from under the stairs, the floor was wet, as if a pot of water had been overturned on it.

"The waters have broken. Why hasn't the midwife come?" Sethu ran away quickly.

He listened carefully for the baby's cry when he came back from school that evening. Amma and Ammayi did not speak to him. No kanji had been cooked. Cheriachan called him, "Come, Sethu."

They went out together. Cheriachan had just won a case against the Irimbiliyath family and received some money due to him as interest. He had notes and coins tucked into his waist. He bought Sethu tea and snacks. On the way back, Cheriachan stopped outside Kandunni's house saying he would be right back. Sethu stayed outside and blew up big leaves from the castor oil plant. Cheriachan came out after a long time, wiping his chin and spitting from time to time as he walked. His round face with the grey stubble had grown red and he smelt of arrack.

"Come on." Cheriachan seemed unsteady on his feet. He said, as they crossed the fields, "Your Cheriamma had a baby boy, but it died."

Everyone liked Cheriachan. When he wanted to marry for the third time and Cheriamma's name was proposed, no one in the family had anything against the fifty-year-old bridegroom. He was the karanavar, the senior most member, of his tarawad and owned a shop facing the Ariyambadath temple. But his business failed and his nephews decided to divide the family property. A dispute arose and Cheriachan surrendered his rights to the property in return for a settlement of three thousand rupees. Then he came to live here. He lent the sum out to the Irimbiliyath mapillas and lost both capital and interest. He filed a suit and pawned first Cheriamma's, then Amma's jewels to pay for the legal proceedings. He won the case, but the sum he received was hardly enough to pay off the debts he had accumulated.

Parameswarettan always gave Cheriachan a rupee or two to buy betel leaves whenever he came home. Cheriamma resented this. Cheriachan would get up early in the morning to escape her recriminations, go to the river and pray till the sun grew hot. After that, he would smear his forehead and chest with vibhuti, come home and pace the verandah. After lunch, he always went to Vadakkethu.

Since she was distantly related to us, all of us called Paru Amma of the Vadakkethu house next door Ammayi. Even Amma, who was older than her, called her Ammayi.

Devu or Sumitra would spread a mat for Cheriachan and he would stay at Vadakkethu until someone called him home for dinner. Ammayi sometimes gave him a cup of tea. She liked to have him there, for her household had no men of its own.

Cheriamma found fault with Padmu for this as well. "Can't your father stay in his own house? Why does he sit in their verandah, to shoo away the crows and chickens?"

The children—Devu, Sumitra and Unni Namboodiri—always played in Ammayi's yard. Cheriachan like to sit quietly and watch them play.

It was at dusk one day that Sethu saw death. Cheriachan had been ill for a month. Sethu heard a scream and ran downstairs.

He saw the sightless eyes open wider and wider. The face seemed to have altered in shape.

Amma asked him to take Padmu away to the illam or to Vadakkethu. But he lingered, staring at Cheriachan's dilated pupils, listening to his laboured breathing.

"I said, get out." Sethu dragged the uncomprehending Padmu away. Even before he reached the areca nut grove, he heard Cheriamma wail. He held Padmu close to him, shivering, and the little girl suddenly began to cry.

They sent word to Cheriachan's house, but no one came. They waited until midnight, then Madhava Ammama said they could go ahead with the cremation. Traditionally, an older person had to be burned with wood from a mango tree, but their sole mango tree still yielded fruit and no one wanted it cut.

Sethu slept at Ammayi's house that night. Sumitra fed Padmu, put her to sleep and then served Sethu.

"I wonder what Edathi is doing at your house," she said. Devu and Ammayi were still at Sethu's place.

Sumitra teased out the tangles in her hair by the light of the oil lamp and gathered it tightly into a knot above her head. She put Padmu to bed with Karthiyayani, who was a year older than Padmu, and told Sethu to sleep as well.

Sumitra and Sethu were the same age, but she suddenly seemed like a grown woman with responsibilities.

Sethu slept on a mat in the hall. He no longer thought of Cheriachan's white eyes widening fearfully. Instead, his mind went back to the time when he and Sumitra used to walk over the hill to school, chaperoned by Devu. Even when she was in the fifth, Sumitra had not worn a blouse. That year, she had stopped coming to school.

They used to stop at the illam fence on their way back from school, leave their books and slates under a tree and worm their way through the gap in the fence to look for fallen mangoes in the illam compound. Bamboo thickets and big trees were clustered there in such profusion that it was dark even at noon.

Only Unni Namboodiri was brave enough to go there to pick up the fallen mangoes. On days when he found a lot, he would give Sumitra and Sethu some. They would creep back through the areca nut grove, taking care that Kunju Namboodiri did not see them. When they got to the fence at the gate on the southern side, they would find Devu waiting with a cross look on her face.

Once he was in the ninth and had moved to the high school four miles away, Sethu had no longer gone looking for mangoes again, although he sometimes went to the old haunt. Now, children never went there at all. They avoided the place because Kunju Namboodiri had been cremated near it. It had become overgrown with shrubs.

For many nights, Sethu had dreamed of Kunju Namboodiri's cremation and woken up with a start. Even when he walked under the jnaval trees in daylight, he felt uneasy although he had forgotten Cheriachan's eyes very quickly. It was Sumitra who had persuaded him to go and watch Kunju Namboodiri being cremated. They had found a place on the rocks, under the jnaval tree. At first, the smoke and the crowd had obscured everything. When the breeze blew away the smoke, they saw Unni Namboodiri with a kindi of water in his hand, the end of his mundu drawn between his legs and tucked behind in ritual fashion.

Sumitra asked, "Do you think Unni Namboodiri would have cried?"

How can a child not cry when its father dies?

But Sumitra was sure he did not cry. Kunju Namboodiri used to beat his son everyday while he taught the boy to chant the Vedas in the bathing shed near the tank. The sound of his blows could be heard in the house. Afterwards, Unni Namboodiri would walk away, the flesh on his oversized body quivering, his face showing no trace of tears.

"Here comes our Hidumban," Madhava Ammama would say. "How many verses did you chant today?"

Although his body was covered with bruises, Unni Namboodiri would bare his big teeth in a grin. Madhava Ammama would tease him, "Eat a black cat, Tirumeni, then the blows won't hurt you."

No, Unni Namboodiri would not cry because his father was dead.

When the areca nut palms in the illam bent over, the children used to swing on them. Once, a palm fell down trapping Unni Namboodiri's hand under it. He pulled his hand out and scrambled up, and everyone saw nails hanging down from two crushed fingers. Even then, he had bared his big teeth as usual in a grin.

Unni Namboodiri sprinkled water, circumambulated.

The crowd fuelled the fire with long sticks of wood and palmyra branches. Sethu suddenly thought of a description of Hell which he had heard as a child, of how the messengers of Yama, the God of Death, threw chunks of flesh into the fire and toasted and fried them.

Sumitra gripped his shoulder and pointed, "Look, Sethu, look." Something in the shape of a huge black ape hung from one of the branches held out to stoke the fire. Sethu saw it for only a minute.

"They're his intestines."

He screamed and fled, leaving Sumitra behind. She had teased him for days, calling him a coward. Often, as he fell asleep, the thing like a black ape would come into his mind and he would wake up, terrified.

The mail train was on the bridge. Relieved, Sethu welcomed the end of another long, hot day of waiting. He pretended he was going for a dip in the illam tank. If he was lucky enough to run into Unni Namboodiri, he could ask him for two annas. But this was the season of temple festivals and Unni Namboodiri was probably at one of them. He loved to ride on the temple elephants. They paid namboodiris eight annas for doing this. But what Unni Namboodiri enjoyed more was being able to sit on an elephant's back as long as he pleased.

If he handled Unni Namboodiri well, he could coax two annas out of him. Which meant he could buy three postcards and Cheriamma's snuff.

Devu was at the tank, washing out the lees of the oil from the big flat bell-metal uruli. She told him that Unni Namboodiri was not at the illam. No one knew when he would be back. He came and went as he pleased.

"I came looking for the goat and saw Kunhathol making fresh oil. How could I refuse when she asked me to help?"

Devu talked like an old woman. Ever since the maidservant at the illam had been dismissed on the charge of having stolen rice, Devu went regularly to the illam to stable the cow, wash vessels and mop the floor. Neither she nor her mother would admit that she worked there. They pretended that she went to help Kunhathol because the latter was growing old.

Sethu heard the rope and pulley creak as he passed the well and saw Kunhathol there. She reminded him of the picture in the Ramayana of the rakshasi who guarded the captive Sita, with her earrings swinging in elongated earlobes, her rough voice and the dark shadows under her eyes. She was fair skinned and thin and her face frightened him.

"Sethu, where has Madhavan gone?"

"I don't know."

"He didn't come this side yesterday."

It was said that once they were ten years old namboodiri women never looked boys in the face. But Kunhathol was different. She talked directly even to Madhava Ammama.

"Did you get through your examinations?"

Sethu stopped. "I don't know yet."

When she sent Unni Namboodiri back to the fourth standard for the third year in succession, Kunhathol had asked Sethu to keep an eye on him. She used to ask him how things had gone after every examination they took. Unni Namboodiri had stopped coming to school after three months. But Kunhathol always said, "Lakshmi's son Sethu is very bright, he'll do well."

Kunhathol said now, "I've been meaning to ask you to bring the music box, Sethu."

"It's out of order. I'll bring it as soon as it is repaired."

Madhava Ammamma had won the gramophone in a raffle. He managed to get hold of some old records. At first, he would not allow anyone else to play them. Kunhathol always asked for "Kalayami sumate bhoosuramoule." She liked "Lakshmithaipe Murare" as well. When Sethu went over to play her the songs, she always gave him a glass of tea and jackfruit chips. She never allowed him to wash his glass and invert it as was the custom. "The girl will wash it when she comes."

He had turned back once as he was leaving and seen Kunhathol take the glass away herself.

Unni Namboodiri had been the only child who survived after she lost five babies in succession. People used to remark sadly, "His mother did not deserve such a cruel fate." Kunhathol was very generous to anyone who asked her for money or food. And yet, destiny had been unkind to her.

People said Unni Namboodiri was mentally retarded, but Sethu did not believe this. He had to use all his wits to coax an anna out of Unni Namboodiri.

Tea was never made at the illam in Kunju Namboodiri's lifetime. He used to come secretly to Sethu's house for a glass of tea. He would bring a packet of betel nuts and give it discreetly to Cheriamma; the tea was in return for this. Cheriamma would ask the cheruman to sell the betel nuts for her and buy snuff with the money.

Sethu put on a shirt, combed his hair, wiped his face with his hand and asked Amma hesitantly,

"Do you have two annas to spare, Amme?"

"What for?"

"I have to send a letter."

"To whom?"

He cursed himself for having asked.

"How many correspondents do you have? Get out now."

He felt something choke his throat. He swallowed hard and went out.

3

There were no letters at the post office for him. He waited while all the letters were sorted and stamped in the hope that his name would be called out. The postmaster came out at last and began to read the list of names, peering through his steel-rimmed glasses. Most of the letters were from the army.

He did not ask whether there was a money order. He hovered around after everyone had left, making sure the postmaster saw him. No, there was nothing for him.

He felt ashamed when he walked back empty-handed, day after day. Once, he came across advertisements inviting requests for free catalogues in a magazine that Parameswara Ettan had left behind. He took four annas from Amma's money box and wrote for them. He was happy for a week. Catalogues addressed to "P. K. Sethumadhavan, Padinjarapattu House" arrived everyday from jewellers' shops and pharmacies. He treasured the wrappers with his name and address on them.

A mile to walk back. The sand was still hot beneath his feet. He kept to the shade of the screwpine bushes. As he turned from the road onto the big field, he saw Unni Namboodiri squatting at

Ammayi's gate, grinning vacantly, opening and closing a five-cell torch.

His first reaction was shock. Had Unni Namboodiri really become soft headed because everyone said he was? He thought of Kunhathol making offerings at the Thriprangot temple so that her son should be right in the head.

He heard a laugh. It was Sumitra, gathering karuka grass near the fence."Is the festival over, Unni Namboodiri? Did you earn a lot of money going on the elephant?"

Unni Namboodiri smiled and held out the torch he had bought at the festival. "Six rupees! You can see very far when you switch it on."

Unni Namboodiri's speech was jerky. Sumitra told Sethu that Unni Namboodiri had been invited to the talappoli festival at Kalladuthoor. Unni Namboodiri smiled shyly, tucked the torch under his arm and walked away.

"Poor fellow!" said Sethu.

"Don't waste your pity on him. He can be smart enough when he wants."

Sethu did not know what she meant.

"Why do you think Kunhathol sent away the servant woman?"

"Because she stole rice."

Sumitra laughed and shook the earth off a bundle of karuka grass.

"Unni Namboodiri is not an innocent little child!"

Sethu walked home full of vague doubts. Amma was seated in the verandah with her legs stretched out, chewing betel, supervising Devu while she swept the front yard.

"No letters?"

"No."

"Hmm." Amma chewed silently. "It's two months now since he sent money. How can I go on? And Parameswaran is like his father, he doesn't care."

Devu asked, "Aren't Parameswara Ettan and his wife coming?"

"Why let strangers know how bad things are with us?"

Sethu went up, took off his shirt and lay down. The sky was the colour of copper. A soft yellow radiance lay over the courtyard. Thunder rumbled now and then and a faint breeze had begun to blow from the western hills.

The twentieth of April. Two months more and he could escape.

When Parameswara Ettan came back from college, he had been a different person. Sethu had been astonished when he opened his box. There were so many shirts, all ironed and faintly scented. Sethu had never worn an ironed shirt. The mapilla who had moved into the room next to the tailor's had an iron. He ironed starched shirts for half an anna. When Sethu suggested it to Amma, she said, "You don't need to be so stylish."

He heard Devu leave. Amma said to her, "Tell your mother to come and sleep here tonight."

Ammayi and her children often slept at Sethu's. Amma would stay up late and liked to have someone to talk to.

Footsteps sounded in the corridor. Cheriamma. She asked from the door, "Where are you, child? I've a bad headache."

"They had run out of snuff in Musaliyar's shop."

Cheriamma looked at him angrily, not believing what he said.

"They'll get some tomorrow. He shook out the jar to show me."

Cheriamma went away.

He heard Padmu chant her prayers and realized it was dusk. He went down and walked up and down the yard.

"Aren't you having a bath, Sethu?"

"No."

"How will you sleep in this heat if you don't have a bath?" In summer, Sethu slept on the floor in the front verandah, and Madhava Ammama on the wooden ledge.

Madhavammama came back late. He said that Govindan the tenant-farmer had brought the paddy to the illam very late that evening. Govindan was becoming impossibly arrogant, Madhava Ammama muttered.

Govindan's sons were in the army. And he had taken over a number of tenancies. You could buy paddy from Govindan only if he wanted to sell. It was futile to threaten him, he had money on his side, and strong young sons.

Amma, Cheriamma and Ammayi from Vadakkethu chattered noisily until Madhava Ammama came. No one would have thought looking at them then that they quarrelled with each other all day. No matter how sleepy she felt, Padmu would sit near the oil lamp, listening to them.

When Madhava Ammama came out after dinner with a wet towel around him, and lighted a beedi, they would lower their voices.

"Padmu, get me some water." It was always Devu who ran to fetch the water for Madhava Ammama.

Sumitra came out with a lamp, her hair tightly knotted above her head and sat down close to Amma. Sethu sat in the dark, leaning against the pillar. Sumitra had her mother's fair skin. Devu was said to be the image of her dead father. Devu looked comical. Her huge ears seemed to wave as she talked. Tall and dark, bony arms covered with hair, Devu reminded Sethu of the black cow which had fallen into a ditch and died during last year's monsoon.

Ammayi always maintained that Devu was much smarter than Sumitra and that she was good with the vegetable and wood accounts.

Amma took pride in the fact that the Vadakkethu women consulted her about all their affairs. It was Amma who had suggested that an opening be made in the fence between the houses.

Amma asked one of the children to spread Sethu's mat for him. Devu brought one and asked Madhava Ammama who was seated on the steps, smoking.

"Aren't you going to sleep, Madhavetta?"

Madhava Ammama grunted something that might have meant yes or no.

A silent flash of lightning illuminated the courtyard and the verandah.

Madhava Ammama said, "I'm going out, sister. Get me my umbrella."

"Where to, at this hour?"

"It's going to rain. If we sow tomorrow morning, we'll need Maimunni's calf. I'd better arrange for it now, everyone will want it."

Amma began to extol his efficiency and his devotion to the family as he disappeared into the darkness. At forty, Madhava Ammama was very hardworking. He did not chew betel, or drink. He had an excellent reputation. When Achan came home last, Amma had broached the subject of Madhava Ammama's marriage. But Madhava Ammama had said, "Sister, I can't get married now."

Amma said to everyone, "He's turned forty, but he won't listen to us." Most people realized that Amma was secretly happy about this, for she always added, "This devotion to the family will last only till he has a family of his own."

A gust of wind blew a trail of dust into the verandah. Lying on his mat, Sethu saw the sky through the areca nut palms, overcast with clouds and fitfully illuminated by lightning. It was going to rain.

Then he heard the faint swish of rain melting into the roar of the wind that tore through the areca nut palms. Sumitra came out with an oil lamp. "Sethu, are you asleep?"

He sat up at once.

"It's going to pour. Your mother asked if you'd like to sleep inside."

No. He loved to sleep here while the rain splashed noisily between the pieces of thatch hanging down unevenly from the roof, and the thunder crashed.

Sumitra smiled into the smoky flame of the lamp and Sethu suddenly thought, how beautiful she is! He had not realized it till now.

Sumitra placed the lamp on the threshold, sniffed her kerosene stained hands, rubbed them on her hair and sat down. Vaguely uneasy, Sethu watched her as she sat in the shadow. Her red glass bangles glittered.

Sumitra stared at the rain and asked, "When are you going next to Kumaranalloor?"

"I have to go and collect my certificate." His heart raced as he said it. How could he be so arrogant and presume he would pass? Bhagavathi, forgive me!

"Can you buy me red chandu for four annas?"

"I don't know."

Inside the house, Devu laughed loudly and Ammayi hushed her.

A gust of wind blew the lamp out. Sethu moved closer to Sumitra in the dark. He longed to touch her wrist, with the glass bangles circling it. Her clothes smelt faintly of washing soap. He hardly heard what Sumitra said. He felt uneasy and afraid. Sumitra seemed so distant! They had gone to school together, been in the same class, but she suddenly seemed older. He finally plucked up the courage to touch her fingertips. He was afraid she would pull her hand away, but she only smiled and said, "That's a steel ring, child. I bought it from the Chettichi."

He held her fingertips tightly and tried to smile back.

"People like us can't afford gold rings, can we, Sethu?" She took the lamp and went in. Sethu sat with his head bent, perspiring profusely, his heart racing.

He grew calmer as the roar of the first rain of the monsoon started. Large raindrops splashed on the thatched roof. A thousand isolated sounds merged into a vast symphony. Branches split with a soft crash. The old walls shivered as the thunder rolled in on them from the distance.

What would Amma say if the mud walls crumbled in the force of the rain? This great mansion!

This broken hovel, with its propped-up roof of thatch, its ghost-filled attic, its rooms that were dark even at noon—a mansion indeed!

He closed his eyes, trying to recapture the image of Sumitra's face in the coppery radiance of the smoking lamp.

4

Koyassan Mapilla of the ration shop subscribed to a newspaper. A boy from Anakkara who delivered soap brought it on his bicycle everyday.

Sethu went to the shop well in time on the day the results were expected. The boy was unusually late. He managed to grab the newspaper before the salesman in the shop put it away. There was a vast sea of numbers. His eyes found it at last, 51931. He checked again, to make sure. Yes, it was there alright. 51931. He had written down a lot of numbers but remembered only Haridas's. Haridas had failed.

He whistled as he walked home, feeling that he had conquered the world. If only someone would stop him on the way and ask; he wanted to tell everyone the news. Parameswara Ettan was at home when he got back. Amma was in the verandah talking to Appan Nair who had bought the house on the hill from the Chettis who made pappadams. He was trying to convince Amma that luck and a good horoscope were far more important than education. "Our Sivayi Pankunni Nair's son failed his tenth, didn't he? He's very rich now. If good fortune is written on your forehead, you don't need to pass a single examination."

Parameswara Ettan had failed the intermediate examination three times and worked in a bank near his wife's place now. Ettan had moved away to a corner of the courtyard, as if he was not interested in Appan Nair's arguments.

Amma and Cheriamma knew that Sethu had gone to find out his results. He had expected them to rush up to him when he came back.

"Where have you been, so early in the morning?" At least Appan Nair had thought to ask him.

"To check my results."

"Did you pass?"

Irritated, he grunted, "Hm."

"Do you have the first rank?"

"I don't know. The mark lists have not come."

Parameswara Ettan came up to them slowly, tearing a mango leaf into little shreds. "Have you sent for an application form for admission to a college?"

He nodded, not looking at Parameswara Ettan. Each time Ettan had failed, there had been a scene at home. Amma had defended him, "It's not that he's stupid. Or that he hasn't worked hard. His horoscope says it's a bad time now."

Sethu stomped up the stairs, threw off his shirt, came down. He ran out, up the hill. Obviously, his family did not think that the fact that he, Sethumadhavan, had passed the examination was an important event.

When he came down the hill, he saw the cheruman children catching crabs by the canal. The old mango tree which belonged to the illam was about to fall into the fields, since the earth at its roots had been washed away. As children, Unni Namboodiri, Sumitra and Sethu used to take turns to sit under the tree to catch the mangoes as they fell, before the cowherd boys could get at them. The mangoes were stringy, but large and very sweet. They used to fall into the seedling beds. The children had to vault over the fence, grab the fruit and run back. If Raghava Kurup, who owned the fields, or one of the workers saw them, they would be severely scolded.

"What are you doing here, Sethu?"

Sumitra. She wore a red silk blouse and a new, unbleached mundu. Seeing that Sethu had noticed them, she said, "I went to the temple this morning." The sandalwood paste she had smeared over her forehead was almost dissolved in sweat.

"Where are you going?" he asked.

"I went to borrow a hatchet from carpenter Raman, but he was not there. The other wretch will never give it to me."

She seemed taller, maybe because she had worn her mundu down, covering the ankles. Sumitra told him how crowded the temple had been; how her eyes had smarted with blowing on the firewood while cooking jaggery-rice.

"Parameswara Ettan is here, isn't he?"

"Yes."

"Is he going back today?"

Parameswara Ettan and Amma must be discussing his future now.

"Yes." Parameswara Ettan rarely came home, now that he was married. And he never stayed the night.

Sumitra's arms and neck were such a beautiful colour. He looked at his own arms which were dark, almost black. He felt too shy to even smile at Sumitra. He was embarrassed whenever he saw his large teeth with the gaps between them in the mirror. He could never keep his prickly hair neatly combed.

Sumitra walked along casually, reaching out to pluck seeds from the kongini bushes on the roadside. He was sure she was not aware of his presence. He would never come out again with his mundu tucked up like a small boy's. She obviously did not think of him as someone who had passed his tenth. No one did.

"I'm going away soon to Palghat, to college."

At the turn of the path, Sumitra said, "I'm going to look for my goats." She clambered up, holding on to the bushes, and disappeared into the jnaval grove. He stood where he was, not sure why she had taken no notice when he told her he was going away. He followed her. His legs smarted where thorns grazed them. He quickened his pace, trying to catch up with her and noticed a long weal on his leg.

Beyond the jnaval grove was a hill covered with rocks. It was a big hill and the whole countryside was visible from the top. Sumitra was nowhere to be seen. He came down again and heard her call out to the goats.

It began to drizzle. The rain gathered force as he came down the hill. He ran down the path and took shelter beneath a clump of bamboo. But the rain was too heavy. He took refuge under the teak tree. It had begun to pour steadily. He heard footsteps splash through the muddy water flowing down the hillside. There was a small sheltered area under a cluster of branches that stood clear of the river. Sumitra ran towards it, cursing the rain.

She wiped her hair and face and said, "What a nuisance. My mundu is completely dirty."

She was soaked. Her wet blouse clung to her skin. He pretended not to notice when her wet arms brushed against his ribs.

A gust of wind moved the leaves above them and dislodged water by the potful.

The rain grew heavier. Sumitra called him to follow and ran towards a little cave that had taken shape when that part of the hillside had been dug out to make bricks to repair the road. The goats were huddled there. She pushed them out and crept in. Sethu followed, trying to avoid stepping on the goat droppings. If they stood up, they would bump their heads. Water mixed with clay coursed down the slope over the cave.

They could see the bean patch in the kitchen yard of the illam and the pounding stone from here.

He stood quietly, his heart beating fast.

She said, "Do you remember being afraid and running away when you saw Kunjan Namboodiri being cremated?"

He smiled. Why had she thought of that now?

He looked at Sumitra from the corner of his eye as she crouched on the ground, scribbling on the wet clay with a twig. He tried to get closer to her but she moved away and asked, "Why are you pushing me?"

He did not reply. He said very softly, "You're all wet, Sumitra." He drew his finger gently down the back of her wet blouse. She did not move. He put his hand on her shoulder and thought he felt her tremble. Slipping his left hand around her neck, he tried to embrace her, but she sprang up. Her eyes, wide as the sky, almost blinded his vision.

"What are you doing, Sethu?"

He got up, still holding her obstinately, mumbling something indistinctly. He did not dare look at her. His head brushed against the wet earth above. The odour of sweat and wet sandalwood was strong in his nostrils.

It was his moment of victory. Her struggling body lay quiet in his arms, which had suddenly grown strong. Her face lay tucked into his neck. Waves of heat and cold coursed alternately through him as he broke away from her.

The old Sethu once more, he looked timidly at her face and could not believe what he saw. There was a soft, moist smile in the eyes that had so recently held fire and, instead of trembling with anger, her lips quivered shyly.

They stood there listening to the sound of the rain diminish.

"It's stopped raining." She vaulted onto the path and ran away. Sethu lingered, trying to capture the scent of sandalwood.

When he walked home through a fine drizzle, he felt that his heart was brimming over with joy like a field overflowing from the Thulam rains.

Amma asked, "Where were you?"

He did not answer. He wanted to tell the world, I, Sethu, embraced Sumitra today.

Parameswara Ettan's leather bag was not upstairs. He must have left.

He did not find it difficult to get through the long, hot days, waiting for his interview card. He began to listen for Sumitra's voice. He would sit by the railings upstairs and call out softly if she passed by. She would stand in the courtyard and look up at him.

He felt too shy to talk to her in front of the others.

And now he was about to leave.

The old tin trunk had been cleaned with a cloth dipped in kerosene. Four shirts, four mundus. Two of the shirts had been tailored when he was in the eighth. Made of coarse, thick, striped material that reminded him of pillow cases, they looked as if they would never tear.

Parameswara Ettan had come the day before. He could not go with Sethu, he had no leave. Madhava Ammama would take him. But Parameswara Ettan had gone alone to college, thought Sethu.

Achan had sent a hundred rupees. Parameswara Ettan had calculated that they needed fifty rupees more. It was Madhava Ammama who had suggested asking Kunhathol. They had just sold some paddy and she would have the cash. She would not refuse if they asked.

He heard Sumitra's voice outside. He closed his trunk and peered through the window. She disappeared around the corner of the house. He waited until she came back and whispered, "Sh."

She shaded her face from the sun with her hand and looked up.

"Come here."

"Why?" Her voice was soft, but he thought she sounded nervous.

"Come on."

She looked around doubtfully.

He called loudly, "Sumitre, I've spread my towel out on that wall. See if it's dry."

"Yes it is." Her voice trembled.

"Bring it here."

Her footsteps on the stairs sent a shiver through him. His heart beat very fast as she came into the room.

"When are you leaving, Sethu?"

"On the early morning train." He placed his hand on her shoulder and said, "Sit down."

"No, I'll stand."

"Sit down, please." He caught her hands and made her sit down. She trembled violently. A hurricane tore through his mind.

"No, no."

He paid no attention.

"Sethu!"

For the first time in his life, he forgot to be shy. Sumitra twisted in his grasp as his burning fingers ran over the flesh at her waist, tender as a banana stem.

He listened to her go down the stairs, heard her voice outside the kitchen and slowly got up. The oil from her hair had made indistinct patterns on the ochre coloured floor. He traced his initials in them: PKS.

He went to the window as her footsteps receded.

No one has the right to touch Sumitra now.

Only I can touch her.

I, Sethu.

PART TWO

1

The small, two-storeyed house had sixteen rooms and had been acquired as a hostel only recently. The main building was exclusively for senior students. There were two other hostels some distance away. Sethu was pleased when the warden said he would give him a room in the hostel called "Premakumar." It was a dilapidated place and the floor was always covered with dust blown in by the traffic that roared past it on both sides. Nevertheless, the name teased his imagination and stirred a lingering fragrance through his mind.

Who was Premakumar? No one knew, not even the old watchman Nagu. The owners lived in some distant place.

When timber lorries from Mannarghat rounded the corner, the screech of brakes and the scrape of tyres often startled Sethu out of sleep. This had once been someone's home and Premakumar must have been the son of the family. Had he woken up like this as well, when the lorries roared past, and tried to recall the image of a young girl, her face beaded with perspiration?

At dusk, the students stood on the verandah and looked at the street, the pulsating artery of the town. Sethu asked himself, was this really the city he had dreamed of, lying on the window ledge at home? At night, when the street was empty and yellow circles of light lay around the lamp-posts, Sethu loved to gaze at the crossroads, wrapped in a dream-like mist.

In the evening, after class, students were not allowed out on the verandah. All the same, they gathered there to watch girls pass by. Bicycles and horse carriages would go past, flooding the road with colour. The young men stood smoking behind the round pillars, praying that one of the girls would look up for just a moment.

Sethu never went to the verandah unless it was empty. He felt awkward about meeting students who would recognize him.

When he arrived two months ago he had been nicknamed "Earrings" because he had been the only boy who wore them. He had worn his little earrings with the red stones for as long as he could remember and had never dreamed that they would be used against him. One Sunday, a group of boys rushed in from the main hostel carrying mugs of water mixed with soot. Someone warned him, "The seniors are going to duck us." Some of the boys were dragged towards the well. Closed doors were kicked open. Sethu did not understand what it was all about. He panicked and ran to the warden's house. Gasping for breath, he said, "The seniors have attacked our hostel." When the warden asked for names, he gave them. He tried not to look hurt when the warden told him coldly that he would look into the matter.

He delayed going back as long as he could. When he finally reached the hostel, everything seemed deceptively calm. But his room-mate Swamy said, "They know." The boy with the red stone earrings had betrayed them. He took off the earrings and, with Swamy's help, hid them at the bottom of his trunk. He tried to convince himself that no one would recognize him, but they came for him at night. They stripped him, hung a garland of slippers around his neck and carried him in a procession around the rooms. He did not cry until they freed him. The pain in his throat became a lump that choked him.

The boys now standing in the verandah might have forgotten him. But he was reluctant to face them all the same.

The girls' hostel was a furlong away. Two of its upstairs windows could be seen from near the three round pillars in the verandah. Shadows moved behind the yellow curtains at night. The boys gathered outside Sethu's room to look at them as soon as the warden finished his rounds.

A woman's shadow.

Malini? No, that's Leelavathi.

Want to take a bet?

How will we find out?

Balakrishnan from Payyanoor had an idea. He exhausted an entire box of Bengal lights each night so that Malini, the shadow behind the yellow curtain, could see his face in their flare.

Balakrishnan, Ganapathy and Sivasankaran formed a little group. They scaled the walls at night to go to the cinema, pursued the girls on bicycles, and smoked. Sethu could not afford these luxuries, so he stayed aloof and decided to be good.

His room-mate, Swamy, was the son of a rich merchant. But Swamy was very careful with his money and kept meticulous accounts in a little pocketbook. Sivasankaran had to try for a whole week to get Swamy to treat him to a cup of tea. He succeeded at last and Swamy wrote in his notebook, muttering angrily to himself, charity— one anna.

Sethu was sent sixty rupees from home on the second of every month. After he paid his hostel dues and the laundry charges, he barely had ten rupees left to manage on for the rest of the month. He wrote to his relatives without actually mentioning money. Dear Sankarankutty Ettan, I hope you are well. I joined college in June and am staying in the hostel. If only one of them would send him some money. They were all happy to know he was in college and some of them even wrote to say so. But that was all.

One Saturday, as he came downstairs, he heard the hostel peon, Ramakrishnan, arguing with someone. A group of students were gathered near the gate around a shrivelled woman clothed in rags. She had a dirty, dark-skinned baby at her breast. The boys nudged each other meaningfully as she nursed the baby unashamedly, fondling it while it suckled her withered nipple and talking all the while to Ramakrishnan.

She was from Kozhinjambara and her Malayalam had Tamil inflections. She had already walked nine miles in search of the baby's father. When she had gone to the workshop he had mentioned to her, they had told her that no one by that name worked there.

He suddenly thought of the heroines of the novels which Haridasan had lent him.

Oh God, Sumitra!

- Tell us, wretch, we'll make you tell us.

- You won't? You slut! You won't?

What if Ammayi tied her to the pillar and whipped her, to make her tell them? He shuddered. His mind wandered when he tried to study.

The men of the Padinjarakalathil family had always had an excellent reputation. Sethu was so quiet, so intelligent. And yet, he had done this!

Swamy studied for two hours every evening, from eight to ten. He would then push the two small tables they studied at together, hang a mosquito net over them, tying its corners to nails on the walls, say his prayers and lie down on this improvised bed. He usually got up at five. Sethu slept late and never got up before seven.

The hostel boys managed to collect a whole rupee for the woman from Kozhinjambara to which Swamy's contribution was an anna. While noting the sum down at night, he said, "Looking for him in a workshop indeed! It's a lie. She should have been slapped for her impudence."

Sethu did not say anything. As soon as Swamy went to sleep, he spread his mattress on the floor and turned off the light. He tried not to think about Sumitra. He heard the roar of the lorries on the road as they approached and then receded.

He thought of the time when the villagers had gathered around the tank where a cherumi's corpse had been found floating. He had been in the fourth class at the time. He fell asleep and dreamt of the dilapidated tank surrounded by screwpine bushes, at the edge of the field, and the corpse floating in it. He woke up with a start and wondered what the time was. His body was bathed in sweat and he could hear his heart racing wildly. The street lights flickered through the iron window bars.

He tried to erase Sumitra from his mind and think of all the girls in his class. Most of them were grown-up. The youngest was Shyamala Nair, who still wore a skirt. He had noticed her the very first day, when the names were called out from the attendance register.

Three hundred and sixty—Sethumadhavan.

Savitri, M.

Savitri, P. R.

Somasundaram.

Shyamala Nair. Large, bright eyes dominated the small face.

The boys talked animatedly when coming back from class. Malini stared at Kunhikrishnan all the time. Nalini always smiled at Chandran. Achamma laughed whenever Rajan said something funny. No one mentioned Shyamala. Sethu said a prayer. Hidden desires can turn into prayers. If ever anyone takes notice of me, let it be Shyamala. He wanted her large eyes to look at him once, at least once.

The day Sivasankaran's money order came, he invited Sethu for coffee. Swamy refused to go with them, so there were only the three of them, Sivasankaran, Prabhakaran and Sethu. Sivasankaran liked to eat biriyani once a week. He was a football player and believed in body building.

They went to the Madras Cafe. Sethu said he did not want biriyani, or chops.

"You're a vegetarian?"

"Yes." It was a lie. Sivasankaran would pay today, but Sethu would have to pay next week.

In his high school days, his mouth used to water whenever he saw meat being served in Balan Nair's hotel. A plate of mutton with the meal cost an extra four annas. The fat old man who sold mats at the local market on Wednesdays always ordered two plates for himself. Sethu used to watch the old man enviously. His mouth would water every time he thought of the flavour and aroma of the coconut fried in the oil used for cooking the chicken that had been sacrificed for the Bhuvaneswari puja.

Controlling himself, he said, "Just a tea for me."

They sat in one of the little cubicles marked out by faded glass panes. Sivasankaran gave the order and went to wash his hands. He came back and whispered, "Shyamala Nair is in the next room."

"Who else?"

"Lots of other people."

Prabhakaran said, "Her father is an advocate."

Sethu cursed Sivasankaran for eating so slowly and with such relish. He wanted to be outside when Shyamala left, wanted her to see him leave Madras Cafe.

They heard the voices of boys in the next room.

Sivasankaran paid, bought a cigarette for himself and asked Prabhakaran whether he wanted one. Prabhakaran hesitated, then bought one too.

"There's no point asking Sethu."

"But I want one." Sethu spoke with confidence but felt that Sivasankaran did not believe him. Sethu went into the street, spitting out the cigarette fumes he could not swallow and saw Shyamala leave with her companions. Maybe they were relatives. They got into a car parked near the lamp-post. A fat man with glasses drove it away. None of them looked at the boys.

Sethu coughed and spluttered, but did not throw away his cigarette. In the hostel someone asked where they had been.

"To town."

"Shopping?"

"No. To the Madras Cafe," said Sivasankaran. Sethu was proud to be part of the group.

Swamy asked him at night, "So you smoke?"

"No."

"Lies. You smell of cigarettes."

Embarrassed, he admitted, "I smoked one. But I won't make a habit of it."

Swamy thought well of Sethu because he spent his free time in the library and did not keep bad company or use bad language. But what would Swamy and the others say if they knew what would happen when he went back home?

He lay awake at night, cursing himself. He had not thought of anything like this the day Sumitra came up to his room. How could he find out whether a sixteen-year-old could father a child? Whom would he ask?

A week later, there was a letter from Parameswara Ettan. In an envelope. Parameswara Ettan seldom wrote letters. Had Amma written to him and . . . ? He went to a deserted corner of the verandah and opened the letter with trembling hands. Oh God, forgive me this once. I'll never do it again. Forgive me for the sin I committed!

He breathed normally only when he had finished reading. His heart steadied in the calm after a violent hurricane. The letter was about next month's fees. Achan could spare only sixty rupees. Could he find out from the office whether he could pay in two instalments? Hoping to see you at Michaelmas.

Of course they knew. They were waiting to get at him when he went home at Michaelmas.

He felt sorry for having been so foolish. How silly of him to have thought that all the beauty in the world was contained in

Sumitra. He had realized how wrong he was when he saw the riot of colours splashed on the balcony of the Pavilion Hall.

2

The Onam and Michelmas holidays coincided this time. Swamy decided to take his trunk home, so Sethu was able to borrow his leather bag. He packed freshly laundered shirts, mundus and a few books. He left on Friday night while the others were still celebrating the start of a fortnight's holiday. It was the first time they were going home after they had joined college.

Sethu pretended to laugh and joke with his friends. He played carroms, and smoked the cigarette they were given after the feast. All the time, he wondered what would happen when he reached home in the morning. Hiding his uneasiness, he stayed with the others, afraid to be alone.

Maybe I won't come back.

He would go away to a place where no one knew him. He was tired of running away from familiar faces.

Man was first prevailed upon to commit a sin by the serpent. When he had looked out through the railings upstairs, the serpent's hood had fanned out in the recesses of his mind. Standing on the uncovered station platform open to the icy wind that hurtled down the western mountain pass, he could not help thinking of the story from the Bible.

He imagined himself being heroic. Don't touch her. It was my fault, Amme.

You!

Yes, I. He would go up to her as she stood with her head bent, tears running down her cheeks. He would take her hand and lead her into the great wide world. He would say to her in his heart, so that only she could hear, I will always be with you.

But he only had to think of Parameswara Ettan's or Achan's face for this bright image to dissolve into darkness like a path visible only during a flash of lightning.

A bell rang. The platform suddenly came alive. There were students going as far as Kasaragode. They whistled, smoked and talked loudly in the mixture of English and Malayalam that identified them as students.

Sethu shrank from the jostling, pushing, kicking crowd in the train. Latecomers were being shouted at, those who had come early and secured good seats were delighted with themselves. People cursed as they dashed against steel trunks which got in their way.

Raghavan Nambiar from Cannanore had managed to secure a few seats by spreading a big towel over them. He invited Sethu to share one. An old man squatted near the bathroom. Sethu pretended not to see the woman who stood next to him, leaning on the window, and hoped that none of those who had studied the poem "Chivalry" in class were around.

Wierd images kept pace with the rhythm of the moving train. The air was full of the stale smell of sweat, beedi smoke and human breath. Balakrishnan from Payyanoor had wedged himself among the straw baskets and steel trunks in the luggage rack above Sethu. He and Nambiar talked late into the night.

The train hissed and panted its way through the darkness like some giant reptile. Sethu watched sparks fly through the window and melt into the night. The woman he had seen earlier was asleep on the wet, dirty floor littered with orange peel. The glass shade of the flickering lamp swung loose. He watched the moths which circled the bulb.

The train would arrive at the station at five thirty. He tried to see himself as a young man returning to his village from a city forty-five miles away.

The station platform, dimly lit by glass-shaded kerosene lamps, was deserted. He was lucky, none of his friends had woken up. They might have asked him his address. He could not bear to think of any of them dropping in. He still remembered the shameful experience of Haridasan's visit from long ago.

He waited on the cement bench until the darkness paled into daylight, feeling very sleepy.

The ferryman recognized him. "Home from school?"

He did not bother to explain the difference between college and school.

It was the first boat of the day and was full of vendors who had come to sell their goods in the local market. He was relieved there was no one who knew him. On its return journey he was the only passenger. The breeze felt cool. The fields lay ready for the harvest.

His heart started to beat faster as he neared home. He summoned up all the courage he had to enter. The old cherumi was sweeping the yard. Amma was seated on the verandah, teasing out the strands of her hair, her betel box beside her. Madhava Ammama sat on the steps, cleaning his teeth. The carpet of flowers laid out the day before for the Onam season had dissolved into the moist cowdung and the flowers lay scattered, disgustingly dirty.

He put his bag down, afraid to look at Amma. He was sure she would explode. Was this the calm before the storm?

"How many days' holidays do you have?"

The fresh breeze that blew over the fields cooled his thoughts as well. He sat down on the the verandah ledge, breathed normally and said, "Two weeks."

He heard the sound of goats' hooves. "This way, little kid, or I'll. . . . " Sumitra's voice. She herded the goats through the western courtyard and noticed Sethu only when she was right outside the house. She came in smiling.

Sumitra pulled down the upturned end of her mundu from her waist and asked, "Have you just come, Sethu?" She did not look like the sorrowful heroine he had imagined. She was the same Sumitra he had seen in June. But she seemed unusually reluctant to meet his eyes. She said to Amma,

"Hasn't Sethu grown taller?"

Sethu smiled. He was sure she had noticed his collar, still stiff after a night's journey, and his cuffs, turned up at the elbows. For the sake of saying something, he asked when Onam was.

Amma said, "Friday. Parameswaran has written that he is going south." To his wife's place, of course.

"We haven't harvested. I don't know how we'll find the money to celebrate Onam. We can do without a feast ourselves, but we have to feed the cherumans and their families the day after Onam. How can we do away with old customs like that? Madhavan." Amma turned to Madhava Ammama who was cleaning his teeth noisily on the other side of the verandah. Feeling nauseated, Sethu took up his bag and went upstairs. At the door, he looked back. Sumitra's eyes were following him.

3

Parameswara Ettan left soon after the Onam lunch. He had come on the morning bus. Amma said angrily, "He can't stay away from her even for a minute, the oaf."

Lying upstairs, he could hear the Onakkali songs from the illam. He had not taken off his shirt after lunch even though he had been sweating. The day after he arrived, Amma had scolded him for wearing a shirt in the house, but he had taken no notice. She had not mentioned it since.

He tried to whistle a tune,

Chale jaana nahi naina milaake.

He had seen only one film in the three months he had been in college. "Badi Bahen." Kunhikrishnan used to whistle some of the songs in it. Kunhikrishnan had seen "Vazhgai" nine times. He had stolen a poster of Vyjayanthimala from some place in town and hung it in his room. He wanted to look at her face first thing in the morning and last thing at night.

Sethu had seen Ammayi and Devu go to the illam earlier in the evening. In the old days, Kunhathol used to teach the women Onakkali dances and songs. Amma, Cheriamma and Ammayi had all gone to her when they were young. Kunhathol still invited the children in the neighbourhood to dance for Onam and Thiruvathira. She gave the adults betel leaves and buttermilk. In the old days, everyone who came to the illam during the Onam season used to stay for the feast, and people came from as far as five miles away. Madhava Ammama said that since Kunhathol was now dependent on the goodwill of her tenant, Govindan, for her annual subsistence, people were no longer interested in coming a long way just for betel leaves and buttermilk. But as Onam drew near, Kunhathol still asked everyone she met to come over to the illam.

Sethu saw a flash of white move around the corner, near the path to the illam. Yes, it was Sumitra.

He hurried down and walked casually around the yard in the hot sunshine. He pretended to himself that he did not want Sumitra to see him.

Madhava Ammama leaned against the pillar, smoking a beedi. Cheriamma came out. "Where's that wretched girl? She's going

to have fever now, running about in the sun after an oil bath."
Sethu had seen Padmu run towards the illam, but he kept quiet.

He went upstairs again and saw Sumitra pass by. Maybe she
was on her way to the illam. She paused under the neem tree and
looked up. She wore an unbleached mundu with a black border.
Her face was flushed. Her blouse with the blue flowers seemed
too tight for her. Had she grown taller since yesterday?

Madhava Ammama was serving lunch to the old mapilla
boatman. Amma would be there as well. In spite of this, he waved
boldly to Sumitra. She smiled into the sunlight and walked
towards the illam fence.

He felt sleepy. But what if he missed Sumitra when she came back?

Who was that, coming through the banana grove, towards
the fence? Yes, it was Sumitra. She looked straight up at the
railings, smiled and walked quickly on. Madhava Amamma asked
her, "Why did you come back, Sumitra?"

"The bitter gourd has been left out to dry in the courtyard and
there's no one at home."

Sethu's drowsiness cleared at once. There was no one at Vadakkethu. He set off for the areca nut grove as if he was going
for a walk in the compound. When he came to the broken fence
outside Vadakkethu, he looked around to make sure no one saw
him. The courtyard was deserted. He cleared his throat and went
in. Sumitra was near the bean patch, her hair spread out over her
shoulders.

"Where's Ammayi, Sumitre?" His voice was rough.

"They're all at the illam. I came back because the bitter gourd
had been left out to dry."

He climbed into the verandah.

"Shall I bring you bananas and chips, Sethu?"

"No." She went into the house and he followed her. It was very
dark. His eyes were blinded, coming in from the bright sunlight.
He waited, trying to get used to the darkness. Sumitra opened
the door of the southern room and the bolt screeched as it moved,
startling him.

He prayed no one would see him now, Sethu who was so good,
who never smoked beedis or went to teashops.

Light filtered into the little room through the rounded bars
above the window ledge. Old mattresses were heaped on the cot.
There was a big box on the floor. An earthenware pot hung from

the ceiling. The odour of worn, oil-stained clothes and incense hung in the room.

They stood close to each other, not talking. When she closed the window, it was pitch dark. Starched cloth rustled as it was ripped away. A mingled smell of sweat, sandalwood and melted camphor closed in on his consciousness.

"Who's that?" Sumitra's frightened voice startled him. Someone coughed outside. She pressed her fingers on his trembling arms and got up. He lay half conscious, his eyes closed. A buzzing noise, like that of bees, filled his ears.

Sumitra came back smiling.

"It was Madhavettan. He wanted the bucket."

"Has he gone?"

"Yes."

He grinned foolishly as they stepped out into the bright yellow sunlight. She smiled at him with a touch of scorn.

"This will last only till you go away, isn't it? Afterwards, you'll forget."

"What an idea!" he said, without meeting her eyes. He could not bring himself to say, "I won't forget." He reached the areca nut grove with a sense of relief. Her huge, kohl-rimmed eyes had made him feel insignificant.

She called out, "Wait."

He stopped. What was she going to say?

"Don't worry, I just wanted to make sure there was no kohl on your face." He waited, as if he needed her permission to leave.

"Go on, then."

When he walked home through the cool, shaded garden, he felt no sense of victory. His mind was still filled with the confusion that had taken hold of him when he looked into Sumitra's shining eyes.

4

People were seated all over the maidan, on the concrete benches and on the grass. At four, they would start to play film songs over the loudspeakers. Sethu loved the few moments before the mercury lamps came on, when human forms moving in the shadow of the fort became indistinct shapes in the waning sunlight. They were the moments when he could hear the vague murmurings of his own heart.

Behind him lay a tomb that belonged to history.

They found a place away from the crowd, on the southern side of the fort, from where they could see the marks made by the cannon balls. Sethu had been inside the fort only once. The first thing that had caught his attention had been the old trees and their tired branches trailing on the ground. When he walked around the red-painted jail, he had heard the footsteps of the prisoners through the mesh-covered ventilators. Later, he had heard blows and the sound of screams. He had come out quickly, trembling with fear.

Prabhakaran threw stones into the moat and asked,

"What are you thinking about?"

"Mm."

College would reopen tomorrow. Many of the students had not yet returned. When he had gone for a walk in the afternoon, Sethu had seen a letter addressed to him, P. K. Sethumadhavan, in the letter box in front of the old-fashioned tiled office building.

It had arrived four weeks ago and was from Haridasan. From Vishakapatnam, where he was working on a ship, the INS Jalaja. His food and uniform were free and he earned sixty rupees a month. After a year they would increase his salary. Haridasan had described his first voyage, from Bombay to Vishakapatnam. There was a postscript underneath the long letter. Our TKP is married. To an agent dealing in rolled gold. I saw him. A horrible creature. He limps like a rheumatic buffalo.

Sethu told his friends about Haridasan. Events from his high school life seemed to belong to a distant past. Last year seemed so long ago!

Sivasankaran boasted about a daring feat he had performed during the Onam break. A Muslim girl lived in a thatched hut next to his house. One night he had cut the ropes that held the thatch in place with a blade and entered her hut. It was pitch dark. He did not know that the girl slept next to her mother. Groping in the dark, he found the mother's foot! She cursed the cat in her sleep. Everyone laughed. Sethu tried to laugh too.

Rajan from Cherpulasserry wanted to become a doctor. His father's brother was an influential executive in Madras. All Prabhakaran needed was a BSc after which he would do Textile

Technology in Benaras. His uncle, who was a dyeing master in one of the big Ahmedabad mills, had advised him to do a course in Textile Technology.

They asked, "What did you do in the holidays, Sethu?"

Achan had come the day before Onam and stayed four days. Sethu wanted a watch and had gone up to the gate with him to ask for one, but had not done so in the end. So there was nothing he had achieved in the vacation. He smiled and said, "I read. There was nothing else to do."

"That's not true."

If he closed his eyes, he could hear the crackle of unbleached cotton falling away from the skin and breathe the odour of incense in the dark room.

He kept quiet.

"You don't have to pretend, we know. How many m's do you have at home?"

"M's?"

"Maidservants."

Sivasankaran was the son of a wealthy landowner in Ottappalam. What did he know of people like Sethu?

"Two," he lied.

"How old are they?"

He had to tell another lie to cover up the first one, "Old, very old."

"And don't they have any relatives at home?"

"No."

"Indeed. I don't believe there's anyone who has not been initiated by a maidservant."

Sethu smiled foolishly. His companions accepted this as an admission of guilt. He hid his astonishment and listened to Sivasankaran and Prabhakaran talk with a casual air.

"I persuaded my sister to give me fifty rupees."

"I went to Guruvayoor in my uncle's car."

"I took away two shirts from my brother's box."

When they got back to the hostel there was a message to say that the warden wanted to see Sethu.

A big built rough-looking young man with a moustache stood outside the warden's house. "This is Krishnankutty," said the warden. "You'll have to share your room with him." Sethu realized only then that the young man was a student. Krishnankutty waited quietly.

"You have a corner room, don't you? We used to put in three students there." The warden made sure he had no excuse. Sethu consented and came out. He cursed his bad luck as he hurried away. Krishnankutty caught up with him in front of the soda factory.

"May I come with you?"

Sethu did not reply.

"I was in a lodge till now. It was so noisy, I couldn't read at all."

"Which year are you?"

"First. History." Krishnankutty had stayed at home for five years after doing his SSLC and then decided to come back to study.

"All I need is a place for my box and books. I can sleep in the common room or the verandah." His voice sounded gentle, though he looked rough.

Most of the hostel students stayed aloof from him but Sethu learnt to like and respect the taciturn and studious Krishnankutty. Krishnankutty usually went for a walk in the evenings. If there was a political meeting, he listened to the speeches. Otherwise he walked three or four miles along the railroad track. One evening he invited Sethu to go with him.

They walked towards the river which had narrowed to a stream that tumbled over the scattered, misshapen rocks.

Sethu felt he had to say something. "Sivasankaran and Prabhakaran are going to Coimbatore tomorrow afternoon to see Tara Singh fight."

Krishnankutty asked unexpectedly, "Do you want to be like them?"

The severity of his tone made Sethu feel small. He did not know what to say. Krishnankutty's eyes had narrowed to slits. "I detest those who like to show off that they have money. They think they are princes. They will know what life is like when they go out into the world in four years' time. Why don't they try to understand?"

Sethu said nothing.

"What use is it to be the leader of a handful of students in a hostel or in class?"

Sethu felt uncomfortable. "I."

"I'm not talking about you. I just don't think poverty is something one should be ashamed of."

"We are not rich," said Sethu.

Krishnankutty's father had a coconut plantation and land that yielded five hundred paras of paddy. He could have become part of the fashionable set in college with just the proceeds from the sale of the coconut palm branches that fell down on the ground. Sethu was astonished to know that he had worked in the Rural Credit Society in his village for four years to make enough money to pay for his studies.

Krishnankutty gazed at the little structure that had been built in the middle of the river, amongst the rocks, for a sanyasi. Before Sethu could ask, he said that all he wanted was to take a BT degree and go back to his village as a schoolteacher. He had fallen out with his father because he was in love with a girl of whom his father disapproved.

His father drank heavily, Every evening, he would drink with his friends. The house was as noisy as a market-place till midnight. "It seems a mark of prestige for rich people like him to behave like that."

"And your mother?"

"She's been mentally ill for nine years now. An incurable condition. She had to be shut up in a room. The maidservants run the house."

Sethu imagined the scene as Krishnankutty described it. The son would be summoned before the group of drunken people. "Here he comes, my beloved son. Mambat Sivaraman Nair's son chooses to fall in love with a woman who works in a princely household!" The son had to stay and listen. Otherwise there would be outbursts, protests, the clatter of crashing china and neighbours would come to find out what was wrong, while the mother, who usually sat praying like an ascetic, would tear her clothes and scream. Rather than provoke all of this, the son would give in quietly.

Krishnankutty escaped to the girl's house whenever he could. He said, "I don't think I am in love. I think of the little house with its mud walls, its thatched roof and its soot-smeared floor as a refuge. It is my father and his friends who made my going there a crime.

"Does it surprise you, Sethu, that I talk about my father this way? When I was a child, he was a God to me. I used to feel so proud when people pointed to me as Sivaraman Nair's son. I began to realize the truth as I grew up. My father has a bell in his room upstairs. The maidservants know which of them is being summoned for two rings, which for three. While one of them is there, the others cannot go up."

Sethu stared silently at the darkening river in order to avoid looking at Krishnankutty's resentful face.

One day, Krishnankutty had confronted his father and moved out of the house to an unused room at the top of the gatehouse. When he went to the girl's house that evening, he said, "I will marry you as soon as I can support you, if you are willing." Her paralysed father, who lay holding pigeons close to his body to bring warmth to his limbs, heard what he said. The girl said nothing.

She was not beautiful or educated. She had left school after the eighth class. She began to visit him often, in his room above the gatehouse. Even at night.

"I've never touched her, although there were many occasions when I could have done so. We talked a lot, that was all." Krishnankutty's voice sounded like the murmur of a deep forest stream.

"I think of her often now. Her letters make me feel restless. Is this love? I do not know. You write poetry in the college magazine. Tell me, is this love?" Sethu made an effort to smile.

Krishnankutty seemed to be at peace as they walked back to the hostel over the railroad tracks. He even attempted to whistle lightheartedly. But Sethu felt restless and uneasy. He thought, I must go to Krishnankutty's wedding, wherever it is and say to his wife, when he introduces her to me, "I've known you for years."

He had realized what a happy experience it was to fall in love and get married at Parameswara Ettan's wedding. Ettan had remained cool and unruffled, although he was the centre of attention. Pretty, fair, Sarojini Edathi loved his brother! Sethu had felt a great respect for him. Parameswara Ettan was very dark.

Sarojini Edathi was Achan's niece. Achan and his relatives had approved of the match but Amma was against it, since she had never been on good terms with Achan's family. Amma's justification was that Achan had given all the earnings from the tea estate to his nephews and nieces. Amma said that Achan's relatives prayed earnestly for Amma and her family to fall ill. When they were all at a relative's wedding, Amma had been coerced into giving her consent for Parameswara Ettan to marry Sarojini Edathi.

Sethu remembered only two women who were at that wedding. One was the bride, the other was the girl who later became his sister-in-law. He loved her, in her blue saree with the silver flowers.

When she came to his house as a bride, it was Sethu who used to go with her to the river. He would look for fallen jnaval fruit that were not crushed and take them to her. He loved to watch her little white teeth, like grains of fine rice, bite into the ripe flesh and turn purple.

When he was in the eighth, Amma and Edathi Amma had a quarrel. Amma started it. "I know that women from Thrissur have an evil reputation."

Sarojini Edathi's voice, usually so soft, grew high with anger.

Amma went on, "You wretch, the only reason I consented to the marriage was because I did not want a woman to hang herself or jump in a well because of my son. Out of kindness. Not because the sorceress from Thrissur impressed me. And people respect me, so they don't ask why my son's wife, who is eight months gone . . . . "

Cheriamma begged her, "Softly, Edathi." Parameswara Ettan and his wife moved to a rented house near the bank where he worked the very next day. Sethu had been resentful of his mother for sending his sister-in-law away. She used to wash his clothes with 501 soap and fold them neatly so that there were no creases. The scent of talcum powder and perfumed chandu had flowed away from the house with her.

He imagined Krishnankutty starting life with the girl he loved.

Entering the road at the railway crossing, they saw groups of girls going back from the temple to the hostel. Their faces were indistinct in the dusk. Krishnankutty asked,

"What are you thinking about?"

"Nothing."

"Are you wondering why I told you all this?"

Sethu grunted noncommittally.

"I have to talk about it sometimes, otherwise I'm afraid my very features might change. I know that constant tension has already given me a cruel look."

Suddenly, the street lamps came on. They looked pale in the dust-laden air, as if they had been startled into wakefulness.

Krishnankutty asked, "Have you never been in love?"

Had he been in love with Sumitra? When he was returning after the Onam holidays, he had seen her waiting for him in the banana grove near the gate of Vadakkethu. He was busy picking his way carefully over the slippery, muddy fields. Had it been painful to walk farther and farther away from her?

He replied, in as expressionless a voice as he could manage, "No."

Although he knew in his heart that he did not want to lose Sumitra.

Krishnankutty took his books and went to the common room. Sethu borrowed an inland letter from Swamy and sat down to write to Haridasan. The hot April afternoon when he had said goodbye to Haridasan by the canal seemed years ago. There was much to tell him. He had not met Haridasan when he went to school to collect his certificates. He must write to him about college and classes, how he had thrown up after dissecting his first frog in the Natural Science practical session, about his friends and the poem he had written for the college magazine.

But in the end all he wrote was, "Dear Haridas, I received your letter and am glad to know you've started on your new job. College life is not bad. Let me know if you are coming home." He had thought of Haridasan as a friend from whom he would never be separated. Long ago. Did he really hope that Haridasan would go on writing to him? He tried to convince himself that he did.

5

The icy December wind of the Thiruvathira season tore down the narrow mountain pass, making the palms shiver. The nights were cold. And the days blazing hot. Sethu did not go home for the holidays. He wrote to Amma that he had special classes which he could not afford to miss. He had to eat out since the college mess had closed down.

He dreaded the thought of the summer vacation. He could forget everything else as long as he stayed in this hostel in the big town, a part of its noise and confusion. It was like hiding in the little cave dug out of the clay of the hillside, sheltered behind the heavy screen of rain, listening to the roar of the wind and the rain outside.

But when he got home he discovered to his astonishment that he had become a respected member of the household. Tea was sent up to him morning and evening. It touched his heart to see Padmu come up the stairs balancing the big bell-metal glass carefully in her hand so that the tea would not spill. Padmu had grown taller this past year. And she had become wary of him.

One day, she said timidly, "Sethu Etta, I need a cloth umbrella."

"Don't you have one?"

"Only an old palm leaf one."

So Sethu Ettan had grown up. Padmu was sure he would get her what she needed. She must have asked Amma and Cheriamma already, and one of them would have said, "A cloth umbrella indeed!"

If only I had an umbrella, Sethu thought, I could have given it to her. He knew he could never save the six rupees it cost. Still, he said, "I'll get you one."

As he walked through the fields that evening, he saw Sumitra's younger sister, Karthiyayani. She was carrying packets wrapped in teak leaves. He went up to her.

"What is there in that stomach of yours?" he teased.

The nine-year-old stood shyly, her short towel barely covering her rounded abdomen. With her narrow, half-closed eyes and protruding stomach, she reminded him of the Chinese doll in the hostel warden's room.

"Where's your Sumitra Edathi?"

"Edathi is at Tirur."

"Tirur?"

"Kunjummalu Amma took her there."

Things became clearer when he heard Amma and Cheriamma talk to each other at night. Kandankulangara Appunni Menon had married a wealthy woman from Tirur. When she went home to have a baby, she had taken Sumitra with her. Ammayi made sure that no one would misunderstand the situation.

"I sent word that no one from our tarawad would ever work as a servant, even if we were starving. Then the lady came herself, big stomach and all, and said to me, would I ask her to be my servant? If you send Sumitra with me, I'll treat her like my younger sister. She's very fond of Sumitra. And it's only for ten days. Though Madhavan didn't like the idea one bit."

Sethu was taken aback to know that Appunni Menon had asked Madhava Ammama for permission. Why Madhava Ammama?

He found that the opening in the fence between his house and Ammayi's had been closed. He stood hesitating at the fence, soap and towel in hand. Amma saw him return and said,

"We've filled in that gap in the fence."

He did not ask why. Amma told him. "Cattle and goats stray in all the time. After all, people can always use the gate."

Cheriamma said to him, "Were you going for a bath, Sethu? The water at Vadakkethu is not good. Ten steps from here and you're at the river. The water there is excellent!"

Ammayi and her children did not come over as they used to.

Amma and Cheriamma talked about Sumitra going away with Kunjummalu Amma in a tone of contempt. They spoke ill of the Vadakkethu family to everyone.

When had this change taken place?

And then things began to fall into place. "He's a grown man, isn't he? And we are his older sisters. We can tell him once, twice, not more."

So Madhava Ammama was behind it. He was at Vadakkethu all the time. He looked after their affairs. Amma and Cheriamma were convinced that the Vadakkethu women had lured him there with a magic potion. Otherwise how could a man who used to turn his face away when even their names were mentioned have changed so much?

Sethu went to the river that evening for a bath. When he thought about Sumitra, he was filled with an unreasonable anger. The Kandankulangara Menons were rich. The villagers pawned their jewels and vessels with them to borrow cash or paddy. And he had heard that Kunjummalu Amma's tarawad at Tirur was an ancient, titled one.

The house must be huge. With deserted corridors and dimly lit rooms. At dusk, the bathing sheds near the tanks would be full of darkness. There would be young men in the house. College students, men with jobs. And Sumitra slept in that house. He would show her when she came back. Why had she gone away to stay with strangers? The more he thought about it, the angrier he became.

If he sat upstairs above the front verandah, he could hear what Amma and Cheriamma said to the village women who came to the courtyard to gossip. They discussed all the village scandals with Andoor Ummuttu Amma, old cherumi Kali and Beepathumma, the fisherman Muhammad's wife. If Amma or Cheriamma were by themselves, each would describe the other's atrocities as well. Cheriamma would talk of Amma's unkindness and Amma of Cheriamma's evil mind. Ummuttu Amma brought a new earthen pot one day and said, as she was leaving, "And when is Madhavan Nair going to begin his sambandham?"

Cheriamma said, "We can't make out what's come over him, Ummuttu. He used to get up and go away every time we talked about marriage. If Edathi tried to tell him that they are not strangers after all, that they need a man in the family, that they're our cousins, he would fly into a rage. Even the sound of her name used to make him furious. And now they've won him over completely with their chicken curry and their cups of tea and all the fuss they make over him."

Amma interrupted, her voice shrill with anger, "It makes my flesh creep to say it. He refused to listen when I coaxed him. Now they behave as if he belongs to them. Edathi Amma pretends to wheeze and look weak, but she knows what she wants."

Cheriamma added, "And the best bunch of bananas goes to Vadakkethu now."

Ummuttu said, "Madhavan Nair would be an excellent catch for anyone. The manager of the illam. He does the work of four. Did you hear, Chathu Nair's daughter, Janaki, has a secret lover."

Madhava Ammama came home very late. Sethu found it hard to believe when he first heard that Madhava Ammama really wanted to marry Devu with her huge ears, her bony face, hairy arms, and thick eyebrows.

Madhava Ammama ate silently and sat smoking in the verandah for a long time, leaning against the worn, cracked pillar. Sethu looked at him wonderingly. He was very dark. His hair, rough as coconut fibre, was growing thin and patches of white showed here and there on his scalp. He seldom smiled. The air whistled through the gaps in his big teeth when he spoke.

Devu did not work at the illam any more. Amma and Cheriamma thought that Madhava Ammama had asked her to stop.

"Where do you want to sleep?" Sethu was startled to hear Madhava Ammama's voice suddenly come out of the darkness.

"Upstairs or downstairs?"

"Upstairs."

Madhava Ammama spread the mattress kept folded on the wooden ledge, lit another beedi and came out. Sethu went in.

How could Madhava Ammama have changed so much?

PART THREE

1

Madhavan threw the stub of his beedi over the wall and stood up.

He watched the shadows of the banana trees dance like living beings and thought he would never be able to sleep. The old wooden boards creaked as Sethu moved around the room upstairs.

He should have asked for some drinking water. He had thought of it when his sister brought the mattress out but had not said anything to her. Somehow, his sisters made him feel ashamed. They seemed to be brimming with unasked questions.

He thought of the time last year, around Onam it was, when he hid behind the thorn bushes near Sumitra's house so that Sethu could not see him. He saw Sumitra leave her house as he was giving the ferryman lunch and then noticed her return. He went into the compound as soon as the ferryman left, paused for a while near the coconut saplings that he had planted when the rains started last year and patted the earth around them firmly into place with his foot. When he finally reached the courtyard of Sumitra's house, he had felt afraid for the first time in his life. His throat went dry and his legs trembled. Had he cleared his throat loudly enough? The door opened. He tried to compose himself. He glanced at Sumitra's face for only a moment, then he began to stare at the branches of a medicinal tree that grew near the goats' shed. Sumitra asked,

"What is it Madhavetta?"

All he could think of was to ask for the wooden water carrier used to irrigate the field, but Sumitra said it was not there. He hesitated for a moment and left. Sumitra must have thought him such a fool—the month of Karkatakam was over, they had stopped irrigating the fields and the apparatus had been dismantled.

It seemed to him just yesterday that Sumitra had been a little child, running around in a shabby red konam, her face smeared with mango juice. Yet, when he saw her now, he felt confused and never knew what to say. He cursed himself. No one had seen him go out or come back, not even Sethu. By the time he got back home, the cherumans had bundled the rice they had been given into packets and left.

He heard the women talk to each other in the kitchen and thought of how foolish he had been.

He did not want to go out again. They would be playing cards in the room over Appu Nair's shop, as they usually did during the Onam season. He decided not to join them. He lay down on the wooden ledge outside and tried to sleep. Someone called from the yard. He opened his eyes. Sankunni's man had come for the dried pepper. What a nuisance! They had discussed it just yesterday.

"Padmu!"

It was so noisy, no one heard him. He called louder.

"What is it?"

"Give me the balance. There's a man come for the pepper."

"You took it to the illam the other day and didn't bring it back."

There was no one he could send to the illam now. Would Sethu go? Madhavan had often called him to help in the past. But the boy thought no end of himself, now that he had finished school. No, he would not ask him.

He told the man to wait and set out himself.

There was a crowd of women on the northern verandah of the illam. He stood uncertainly behind the pounding shed, under the withered mandaram tree. Kunhathol noticed him, and came down, "Yes, Madhavan?"

It pleased him that he was no longer regarded as a stranger at the illam, now that he looked after its affairs. Kunhathol never used a condescending tone to him, never treated him as if he were only a manager. She talked to him directly, without reserve. When he settled accounts with her after the areca nuts and bananas were sold, Kunhathol would push aside a heap of notes and coins and say, "Madhavan, put this away." He did not draw a regular salary. Kunhathol did not know how to keep accounts and Unni Namboodiri was not interested anyway. Still, Madhavan had never once thought of taking even a five rupee note for himself.

"Can I have the balance, Kunhathol?"

"It must be in the front verandah or under the stairs. Ask Unni to find it for you."

He crossed the muddy vegetable beds and avoided looking at the women doing Onakkali dances in the yard. Was that Sumitra's voice?

That fool Unni would be stretched out on the wooden seat in the verandah, replete after the Onam feast. The rascal! He hated the sight of him. He should have been Kunhathol's mainstay in her old age. Instead of looking after the areca nut palms, he spent his time wandering around on the backs of elephants. Of course, if someone else confronted the tenant farmer Govindan, on behalf of the family, extracted some paddy from him and put it away in the granary, Unni Namboodiri was ready enough to eat it.

The goats lay on the front steps, chewing cud. Unni Namboodiri was not to be seen. The door of the inner room was open, so Madhavan peered in. The balance was not there. Perhaps Unni Namboodiri was asleep in the thekkini? No, there was no one there. Whom could he ask? They were all so busy.

He found the balance under the stairs. As he went back through the dark corridor, he heard voices behind the door of the southern room. He waited a moment, listening. The door opened slowly and he made out a face with bony cheeks and large ears.

Devu!

He had no time to move away. He saw a scream freeze in her throat. As she crept forward and passed by him, the door opened fully. Teeth stained with betel juice gleamed in the dark. Unni Namboodiri's voice seemed to come from a great distance, "What is it, Madhava?"

He left without answering. Skirting the noisy crowd in the northern yard, he hurried home, his tightly curled fists trembling with fury.

Kunhathol called out to him but he did not respond. He only walked faster.

2

All day a fire smouldered inside him. He screamed at an old cherumi who was picking up areca nuts from the ground and chased her away, threatening to break her legs if he ever saw her there again. She muttered something angrily, running her hands through her tangled hair.

He shouted at Sankunni's man who was still waiting, "Go and tell the old fool I've no time today. What a day to have chosen! I can always find another buyer if Sankunni doesn't want the pepper."

His sister scolded him, "Just when we have so many expenses. Why can't you weigh out whatever there is and get the money for it?"

"Don't try to teach me how to do things. If you're so efficient, why can't you do it yourself?"

She mumbled something and went in. She must have been surprised. He had never shouted at his elder sister before. The younger sister came up to him as he was going out.

"Are you going out?"

"No, I'm coming in."

"What's the matter with you? I only asked because I wanted you to bring me snuff for half an anna if you're going out."

On his way to the bazaar, he kept asking himself, should he tell Devu's mother at Vadakkethu?

He thought of Devu with a feeling of disgust. Of her bony frame and black hairs bristling over her arms. He was not really concerned about her though. What worried him was that she would bring the Vadakkethu family a bad name.

"Didn't you hear, at Vadakkethu?"

"You know, where our Madhavan Nair. . . ." He added, fearfully, "Whom has he married?"

"The Vadakkethu. . . ."

"You mean our. . . ." He could not think beyond that point.

He sat down on the platform outside Veerankutty's tea shop and gazed at the people passing by.

"Will you have tea, Madhavan Nair?"

"No."

Nanu Nair, the manager of Kandankulangara, remarked, "You didn't come to play cards today."

"I fell asleep.

"I stopped playing when I lost four rupees."

Fishmongers who had spread out their catch in front of Bappu's shop some distance away screamed to attract buyers. The bazaar was coming alive.

Veerankutty knew that Madhavan Nair liked fish.

"There's good veloori today."

"Ah!" He continued to stare at the chameleons entangled on the fence across the road even as they separated. He recognized the figure walking over the fields even at this distance. Unni Namboodiri. He thought Unni Namboodiri would hurry past when he saw him. But he stopped and grinned, displaying all his reddened teeth. He looked like a sacrificial goat waiting to be thrown banana peels. A short, clean towel ineffectively hid bits of his scab-covered body. He held a long torch in his hand. Madhavan cursed him silently, "The rascal!"

Appukuttan called out, "Where to, Unni Namboodiri?"

"Nowhere in particular."

"If you want to taste good bazaar tea, Unni Namboodiri, you must drink mapilla tea."

Madhavan pretended not to notice Unni Namboodiri looking at him through the corner of his eye.

Veerankutty urged, "Come on, Unni Namboodiri, don't worry. Madhavan Nair won't tell on you. Will you, Madhavan Nair?"

Unni Namboodiri stood where he was, playing with the torch.

Madhavan got down from the platform, lit his beedi at the fireplace and left.

It was very noisy in the room above Achu's shop; they were obviously still playing cards. Someone had spread out straw to dry on the stretch of road beyond the shops. These people thought the public road was like their own yard. By the river, he heard the sound of axes hitting the roots of the banyan tree that had fallen down in the gale in Karkatakam.

People were sure to ask him questions if he hung around the shops. He suddenly wanted to distance himself from everyone. He went down to the fields. The big path was wide enough here for vehicles. It led to the Kandandulangara gatehouse. Two fields more and he would be at the Vadakkethu gate. He kept his eyes on the ground.

Did someone call out? No, it could not be. Then he heard distinctly, "Madhavetta, can you come this way?"

Sumitra was standing on the steps that had been freshly smeared with cowdung. He thought she would come down into the field if he did not go up. So he walked towards her gate.

She looked as if she had just had a bath and changed out of wet clothes, as she stood teasing out the tangled strands of her hair. Her arms, which were the colour of a faded banana stem and her neck with the black thread around it still looked moist.

"Amma said we have to make an offering to the gulikan tomorrow. She asked if you could come home."

He did not know what to say.

"We promised the offering when the goats fell ill. It's been arranged for tomorrow."

He was tempted to ask, do you need me when you make an offering to the gulikan at Vadakkethu? He stared at the muddy water collected in the footprints between the stumps of paddy in the field below. How could he refuse? He could not offend Sumitra.

"I was just about to send Karthu to call you when I saw you."

So she had seen him come down into the field as she stood in the courtyard, and recognized him from that distance.

He looked at her again and suddenly became aware of his hairy chest and tucked-up mundu. When he went next to Kumaranalloor, he should buy himself a few sleeved vests, he told himself.

"Shall I call Amma?"

"Tell her I'll come."

He waited for a minute, wondering whether Sumitra would say something more. As he turned to walk away, she asked,

"You didn't buy any fish today?"

"But it's Tiruvonam."

"You brought us narimeen last year, the day after Onam."

Aboobacker had brought two of them, huge ones, in return for having arranged for him to lease a small bit of land near the illam to grow tapioca. When sliced, they had a whole pot full. His elder sister had sent across four slices to Vadakkethu through Padmu.

He told himself as he changed direction, I'm not going to Aboobacker's, I'm going to have a look at the banana grove. There were five clusters of bananas that had been too unripe to cut down. He examined them, then took the long way back home, past Aboobacker's. Aboobacker had gone to Kuttippuram that morning. A net was lying in the yard. He asked Aboobacker's son,

"Don't you catch any narimeen these days?"

"I heard there were some on the northern side of the river."

"Hm."

He thought of the koothu last year at Ariyampadathu, as he walked to the illam. The seventh day's koothu. They were going to act the killing of Indrajit. Nanu Nair and Achu had told him that evening that they were going.

"Are you coming?"

"Let me see."

After dinner, he had decided to go. He put on his shirt and asked for the torch. Edathi Amma from Vadakkethu was in the kitchen. She asked,

"Where are you going, Madhava?"

They had come to sleep at his place.

When he told them he was going to Ariyampadath, they wanted to go with him. He cursed himself for having told them. Achu and the others would have left. He had to wait till the women and children got ready. He felt embarrassed, walking in front of them with a torch.

They spread the mat they had brought under the banyan tree in front of the koothambalam. Madhavan did not sit down. He looked for his friends but did not find them. Feeling tired, he came back. Some of them were asleep on the mat. Edathi Amma was dozing. She moved aside to make place for him.

Pests! Was it for this that he'd dragged them here? It irritated him to see them all lying there, fast asleep.

He leaned against the banyan tree, stretched out his legs and listened to the koothu performer's rhythmic, skilful word-play.

When the heavy sky cleared for a minute, he was surprised to see Sumitra lying asleep near his feet. She seemed like a marvel he had never seen before. Her breath moved in gentle waves over the bluish leaves and branches on her blouse.

He no longer heard the poet-performer's chant. Sumitra lay like a princess in the little island of light amidst the darkness. And he was her strong bodyguard, keeping watch over her.

That was the first time he had wanted to look at Sumitra without her being aware of it.

He heard someone washing clothes as he reached the illam. And a child crying continuously.

Kunhathol must be in the kitchen. Good. There was no one in the northern courtyard, where the women had danced that morning. He cleared his throat.

"Who is that?"

"It is me, Madhavan."

Kunhathol opened the door from the kitchen to the verandah and stood half hidden behind it.

"Did Govindan say anything about the rest of the paddy, Madhava?"

"I haven't seen him. I'll ask again."

"Instead of the usual two hundred paras he brings in Chingam, he's brought only fifty. It's going to be difficult if things go on this way."

He waited quietly. How was he to broach the subject?

"You must have lunch here tomorrow, Madhava."

Yes. He always had lunch at the illam the day after Onam. And Kunhathol always threw a five rupee note into his hand when he came away, "It's to buy new clothes for Onam. Unni doesn't know how to choose. Get something really nice."

He hesitated. Through the blackened railings, he could see the flames in the kitchen flare up and die down.

"There's something I'd like to say."

He wondered whether his voice sounded unusually rough. The dark circles below the eyes in Kunhathol's withered face seemed to deepen.

"What is it?"

The half-framed phrases in his mind splintered into bits.

"You must get Unni Namboodiri married."

Kunhathol's face brightened. "Yes I've been wanting to talk to the namboodiri at Kizhakkiniyath about it."

"Whoever arranges it, the sooner the better. Otherwise." He checked himself.

"What is it Madhava? Tell me, whatever it is."

Her voice sounded more hurt than anxious.

"Nothing."

He curbed the words that bubbled on the surface of his mind and said, "Let's see if he will look after the affairs of the illam at least when he's married."

He left at once. Midway down the garden he turned and looked back. Kunhathol stood with her hand on the door like a shadow that had taken refuge in the darkness.

He thought angrily, the illam would be destroyed, the mapillas would encroach on the land. He prayed that the old woman would die before that happened.

As a child he had heard the story of Varahamoorthy's curse, of how he went around carrying red-hot copper vessels to burn people's faces and a mattress soiled with menstrual blood to pollute their souls. He would dig the earth with his tusks and make tanks out of the spots where the illams stood.

Unni Namboodiri's illam had once stretched they said, from carpenter Raman's place to the upper boundary of the Kandankulangara property. It had been reduced now to one-fourth its former size.

The mapillas now ran a weaving factory in one of the illams on the banks of the river. The namboodiris who lived in the illam on the hill had been the wealthiest landlords in the region. A property dispute and the legal proceedings that followed had drained them. They had been forced to demolish the new outhouse and divide the proceeds from the sale of the tiles and the wooden rafters amongst themselves.

And here? Madhavan felt that Unni Namboodiri was the destructive seed of Varahamoorthy's curse in his own illam.

His mother had told him when he was a child that all the lands and fields in the countryside had belonged to the namboodiris of the Panniyur Gramam. They had prospered by the grace of Varahamoorthy's blessing. The folk of Shukapuram tried to take this grace away from them, but did not succeed. Then they engaged spies, who covered the idol of Varahamoorthy with a red-hot copper vessel in order to subdue its power. But the vessel exploded. The priest then placed a cloth soiled with menstrual blood on the idol to help the Shukapuram folk. It was then that Varahamoorthy had leaped out, shouting "Despicable ones!" Now his curse was taking effect.

The wind had died down. Wildcats bared their teeth in the overcast sky.

Madhavan tried to sleep and tossed and turned restlessly.

Because he went to Vadakkethu once in a while, everyone said, contemptuously, "He's there all the time. What on earth has

happened to him?" Even his sisters thought he went there because
he was consumed with desire for the one with the lean, bony face
and the disgusting black hair on her cheeks and lips. He was
furious with them.

It was the emaciated, asthmatic Edathi Amma of Vadakkethu
who had started the rumour.

-Madhavan sent us a bunch of nenthran bananas.

-Madhavan says.

-Madhavan, Madhavan, Madhavan!

She would sit on the verandah and call out to Devu, "Give him
a mat, Devu."

Devu never came out. His blood boiled when they hinted that
she was too shy to face him.

"Things have changed after all," Sumitra teased, breaking off
the little white chillies that grew near the fence and tossing them
into the ends of her mundu. For a moment, he forgot that Devu
was behind the door, waiting for him to say something while she
mixed a tablet into the juice of herbs.

They were sure to lose patience and broach the subject one day.

"Madhava, I've been wanting to talk to you for a long time."

"About what?"

"We can't go on like this. Everyone wants to know when it's
going to be."

"What are you talking about, Edathi Amma?"

"About Devu."

And then . . . it would all explode like the sudden gusts of wind
. . . that broke out in Thulam. Wait and see, he said to himself.

3

Ever since Unni Namboodiri's marriage had been decided, people
talked only about Karakkattu Mana, an illam which lay to the
east of the village. It was as if the bored villagers had suddenly
come upon a treasure.

Unni Namboodiri was lucky. His mother's goodness had
brought him good fortune even though he was a simpleton, said
Amma. An illam with a large income. They still had elephants.

Sethu overheard Sankunni the trumpet player describe the Karakattu elephant to Madhava Ammama.

Unni Namboodiri came to Sethu's house as soon as his marriage was fixed.

"What's the news, Unni Namboodiri?"

Unni Namboodiri smiled and kept his eyes on the ground, his mouth full of betel leaves.

"How much money are they giving you?" asked Cheriamma.

"Two thousand."

"Did you see the anterjanam?"

"Of course not!" Unni Namboodiri was not interested in such things. He said the deity had been carried on the Karakattu elephant's back at the Thirumanthamkunnu temple festival last year. Unni Namboodiri had been riding on the back of Kollengode Ayyappan at the time.

"He won't move an inch, no matter how many fireworks there are. And he's never hurt anyone."

Madhava Ammama had just got back from the illam. "Have you seen the Karakkat elephant, Madhava? He's really something to look at."

Madhava Ammama grunted non-committally.

"I believe he goes straight into the shed when he's in rut!"

Madhava Ammama gazed into the jnaval grove and said, "Even animals have brains, only Unni Namboodiri doesn't have them."

Unni Namboodiri laughed. He played with his torch, switching it on and off. He carried it with him even during the day.

Cheriamma tried to advise Unni Namboodiri. Once he was married she said, he should attend to the affairs of the illam, not go around festival grounds on elephant back. The anterjanam was from a good family, he should not make her suffer. Unni Namboodiri grinned vacantly. When he left, Cheriamma asked Madhava Ammama,

"Will they really give a dowry of two thousand rupees?"

Madhava Ammama pretended not to hear.

Cheriamma was irritated. "You're the chief manager of the illam, aren't you? That's why I asked."

"I don't know, I didn't ask. Why don't you go and find out if you're so interested?" And Madhava Ammama walked towards the hill, where the cherumans could be heard cutting firewood all day for the feast.

Besides the other namboodiris, two nairs had to go with Unni Namboodiri. Kunhathol had asked Madhava Ammama to go, but he had said he would send Narayanan Nair and Sankunni.

"I can't leave the place. There are so many things to attend to."

The illam was full of people the day before the bride was brought home. Someone said, "They have elephants and wealth enough at Karakkat illam, but they're getting rid of a bride whom no one wants."

"So what's what it is. I was wondering who would give this idiot a dowry of two thousand rupees."

Amma tried her best to persuade Sethu to go for the wedding feast, but he did not want to go. "There'll be such a crowd. I can't be bothered with all the pollution rules of these namboodiris."

"But the old lady came up to the fence two or three times to invite you."

He was adamant. Amma went so far as to threaten him with a Brahmin's curse.

And so he went, with great reluctance.

The garden was full of cheruman families waiting for the common feast. The nair women who had come with the bride chattered loudly in the northern courtyard. The nair men ran around organizing the feast. Sethu went to the front verandah, silently cursing his mother. Catching sight of Kandankulangara Chinnan Menon and his son, he went up to them. There was a crowd of namboodiris on the verandah, talking loudly enough for the whole world to hear. Pots and other cooking vessels clattered in the thatched shed on the southern side.

Madhava Ammama was the chief supervisor. He came up to Chinnan Menon "It won't be long now. I've made all the arrangements."

Sethu thought about the new bride from Karakkat. Someone had come home yesterday and said that she was short and waddled like a duck, that people had nicknamed her Ovuthangi, she who supports the trough. Who was it who had first thought and then named her after the ugly figure under the mouth of the stone trough in the Siva temple, through which the thirtham flowed?

Someone had been asked to give the signal as soon as the bride's party crossed the river. Madhava Ammama had arranged for a group of nair women to welcome them with ululations. Madhava Ammama was everywhere.

Chinnan Menon said to his son, "Let's go, Unni. If we wait for the namboodiris to finish lunch, we'll have to starve till the evening."

One of the helpers said, "It's not everyday that you have to do it, it's just this one time." Sethu thought that he probably had not recognized Kandankulangara Menon.

The namboodiri women and children had to eat first, then the namboodiri men. The nairs who had been invited could eat only in the third lot. Sethu decided to leave with Chinnan Menon and Unnikrishnan but Madhava Ammama appeared at that moment.

"Come, Menon, and both of you. I've arranged for a few leaves to be laid on the thekkini floor before the crowd comes in. Is there anyone else?"

The thekkini was usually reserved for the namboodiris. This was the first time the custom had been broken and a few distinguished nairs allowed to eat there. As they came out after their meal, ululations echoed in the air. Unni Namboodiri had arrived with his bride.

Sethu walked back across the field with Menon. Menon asked, "Which class are you in now?"

"I'm doing my Intermediate."

Amma wanted to know all about the feast. The wedding at the illam had been the only topic of conversation for the last nine days. And now it was over.

Sethu went upstairs and stood by the window, looking out. The ululations had died down. The feast must have begun.

He wrote a long letter to Krishnankutty.

I realize what boredom means. Each day starts exactly like the one before and ends like it as well, each tomorrow promises to be the same. He wondered whether he should add that even Sumitra was no longer at home. The sentence lingered in his mind for a moment, then he dropped it.

He posted his letter and browsed through old newspapers in the ration shop. He knew there would be no letters for him, but he waited all the same until the postman came and Velayudhan Master read out all the addresses. He walked over the paddy seedling beds to the broken-down temple.

Its god was asleep.

He suddenly wanted to write a poem to the god who lay dreaming of old times, when puja was performed and naivedyam offered to him. Young girls walked past carrying gleaming brass pots of rice and bundles of firewood, their long, wet hair fastened at the tip in a little knot, a sandal paste mark on their foreheads. The pradakshinam pathway was covered with tangles of grass and buffaloes grazed there, with periodic snorts and grunts of satisfaction. He sat down on the stone pillar that was half buried in the sand.

Elusive words fluttered through his mind like chattering sparrows. He realized that the cheruman children who were playing dice in the dilapidated prayer hall were staring at him and got up, feeling self-conscious.

"Are you going, Cheria Thampuran?"

He pretended not to hear.

"Throw us a beedi, Cheria Thampuran."

"In the glow of a thousand little earthen lamps."

No. The thoughts of the god who lived now on memories of the past refused to be trapped in words.

And the image of a young girl, eyes glowing with the radiance of a thousand lamps, would never find a place in the thoughts of a god.

He reached home as it began to grow dark. Padmu brought the lamp out and lit the three wicks which faced west on the front steps.

Nanu Nair came in, joined his palms before the lamp and smiled at Sethu. Amma was on the verandah, fumbling in her betel box.

"I've been wanting to come over. I thought I would talk to you when I came this way for the wedding feast."

Amma closed her betel box and waited silently. Sethu walked up and down the courtyard a couple of times and stopped near the crumbling wall.

"I'm not a fool, Nanu Nair." Amma's voice rose suddenly. Cheriamma rushed out, anxious not to miss anything. She had just finished her bath and was still knotting the ends of her rowka.

"I know what is happening, I've got eyes and ears."

Who was Amma angry with?

"These things should be done at the right time. You're older than he is, it's up to you to think it over and decide."

Sethu realized that they were talking about Madhava Ammama. He felt embarrassed when Amma repeated her grievances against him. He was always at Vadakkethu, drinking tea and talking to them.

"Just think of it, he even ate there on that little Karthu's birthday."

Cheriamma chimed in, "Don't we have a little girl here as well? But no, she wasn't invited. Only he was."

If there was good fish in the market, it always reached Vadakkethu.

Amma warned Cheriamma. "Keep quiet. I'll do the talking."

In order to provoke Amma, Cheriamma promptly changed sides. "He's forty years old after all, and knows his mind. If he wants to start a sambandham there, let him. Do you know, Nanu Nair, it was Edathi herself who kept on at him to visit them in the first place?"

"I'm not denying that, am I? It's true that I did. I thought they were harmless, that they had no one to help them. It wasn't that I thought much of them. I just pitied them."

"And has that changed then? They're still harmless and have no one to help them. Even now."

"That's what you don't realize. They have trapped Madhavan. It makes me mad to see them behave like Urvashis. If he starts a sambandham there now, they won't walk on the earth anymore."

"Look," said Nanu Nair. He cleared his throat and spat. He got up, moved his mat nearer Amma, lowered his voice and said,

"Madhavan is not moving in the direction you think."

Amma concealed her surprise.

So Madhava Ammama had sent Nanu Nair as his messenger, to get his sisters' consent. Achan could always be informed in a letter. And the Vadakkethu family could be asked to decide on a suitable date.

Cheriamma expressed the thought in Sethu's mind. "So Madhavan wants it. How can you blame a man for that?"

"But what does he see in her? She had no looks at all to boast of, the wretch."

"It's not the older one he's interested in."

"Then?" Had his voice joined Amma's and Cheriamma's? Sethu checked himself.

"There's the second one."

"Who, Sumitra?"

"I don't know what she's called, Sumitra or Kaikeyi."

The soft breeze that had wafted through the areca nut palms into the yard suddenly ceased. No one spoke. Sethu waited, listening to his heartbeats.

He felt relieved when he heard Amma's voice after what seemed to him endless days and nights.

"My God! What's happened to him?"

"I spoke to him. They won't like it either, giving away the younger one while the older one is still unmarried. Do you know what he said? That he can get Devu a husband."

Sethu pretended he had not heard anything and quickly went past them upstairs.

It was dark, but he did not ask Padmu for a lamp.

He lay down on the window ledge, full of resentment and blind revenge.

An enemy, a rival in Madhava Ammama! With his yellowed teeth, the stench of beedis, his black, hairy body.

He had pitied him once. But Madhava Ammama seemed like a rakshasa now. The rakshasa of his childhood stories, brandishing a spiked club and standing guard over an inaccessible stone fortress.

He went to bed feeling helpless and angry. He would never be the prince arriving at the door of the fortress with the seven magic stones that would release the princess. Never.

He thought of Sumitra lying on the ochre floor, her sandalwood coloured skin, her moist parted lips and her closed eyes.

It hurt him to think that she knew nothing of this danger, shut away in Appunni Menon's wife's house in Tirur.

It was the first time he had tasted the bitterness of jealousy, the anger and hurt of love that only an eighteen-year-old can understand.

He remembered how Sumitra used to follow him like an inimical shadow when he ran round the mango groves and jnaval trees as a little boy, his shorts with the broken buttons tucked into his waist thread. She would pick up a crushed mango with her witlow-covered fingers and hand it to him lovingly, and he would feel disgusted. She used to bathe in the bathing ghat next to his, wearing a faded red konam. If she came up to him, he used to move away. And then one day he had come upon her on the hillside and the years had dissolved. She was no longer the inimical shadow, she had become the beautiful princess of the fairy tale who had broken out of a curse.

After that, she had grown distant, and moved away from him. And he had been afraid even to call out her name in his hoarse voice which had just begun to break.

When life became a dream and she the world, he had waited outside. The little enemy of yesterday who had turned into a woman overnight was growing away from him and he could only watch resentfully.

There was no one he could speak to. No one would be interested in the dreams of an eighteen-year-old.

The palms seemed to wield iron clubs in their huge hands. He shuddered.

4

The night crept by slowly. Early morning, he heard the bleating of goats outside. He shook off his sleep and got up.

Yes, it was Sumitra's voice.

He gripped the window bars and listened. Amma asked coldly, holding her anger in check,

"So, when did you get back?"

He did not make out her reply. He rubbed the sleep from his eyes and hurried down only to find that Sumitra had gone up the hill with her goats.

Amma must have been surprised to see him up so early. Ever since he had come home from college, he had grown used to lying in bed till the sun became really hot. Padmu, who always got up with Cheriamma, was in the yard, following the old cherumi with her little broom and dustpan. He shouted at her for no reason,

"Go in, girl, don't make the place dirty." She looked at him, her huge eyes filled with fear, and walked away slowly.

He did not bother to have a wash. He wiped his face with the end of his mundu, ran his fingers through his hair and quickly went up the hill.

Sumitra's goats were looking for fresh stalks in the thickets. The old mother goat with full udders gave Sethu a baleful look and moved off. Sumitra was not to be seen. Nor did he look for her. He wanted to come upon her by chance. He walked past the clump of jnaval trees, down the lane and wandered right up to the palms. Then he turned and walked back to the compound near the illam which belonged to a mapilla. He had fenced it to grow root crops. Sethu picked up some stones, threw them at the goats and returned home.

Since the Vadakkethu fence had been closed, he would have to go round the fields if he wanted to see Sumitra.

I don't want to see anyone, he said to himself. Sumitra means nothing to me.

He sat upstairs reading till it was time for lunch, listening all the time for her voice.

It always distressed him when Padmu came and called him for lunch. After all, it was not so long ago that he used to watch Parameswara Ettan eat rice with resentment and hurt, knowing that he himself would be served only kanji. Now that he had grown up, rice was cooked for him every afternoon and the kanji bowls for the others would be set out only after he had finished his meal. If Padmu passed by while he was eating, the rice would taste of pebbles and Sethu would not be able to eat anymore.

He often thought of what Krishnankutty had said, that poverty was not a crime. But Amma and Cheriamma were always trying to hide that crime from him here.

My friend, I have become a stranger in my own house for no reason I can think of.

Everyone in the house prepared for an afternoon nap, mopping up their own bits of floor. He went out again towards the hillside in the afternoon sun.

He could see a portion of the Vadakkethu courtyard and the floor of their dilapidated cowshed if he stood in the shade of the palms near the Brahmarakshasu shrine.

He would summon her there by an act of will.

He remembered something he had learned in class. If human beings prayed for centuries to divine images made of stone or wood, their faith would invest the lifeless statues with a sacred power.

Whether it was the strength of his faith, or the acuteness of the electrical impulses in his brain he did not know—Sumitra came up the gravel path, sweating in the hot sunshine. He wanted to laugh in the arrogance of his victory.

"What are you doing here, Sethu?"

"Nothing."

"We're redoing the floor of the thekkini. I'm going to get the polishing stone from Paru's."

Had she put on weight? The red edging of her yellow satin blouse was soaked with sweat. She walked on and he called out to her.

He wanted to ask her about the big house in Tirur. About the people who lived there. Was the little gold chain with links shaped like beaten rice lying flat on her throat a gift from Kandankulangara Menon's wife?

He fumbled for words.

"When are you leaving, Sethu?" she asked, and he found his chance. "Are you in such a hurry for me to leave?"

Sumitra laughed, ignoring his reproachful tone.

"What is there to laugh about?"

She shook her head, still laughing.

"Though you're in college and all, you're still a baby, Sethu."

He burned with anger.

"I heard about Madhava Ammama's wedding."

But no, Sumitra did not look guilty, as he had thought she would.

"Oh yes, I know."

"Why does Madhava Ammama come so often to your house?"

"Who knows?"

"I'm sure it must be to see you."

Sumitra laughed loudly again. She walked a few paces, turned, spat and came back wiping her chin. He thought her eyes looked moist.

"I'll die of laughter, Sethu, listening to you."

He drew himself up and stared at her, willing his eyes to tell her, look at me and see if you can laugh.

"I thought you might have left by the time I got back. Karthu told me you were still here."

"When is the wedding?"

Sumitra seemed to be confused for a moment. Then she said calmly, her smile unchanged,

"Soon. You'll come, won't you?"

He wanted to shake her by the shoulders and ask, what did you see in that black-skinned man with his yellow teeth who smells of beedis? But he walked away, his head bent, as if it had been a casual encounter. He knew she was behind him. She called out to him as he turned into the lane.

"Look, Sethu."

He stopped, but did not look back.

"It won't be a grand wedding, but you must come."

He did not reply. He hurried away, murmuring the lines of a poem by Changampuzha which described women as the root of all destruction.

He sat upstairs and watched the daylight grow dimmer and another night creep up. He had finished one of the two books he had taken from the college library. He started on the Hardy novel. When he got to the part where the wife was about to be sold, he heard Amma and Cheriamma talking animatedly downstairs.

"What star was it yesterday? Put on water for tea, Padmu. And give Sethu Ettan the almanac."

Sethu came down. Pankutty, the son of the vettuvan who stayed in the little thatched hut in Achan's compound had come.

"Sarojini has had a baby girl Sethu, yesterday evening at six thirty. The star can't be Pooratam then, it has to be Uthratam."

Sethu consulted the almanac. To Amma's relief, it was Uthratam. "Pooratam is not a good star. We'd always be worried about its evil influence."

Cheriamma was instructed to make tea and uppuma. Amma called Sethu inside, "Do you have any money, child?"

Sethu was irritated, "From where?"

Amma murmured, "I have to give him at least five rupees, don't I, when he brings news of a childbirth? I'll send Padmu to the illam. Give me a clean, washed mundu if you have one, to give Pankutty."

He began to argue with Amma and she hushed him, "Sh . . . softly, don't let him hear. I don't want a very new one, just something that's not too old."

Amma walked up and down restlessly until Pankutty had eaten and left with his five rupees and a clean, washed mundu.

While he had dinner that night, Amma said, "Why don't you go there tomorrow?"

"Where?"

"To Achan's house. If no one goes to see the baby, they'll blame me."

"You go, Amma."

Amma stayed silent for a moment. "Hm . . . that's all I need to do now. You have nothing to do, Sethumadhavan, why can't you go?"

He had been to Achan's house only once, after Parameswara Ettan's wedding, five years ago.

He thought of Nalini Edathi, Valia Oppu and Cheria Oppu and suddenly wanted to go. Amma went out early morning and managed to borrow ten rupees from somewhere but he still pretended he was not interested. Even when she instructed him to give the midwife a rupee, he complained, "What a nuisance all this is!"

But secretly, he wanted to show his father's sisters that the little boy of five years ago with his thick striped shirt and oil-streaked face had grown up.

As he set out with a packet containing his clothes, Devu called from the gate, "Where to, Sethu?"

"To Thrissur."

He did not look that side. He did not care whether Sumitra heard or not.

As he hung onto the iron railings of the ferryboat amongst the fishmongers and the porters, sweating profusely, he thought about Nalini Edathi.

Nalini Edathi had been in the tenth when he went there five years ago. She had gone to Cannanore for a teachers' training course but had not completed it. The family had heard that she had fallen in love with a Christian boy who was her classmate. Edathi Amma had been the first to know. Parameswara Ettan had gone to bring her back but she had refused to come. He had overheard whispers that she had run away to live with the Christian boy. Achan had been sent for by telegram, so that he could get her married when she came home on vacation. But Nalini Edathi would not come back. Achan and Parameswara Ettan had gone and brought her back by force. Achan had ordered that she be shut in her room. There was no wedding. Afraid that his niece might run away, Achan had appointed a watchman. And after that no one talked about Nalini Edathi. Sethu had often wanted to ask Edathi Amma about her, but Edathi Amma had not mentioned the existence of a younger sister.

Loud-voiced Nalini Edathi always wore a big pottu and bangles from wrist to elbow and could whistle like a boy. Sethu had loved watching her embroider coloured flowers on lengths of off-white material.

After they passed the big heap of rocks, the broken-down temple and the tile factory and the road began to wind upwards, he

called out to the conductor to stop. But the conductor, busy exchanging witticisms with the commuters in the seats at the back
while he scratched himself obscenely, his trouser leg lifted, paid
no attention and continued his attempts to amuse the passengers.

The kind driver stopped but only when they reached the foot
of the hill. Sethu escaped from that pit of hell.

5

Here was the familiar lane, slippery with sand, and the great
banyan tree. Coconut palm branches, coconut shells and banana
stems lay heaped under the banyan. He used to run through the
peon's house whenever he came back from the bathing ghat in
the temple at dusk, to avoid the banyan tree, because black magic
was often performed there.

It was a big house. He was proud of the way it lay spread out
in the middle of the coconut grove. The branches of the mango
tree in the courtyard reached right into the upstairs verandah
with its black wooden railings.

This was not his house, though. He was a visitor here.

As he crossed the empty courtyard and climbed into the verandah, someone called out, "Who is it?"

He moved aside to make way for the woman who came in
with a heap of dry clothes she had gathered from the clothesline.

"It's Sethu, isn't it? God! I didn't make you out at first!"

Nalini Edathi.

She looked much thinner and the borders of her mundu and
veshti were worn and faded.

Cheria Oppu came out. He was happy to see his father's sisters;
they were so dignified. They had their baths in the ghat of the
kovilakam every morning and wore clean white clothes and
sandal paste marks on their foreheads. He felt so ashamed of
Amma and Cheriamma who wore short little towels under which
their shabby undergarments showed.

"So now you've become a big person, going to college and all.
Still, you could visit us now and then."

"Where's Valia Oppu?"

"She's gone to have a bath. Give me that packet now." Nalini Edathi took the paper packet he had with him and brought him water to wash his feet.

Valia Oppu came back.

"Have you seen the baby?"

The dark little room was heavy with the smell of Dettol and wet clothes.

Edathi Amma raised her head to ask, "Why didn't Amma come, Sethu?"

"She said she would come later, with Ettan."

The woman who looked after the baby brought the child out, wrapped in a dirty cloth. It seemed to him that its half-closed eyes were afraid of the light.

"Look who's come. It's Sethu Ammaman!"

"Where are Unni and Shyamala?"

"They've gone with Ettan. I won't have a minute's rest if they stay here," said Edathi Amma. "Is the upstairs door open, Amme? The folding chair has been put away. Its supporting rod is under the cot."

The room upstairs was Edathi Amma's. Nalini Edathi pushed the closed windows open.

"Sit down Sethu. Did you come by bus?"

He saw himself in the big mirror as he stood at the window holding on to the squared bars. A big framed photograph of Ettan and Edathi Amma hung above the other window.

Valia Oppu came up with mangoes in a silver plate and tea in a bell-metal glass.

Nalini Edathi took off the blanket that lay over the cot and shook out the mattress.

"Where's Ravi?"

"He's gone out. He'll be back soon."

Cheria Oppu's son Ravi and he were the same age. They used to be childhood friends. Ravi called Sethu Ettan because Sethu was three months older.

Nalini Edathi had changed a lot in five years! She had lost so much hair that her scalp showed in places. Her arms, which used to be covered to the elbow in coloured glass bangles were bare. She was as faded as a flower bed soaked in rain, and choked by wet sand.

"I wanted to write to you ever since I knew you were in college."

"Didn't you ever go back and write your exams, Nalini Edathi?"

Nalini Edathi gripped the panel of the door, bent her head and tried to smile.

"Exams! I'm too lazy now to even note down the number of clothes I give to the washerwoman. It's all over."

Sethu did not say anything.

"When you finish your studies and begin to work." Nalini Edathi turned her face away. "That's what I wanted to write about. It occurred to me suddenly one day. Edathi feels ashamed to take me with her. If you ever need someone to come and look after your children one day, you must send for me."

Sethu stood very still. She went out with the old sheet and pillow case. When she came back with fresh ones, he was still at the window.

"Don't worry, I'm not mad or anything like that. Do you wear trousers to college, Sethu?"

"I don't have trousers."

"It's Easter today, I saw in the calendar. When I was in Cannanore. . . ."

She stopped speaking and looked as if she wanted to shake something out of her mind. "What nonsense I've been talking. Sit down, Sethu."

He heard a shout from downstairs, "Sethu Etta!"

Ravi had arrived. He heard the stairs and the boards of the ceiling tremble as Ravi bounded up.

Ravi surprised him by having grown much bigger than him. The collar of his striped shirt, made by the village tailor, was too broad. He was bathed in sweat. His shirt was unbuttoned and the dirty vest underneath showed. He looked a bit of a boor. Sethu noticed that Ravi still wore his big red-stone earrings.

Sethu shrank away when a heavy hand fell on his shoulder.

"I'm taller than you, Sethu Etta." They stood next to each other to see who was taller. Ravi opened Sethu's parcel and examined its contents. He brought the clean, ironed shirts to the window and asked the price of each.

"Will you pass this time?"

"I'm fed up of studying, Sethu Etta. I'll kill the headmaster if he doesn't promote me this time. We have the cinema here now, near the river. Do you see many films in Palghat?"

"Sometimes."

"We'll go this evening."

"What is playing?"

"Gulebakkevali.' I heard it's good. There's a fight with a tiger."

"We'll think about it."

"What's there to think about?"

Ravi sat on the bed and talked about school. All he wanted was to somehow get through the tenth. He was the only son, and there was so much work at home. There were coconuts to be plucked and they grew tapioca by the sea.

Ravi went out again after they ate. He had to supervise the drawing up of water by a wheel for irrigation. He had to count the palm branches that had been cut down before buyers came for them. He said he would be late coming back.

Valia Oppu and Cheria Oppu came and talked to him by turns. Nalini Edathi brought him tea in the evening, and then settled down on the floor by the door. It distressed him to see her sit so quietly, with her head bent and her fingers running restlessly through her hair. She looked up with interest when he described the fort Tippu Sultan had built on the outskirts of the town he lived in now. The familiar gleam came back to her eyes when he told her the story of the secret underground passage which led out from the fort.

Long ago, there had been a military chief in charge of the fort, who had a lame daughter, a beautiful girl. She could not walk without help. Sardar Khan sighed whenever he saw his daughter who spent her days and nights playing the sitar. A prisoner came to the fort once. One night, she managed to get hold of the key to the secret passage and she somehow hobbled to his cell and helped him escape. They were caught and shot dead by the sentries. The passage had remained sealed from that day.

When he finished the story, Nalini Edathi asked, "Is that true, or did you make it up, Sethu?"

"People say it's true, people who know its history."

Nalini Edathi fell silent again. She leaned back, closed her eyes and then opened them again after a while, as if she had been asleep.

"What was the name of the prisoner in the story?"

"I don't know."

"He was a Hindu, wasn't he?"

"Hm."

"Do you go for films, Nalini Edathi?"

"Films! What a thing! When I was in Cannanore." She stopped as if she had had second thoughts about what she was going to say.

He described the maidan outside the fort, where he spent the evenings. And the girls in his class. He longed to see her laugh as she used to.

Someone was coming up the stairs, someone with a very soft footfall. He heard the tinkle of glass bangles in the corridor.

"Nalini Edathi, aren't you coming for a bath?"

"Take this glass down, Thangamani."

The girl who came in looked timidly at him. She was slightly built and wore a light green skirt with a white blouse.

"Don't you know Sethu?"

She shook her head, biting on her glass bead chain. Did she mean yes or no? Sethu tried to give shape to a shadowy memory.

"Haven't you met Thangamani, Sethu? She's from Cheriamma's place at Pushpoth." She had come from Pushpoth that morning to make an offering at the Siva temple.

"Which class are you in?"

"Ninth."

When Thangamani went down, he asked Nalini Edathi whether Pushpoth Govinda Ammaman was still at Tiruppur.

He had been to Pushpoth once, as a child. His paternal grandmother's younger sister had been in difficulties after the family partition. Her sons had no jobs. Her eldest daughter had married a teacher in a mapilla school who earned a salary of ten rupees. When the proprietor of the school refused to pay him even this pittance regularly, he had quarrelled with him, left the village and became accountant to a Chettiar in Tiruppur. Later, he had found employment in a mill and began to make good money.

Amma preferred her mother-in-law's younger sister, Pushpoth Cheriamma, to her mother-in-law.

Everyone was terrified of Govinda Ammaman. He was a hot-tempered man even now. When he came home on holidays, he would begin to drink early in the morning. Even his children were afraid of him. But he always brought plenty of money every time he came home and spent lavishly, both in his own house at Tirumanayur and in his wife's house.

He used to visit Sethu's house in the old days. Amma used to make chicken for him and send someone secretly to buy arrack.

"Whatever people say, he's so meek and gentle with me," Amma would say after he left. Govindammaman always gave Amma some money as he was leaving. Sethu could still recall the scent of the one rupee note he had once given him.

But Govinda Ammaman had not visited them for many years now.

Achan had gone to Tiruppur looking for a job, when he lost his job in the Anamalais. He had stayed with Govinda Ammaman for a month. They had quarrelled before they parted. Achan had come back with scandalous stories: Govinda Ammaman had two young girls to work for him and didn't want his wife and children in the house.

Sethu had wondered whether Govinda Ammaman would send him some money if he wrote to him from college. But in the end he did not have the courage to write.

When Sethu had come here for Unni's anna prasanam, Oppu had come from Pushpoth. She had invited him to go back with her. "There are lots of children there."

He had hung his head shyly. Oppu asked Parameswara Ettan, "Shall I take Sethu with me?"

Ettan had said, "He has to come back with me today, he can't miss school."

So he hadn't gone then. He had been to Pushpoth when he was six years old. He remembered Pushpoth Cheriamma very faintly. She wore a gold sovereign on a thread around her neck and was twice his grandmother's size, although she was younger. She walked with difficulty. He remembered playing hide-and-seek with the children. He had heard that the house had later been demolished and rebuilt.

When he came down, Thangamani and Nalini Edathi had still not gone for their bath.

"Don't you want a bath, Sethu?" asked Valia Oppu.

"Later, at dusk."

"Go down to the bathing ghat at the kovilakam, the water is excellent there."

"No, I prefer the tank." He felt shy now about bathing in an open place, having grown used to the hostel bathrooms.

Cheria Oppu asked, "Shall I make you some coffee?"

"No, I just had some. Why hasn't Ravi come?"

"He'll come now. Do you like sweets made with dates, Sethu?"

Of course he did. After coming here, he felt he loved the whole world.

Cheria Oppu said, "We'll go to the temple after dinner; there's a niramala today."

"All right."

The white sand between the coconut palms glittered in the evening sunshine. Crow pecked at the fallen jackfruits under the trees near the northern fence. A faint breeze rippled through the palm leaves. He could hear the indistinct murmur of the sea in the distance. A pleasant restlessness stirred inside him.

The clock in the verandah upstairs chimed. Six o'clock.

Thangamani spoke to Nalini Edathi somewhere inside the house. What a soft voice she had!

"Deepam!" Sethu turned and looked at her as she stood holding the lamp high for him to worship. But he did not join his palms, it seemed an undignified gesture for a grown-up boy who went to college.

He saw the long vibhuti mark on her small forehead in the bright yellow radiance of the oil lamp.

She set lighted wicks in the shrines in the courtyard and returned to the house.

"Aren't you having a bath, Sethu Etta?"

"I'll wait for Ravi."

Nalini Edathi came in from the yard and sat down on the steps. "I have such a headache every evening. I can't sleep all night. Go and have your bath, Sethu. Cheriamma said you're going to the temple for the niramala."

"Yes, Cheria Oppu said we could go."

"Thangamani, get the soap and a towel for him, child."

He went in to take his shirt off. Ravi had come back by the time he came out again.

"Sethu Etta, I'm coming for a bath as well."

Ravi helped Pankutty, the son of the farmhand, unload the burden on his head, paid him and instructed him about next morning's jobs. He asked his mother and aunt to tell him the arrears in the accounts the mapilla coconut buyer had given. Sethu was amazed to see the ninth standard schoolboy behaving like the manager of a tarawad.

Ravi pulled off his clothes, rolled them and threw them to Nalini Edathi. Wrapping a towel around his waist, he swung his arms and began to do exercises. "Get me some oil, girl," he called out.

Sethu could not make out Thangamani's face behind the thatch screen, but he thought silently to himself, "The oaf, calling her `girl' like that."

They walked towards the river.

"How many years more do you have at college, Sethu Etta?"

"Many more. And I have to pass every year, you know."

"How can *you* fail, Sethu Etta? Impossible! I plan to start a shop. I've found two rooms near the Panchayat office. No office job for me."

"Why should you have an office job? You have coconuts and paddy. It's those who don't have such things who have to hunt for jobs."

"I'll come and see you when you're in an important position."

Sethu thought with panic, how far away that time is.

The only ghat in the river which was deserted was the one where the elephants were bathed. So they went down to it. The water was lukewarm and only came up to their necks at its deepest. They could hear the men of the kovilakam talking loudly as they bathed by the light of lanterns in the tiled bathing ghat nearby.

"How many are there in your class?"

"About forty, mostly kids. I feel so ashamed, Sethu Etta. I'm glad Thangamani is in the other division."

"Are there any girls?"

"A few. All horrid creatures!"

Sethu tried to turn the conversation to girls, but Ravi did not seem to be interested. He talked about the giant fish in the temple tank, and the bats that hung on the banyan near the gate of the kovilakam, easy targets for a gun. Now and then, he reminded Sethu that they were going for a film.

A lantern had been lit by the time they got back and leaves laid for dinner.

They walked in the yard after dinner and Ravi asked softly, "Do you smoke, Sethu Etta?"

"Hm?"

"I just wanted to know, that's all."

"Sometimes. They give us cigarettes after a feast in the hostel. But I don't make a habit of it."

"I'll bring you some tomorrow."

He did not say anything.

Cheria Oppu asked, "Aren't you ready, Sethu?"

"What madness, Amma, as if Sethu Ettan wants to go to the niramala in the temple. We're going for a film. Anyway, you can't go into the temple. We are still in the period of pollution, with a newborn baby at home."

"Don't try to teach me. We were not going in anyway. And how can Thangamani and I go by ourselves?"

Sethu said to Ravi, "Why don't you come with us?"

"Not me." Ravi whispered, "Let them go. We can go for a late night show."

In the end, he had to disappoint Ravi. He put on his gleaming, ironed poplin shirt. His mundu was quite clean, but he changed it anyway. He took a little talcum powder from Edathi Amma's table.

"Do you need any small change?" asked Edathi Amma when he went to tell her he was going.

"No."

"Take a torch with you."

Beyond the lane was a sandy track, and then a few shops and a couple of banyan trees. After that an empty road stretched through a coconut grove.

Cheria Oppu led the way, talking about Amma. Why didn't she visit them sometimes? At least to mollify the villagers? After all, she said, none of us have harmed her in any way.

He followed the beam of the torch, listening to the footfalls of the girl who walked at arm's length from him. She looked more grown up now, in her flowered half-sari, with her hair in two plaits. A faint whiff reached him from the strand of jasmines wound in one plait.

A group of women with flaming torches in their hands came in from the lane and joined Cheria Oppu.

"And who is this?"

"Sethu, my older brother's younger son. He's in college in Palghat. He just came in today."

Sethu slowed down and fell back. Thangamani did not seem to want to join the other women.

"Walk carefully, the road is full of stones."

Her eyes gleamed softly in the shadows.

He wanted to talk to her.

She seemed like a bud with all its sweetness folded within it.
This was poetry, surely.

The clouds moved away and the sky cleared suddenly. In the bright moonlight, the long shadows of the palms and the road smiled at them. The flowing moonlight was like a marvel, unbelievable.

Why did the thought of Sumitra come to him now? He scolded himself. Sumitra matters nothing to me. A beautiful girl who had emerged from all the poems he had ever read was here beside him.

As they crossed over the makeshift bridge of coconut trunks, he said, "Carefully, hold my hand."

Her fingers felt fragile. He caught a scent of talcum powder and jasmine.

He did not release her hand when they reached the other side.

Above them, the sky was clear, and a sea of moonlight flowed beneath. A distant thudding of drums from the temple sounded like the beats of a giant heart and grew louder and louder with every step they took.

He held her hand, savouring the scent of freshly opened jasmines and thought, I had been waiting for this moment all my life.

Had the world been waiting for me, with moonlight and fragrance and the thudding of drums?

For me, and for you?

6

The thought of leaving next day distressed him.

And so we have to part. Till we see each other again.

The fields and coconut groves were left behind, and the sandy track merged into the tarred road. As he waited for the bus with his paper parcel under his arm, he had a strong feeling of loss. He shrank into the smallest possible space in the bus in the middle of a disgusting stench of human beings and no longer heard the sounds around him. All he heard was the tinkle of bangles. The scent of jasmines and talcum powder flowed around him like moonlight by the river. His fingers held the memory of touch, the feel of her left shoulder.

He slid into a near-coma induced by the heat and the rocking of the bus. Each minute of the past few days swam before his eyes like bubbles distilled from the indistinct colours of sunset clouds.

And so we have to part, till we meet each other again.

A guest must always leave before the novelty of his presence wears off. Valia Oppu and Cheria Oppu had tried to persuade him to stay on. Edathi Amma had said repeatedly, "College hasn't started yet. Stay for a few days."

Nalini Edathi had hidden her sadness and murmured, "After Sethu came, I felt I had someone to talk to."

"I'll come again."

"Write sometimes. I've often thought of writing a letter to myself and posting it."

"I'll write."

Thangamani had wanted to leave the day after the niramala, but they had persuaded her to stay. She had stood undecided on the verandah, drawing her nails over the cement flower patterns on the pillars.

"It may not be as comfortable here as at Pushpoth, but we are your aunts after all," Cheria Oppu had chided her.

Sethu had waited anxiously near the window until he was sure she would stay.

Time was not a strangling curse here. Every moment was filled with hope. Could he hear soft footsteps in the kitchen and the corridor? When the women laughed loudly at the foolishness of one of the maidservants he could make out her soft laugh distinctly amongst the others. He felt a shiver of delight run through him when he ran his fingers over the folds of the skirt she had hung up to dry on the upstairs verandah.

This must be what they call love.

I can murmur to the world, I have a secret. I am in love with a fifteen-year-old girl who is like a poem.

I love you!

All of them sat talking late into the night in the kitchen. Valia Oppu dramatized everything she said. If she talked about Asharichi Paru, she would pretend to be a trembling old woman with a stick. Nalini Edathi always listened to everything quietly and appreciatively.

Sethu could not stop laughing at the story of how the watchman's wife had fought with her husband and jumped into the well. There had been very little water in it. Her husband Raman heard her scream, ran up and asked, "Is there a lot of water?" No. "Did you hurt your hands or legs?" No. Raman rolled up his mat and pillow, came here to the house, and said, "I'll sleep on the ledge in the pounding shed tonight. At least I can sleep peacefully for one night without having to listen to her cries and screams!"

He listened for the soft laugh from the darkness beyond the kitchen door.

Nalini Edathi brought a lamp upstairs. "You must be sleepy, Sethu."

"No, I usually sleep quite late."

He heard Thangamani's footsteps in the corridor.

"Not asleep, Thangamani? Come and sit with us." Thangamani sat down just behind Nalini Edathi.

"Is Ravi asleep?"

"I mopped the verandah for him. He likes to sleep on the bare floor."

Once, coconuts had been stolen from four palms at the edge of the compound. Ever since, Ravi slept on the front verandah with a five-cell torch and a stick beside him.

Nalini Edathi said. "Tell us the story of one of the films you've seen."

"I don't remember any of them."

Thangamani said softly, "You must," and leaned on Nalini Edathi's shoulder.

The lamp in the verandah outside grew dimmer as the wick burned low. Leaning against the wall, he stretched out his legs, drew on a cigarette and told them a story. About the prince who fell in love with a gypsy girl who danced by the roadside.

Nalini Edathi's responses grew fainter.

"She's fallen asleep."

"Go on with the story," Thangamani insisted. She took her hand carefully away from Nalini Edathi's shoulder so as not to wake her and came up to him.

"Have you heard the song, `Suhani Raat'?"

"No."

That was what the prince had sung, when he came for the tryst by moonlight. Sethu knew his voice was rough. He could not sing, he could not even recite a line from a song properly.

Still, he said, "It's a beautiful song.

'Suhani raat dhal chuki, na jane tum kabaoge.'"

By the time the villain had fallen on the unsheathed knife and the hero had escaped, Thangamani's slender fingers were in his grasp.

Nalini Edathi woke up with a start. "I fell asleep. It must be quite late. Go to sleep now, Sethu."

Nalini Edathi picked up the lamp and it went out. It was pitch dark.

"Be careful, Thangamani, when you go down the stairs."

The darkness gave him courage. She fitted neatly in the circle of his arms. He held her close as they walked to the staircase. Then he touched her shoulder gently and said, "Go to sleep now."

He stood in the dark as she went down. Outside the window, moonlight played on the sand with the shadows of the mango trees. He closed his eyes and breathed in the fragrance of burnt camphor, of sandalwood paste and soap that lingered around him.

He said goodbye to Edathi Amma at the door of her room. Thangamani was about to leave as well. His father's sisters urged him to visit them more often and Ravi went with him to the gate.

Thangamani was just behind him. The lane was covered with elanji flowers. He stopped at the steps leading up to the coconut grove at the end of the lane.

"I'll go then."

"When will you come again, Sethu Etta?"

"Soon."

"Come when you come home next."

"I will."

"I'll tell Amma that you've promised to come."

He reached home late in the evening. Amma looked displeased. "Why did you stay so long?"

He felt intensely irritated. Did he have to be shut in here all the time? He had escaped only for three days, after all.

As he sat in the dark verandah with its chipped floor and worm-eaten pillars, he was overcome by disgust. One could hear the ant-eaten wood disintegrate slowly all the time here. The unpleasant odours of wet clothes and damp darkness clung to every corner of the house.

No one had even had the good sense to light a lamp. Where was Padmu? She finally appeared with a smoky little kerosene lamp, which she placed on the threshold. He sat silently watching the twisted soot patterns it made on the wall.

He imagined Thangamani coming here, and the thought filled him with panic. Her Sethu Ettan's house!

"Bring me a towel, girl."

Padmu shouted something to his mother.

Someone was washing clothes in the illam tank. He went down to the courtyard. Cheriamma said to him, as she brought in the dry clothes from outside, "There's a crowd of women at the illam tank, it won't be free for quite some time."

Padmu brought him a towel and a soapbox which contained two worn chips of soap.

"Do you want oil?" asked Cheriamma, but he did not reply. A faint breeze stirred through the fields. It was not quite dark yet.

He walked a little way and stopped. The lights were coming on in the shops. He heard a cart creak along the road.

This time yesterday, he had been strolling under the mango trees, like a prince on whose commands the household waited. His heart had beat faster every time a particular footstep drew near him.

And now, after three days of freedom, he was back in prison.

It looked like rain. It started to drizzle as he reached the gate of Vadakkethu. Darkness descended suddenly into the areca nut grove.

The front verandah at Ammayi's was enveloped in darkness. A lamp glimmered outside the kitchen. Karthiyayani was seated near it, picking stones from rice.

"Is it Sethu Ettan?" He stopped. Sumitra came out with a lamp in her hand.

"When did you come, Sethu?"

"This evening." He moved into the verandah, out of the rain and ran the towel over his hair.

"Does Sarojini Edathi's baby look healthy?"

"Hm." He grunted non-committally.

Sumitra peered at him in the red glow of the lamp.

"Where's Ammayi?" Sumitra told him that one of Ammayi's cousins had started her pains and Ammayi and Devu had gone to help.

"Are there any proposals for Nalini Edathi?"

"I don't know."

He put everything else out of his mind and concentrated on the fact that Sumitra was alone.

"Do you want an umbrella?"

"No."

"Here, take the lamp then. Be careful when you walk. Just yesterday we saw a snake near the screwpine bushes."

He pressed her fingers as he took the lamp from her hand.

The lamp's feeble glow intensified the darkness around. He even felt a little scared as he passed by the screwpine thicket. The tank seemed a bottomless pit of darkness. It used to be a well once, they had deepened and widened it.

He screened the lamp so that the raindrops which spattered the steps of the tank would not break its glass, and went down to the water. He sat down on the washing stone and dangled his feet in the water. It was very cold. He wiped himself all over with a wet towel and climbed up. Suddenly scared that someone was watching him from the darkness outside, he blew out the lamp.

"Sumitre!" he called out, trying to keep his voice steady. "Sumitre, the lamp has gone out. Get me a match."

Drops of water fell steadily around him. Was it raining again, or was it water dripping from the acrea nut palms?

Maybe Sumitra had not heard him. Maybe she would not come, even if she had heard. She was not the old Sumitra anymore. She would soon enter his house as his uncle's wife. That was why she had looked at him with such contempt. She had had the same look when they had stood under the palms the other day and talked about the wedding.

He saw the glow of a lighted wick weave its way through the thick darkness. Was it Karthu? He didn't care if it was. All he needed now was a light. His own, he told himself, had gone out in the wind.

It was Sumitra.

He took the wick from her, pretended to burn his hand while he lit the lamp and dropped it.

The little island they stood in was suddenly enveloped by waves of darkness. He felt a hurricane tear through his ears as he gripped her brutally.

The darkness whispered, "Don't Sethu, don't."

"So you've grown arrogant now. Did you ever think of Sethu while you stayed in the big house in Tirur? Who gave you that gold chain? It's the smell of beedi smoke that you like, and yellowed teeth, is it?

"Don't, Sethu, don't." Leaning against the wet, moss-grown stone wall, she murmured, "Don't" over and over again, not really making any effort to free herself.

No, you won't be able to push me away.

The wind unleashed itself dementedly around them and its moan rose to a roar. The areca nut palms swayed like possessed women seated in front of a sorcerer with their hair streaming wildly. Needle-fine rain spattered them. The scent of wet earth was all around them.

He came to himself when he saw her eyes shining like gleaming fish in muddy water.

"My elbows are badly grazed." Tears and laughter were mingled in Sumitra's voice.

Soaked to the skin, they sat shoulder to shoulder on the steps of the tank. She was very quiet. He wanted to dry himself quickly and go away, but his left hand was imprisoned in both her hands. Her fingers made wet trails across his wrist.

He broke away from her and got up. She came to him suddenly, gripped his shoulder and said. "You want to hurt me, don't you?"

He stood like a coward, the strength drained from him. Her face sank into his shoulder and he felt her hot tears.

A lighted torch moved across the courtyard.

"Who is in the tank, children?"

It was Madhava Ammama's rough voice. He wanted to escape, fast. But Sumitra did not seem to have heard. He raised her face and saw that she was still crying.

Forgive me, Sumitre. But no, the words stuck in his throat. All he could manage with difficulty was, "I must go now. I'll see you."

He patted her cheek lightly, took his soapbox and hurried through the darkness. He jumped over the low half-wall into the fields. Until he reached home, he was afraid that someone was following him. At his own gate, he slowed down. He was drenched. He wrung out his towel and dried himself.

Suddenly, he hated himself. Thangamani, forgive me. He thought of the rivers of moonlight and of her long, slender fingers. And whispered to himself, Sumitra is nothing to me.

Before you, I am a god.

Still, the bitterness of having seen Sumitra cry for the first time hung heavily in his mind. No, I won't do it again, I promise.

Forgive me, all of you!

His heart and body seemed as limp as a pile of rags.

Sethu wanted to weep.

Part Four

1.

Visitors began to arrive from early morning. The first to come were those who merely wanted to make a formal visit, have tea, chew betel leaves and leave. There was no way he could escape them. Even people who had avoided him until the day before came to exchange small talk.

Relatives began to pour in by noon. Madhavan could not find a hiding place, so he came and sat in the verandah with a wooden expression born of helplessness on his face. Another group arrived at the gate. Unnichiri Edathi, who had gone away in Muthassi's time when the family property was divided, and her children. Seventy-year-old Unnichiri Edathi held her long-handled palm leaf umbrella high over her head and walked erect like a man. She lived three miles away across the river and had come with her daughter and three grandchildren.

Narayanan Nair, who had come to help for the wedding, was busy cutting and stacking banana leaves at the other end of the verandah.

It was very noisy inside the house.

His eldest sister came out, "Where's Madhavan?"

He heard her but did not move.

The easy chair in the inner room creaked and his brother-in-law said, "I saw him here a while ago."

Don't worry, I'm not going to run away, he muttered angrily.

"Ah, you're sitting here then? What a thing."

What do you want me to do? Jump? Turn somersaults?

"Kavungal Chathu Nair hasn't turned up yet. Did you tell him?"

"I didn't see him." He kept his eyes on the gravelled courtyard.

"I sent word to him twice. How can Kunhukuttan manage the cooking by himself?"

He lost his temper. "What can I do about that?"

"Nothing. What do you care, anyway? True, we've invited only members of the family, but we have to give them a decent meal. And Parameswaran's father is here as well."

If he sat there longer, he would have to listen to his sister describe how hard she worked, how she had to bear the entire responsibility. He got up, pretending he had to attend to something important.

"Madhava!" That was his brother-in-law. "Have you arranged for a petromax?"

"No." It cost six rupees to rent a petromax. And the kerosene was extra. It was easy for his brother-in-law to give orders, lounging in his easy chair. He obviously wanted to make sure nothing was wanting.

There was more noise than actual activity. He stood at the edge of the yard, trying to convince himself that this was not his affair, that it had nothing to do with him.

"Where's Madhavan?" It was his younger sister. She sounded as if her nostrils were blocked with snuff.

"Come here, Madhava."

"What is it?"

"Open the storeroom and get me some areca nuts." She lowered her voice and muttered, "The wretches. They chew endlessly, like goats. I had just put out four bunches of betel leaves a minute ago and now there's nothing left." He opened the storeroom and took out the big jar for her.

As he walked away, he thought, all he had wanted was something very simple, but it has turned out as elaborate and crowded as Parameswaran's wedding, which he had conducted himself, and for which he had worked really hard. The invitees had been served in two lots. He had eaten only with the cooks, after everyone was fed, and he had stopped feeling hungry. This would be one more time when he would be famished, and would not be able to eat in time.

He suddenly remembered that Parameswaran's wedding had been much like this one. His sister had been against it at the beginning and had scowled angrily when it was fixed. But she had changed her attitude as the function drew near because she had wanted to show off that she was in charge.

His sister had agreed when he had told her that he did not want all the pomp and rituals. The Vadakkethu people wanted a simple wedding as well. A small group would come late in the evening and they would leave for the wedding after the lamps had been lighted. There would be an exchange of rings and the Vadakkethu family would prepare a modest feast, that was all. Even when his brother-in-law arrived four days ago, these had been the arrangements.

"What a waste, having a feast and celebrations. People stuff themselves and then complain there's not enough salt or spices in the food."

His sister said, "I've told Parameswaran's father and he's agreed that it will be a very simple wedding."

But by the evening they had decided to invite all their relatives. Members of the extended family lived across the river and on the other side of the hill. They could not be left out. "How can we forget our blood relations?" argued his sister. And then they decided to invite people to accompany the bridegroom to the bride's house. They justified this as well. "After all, as Parameswaran's father says, we don't have to go by bus or train to invite them. All we have to give them is a glass of tea."

He waited uneasily, listening, holding on to a rafter. The sharp odour of cheroots clung to his brother-in-law.

Unnichiri Edathi squatted on the floor, chewing betel.

"Hasn't Parameswaran come?"

"He's expected."

"What about the younger one? I forget his name."

"Sethu? He has to study, so he won't come."

"Madhava, what are you doing there?"

The old woman was sharp-sighted, though she was over seventy. She moved forward to look at him.

"You're doing a wise thing, son. They're not strangers and you can count only on neighbours for help. This marriage will bring you good fortune."

Good fortune! A wedding that would bring him good fortune, indeed!

He wanted to be alone. He could not go out. Everyone he met on the road would ask questions. And it would not be proper to sit in a teashop or the bazaar while preparations were going on for his wedding. The house was full of guests. A fire had been lit in the courtyard and the children were gathered around the big flat uruli placed over it in which uppuma was being made. It was only this morning that his sister and brother-in-law had decided that those who were accompanying the bridegroom had to be served something besides tea.

His sisters competed with each other to be everywhere, in the yard and the kitchen and the living room. They had decided to open the fence between the houses once again. Although they had been the ones to complain resentfully that Madhavan had been bewitched.

In the end—

"What have you decided, Madhavan?" He had detected anger and spite in her voice.

"I've made my decision, sister," he had said, not looking at her face. He had expected an explosion, but there had been only silence. His sister had said,

"Tell Achuthankutty Panikker that I need to see him tomorrow. We have to find an auspicious date. And it's only right and proper that you write to Parameswaran's father yourself today."

His sisters had taken on the entire burden of the wedding from that point.

He took a sip of the bitter tea which Padmu had brought. In the courtyard, someone was clearing his throat to attract attention. It was Vilakathra Kunhan, who had the right to carry the steel box containing the married couple's things.

The sun had gone down and the shadow of the verandah stretched to the compound wall.

"It's getting late, Madhava. People will soon start arriving. Go and have your bath, Madhava."

It was as if he was an irresponsible child again to be advised, scolded and ordered around.

He got up.

"Padmu, bring him a towel."

Unnichiri Edathi reminded him that he could not use oil today, his wedding day. The sastrams forbade it.

All right then, he would do everything according to the sastrams.

2

As he stepped over the stile he noticed someone in a white shirt and mundu in the field next to the banana grove. Yes, it was Parameswaran. Madhavan kept his eyes on the paddy seedling beds to avoid him.

He was relieved to see that there was no one at the river. At last, he could escape their mocking eyes. He stopped by the path which led to the river. What if he crossed over now, and went through the fields and the vegetable gardens to the bridge? Beyond it was the railway track which went on its endless journey to unknown destinations.

No, there was no escape now.

And he could not find fault with anyone, except himself.

He felt ashamed when he thought of how he had stood in front of Sumitra, feeling shattered, unable to raise the slightest sound of protest.

It was the day he had heard that river fish was being sold near the bathing ghats. On his way there, he saw Devu and her mother leaving the house. He bought the fish, wrapped it in a teak leaf and went home, his mind in a whirl. What if he went to Vadakkethu to see Sumitra? At first he thought, better not. She might think he had deliberately chosen a time when she was alone at home. But he was restless. Finally he went, hesitantly.

He knew there was nobody at the bathing tank, but he still called out to make sure.

Karthiyayani opened the door and brought a lamp into the verandah.

"So, you've shut yourself up in the house," he teased her.

"Edathi and Amma have gone to Vadakkumuri." He sat in the shadow, just outside the tiny circle of lamplight.

"Shall I bring you a mat?" He stared into the dark, straining his ears for the sound of footsteps.

"Bring me a glass of water." He dared not ask where Sumitra was. He drank a mouthful of the water she brought. Surely Sumitra must have heard his voice. Karthu went inside again.

He looked vacantly into the dark. Sumitra came out, "The tank is free now." She shook out her mundu, tied it tightly around her again, and stood leaning against the wall.

He was not sure how to say what he wanted. He had tried to talk to her so many times, but he always became tongue-tied when he came face-to-face with her.

She repeated, "There's no one at the tank."

He got up and waited for a moment in the courtyard as if he had forgotten something. Sumitra was about to go in, so he called quickly.

"Sumitre!"

"I've . . . well . . . been wanting to say something to you." He stopped and looked at her, drawing a deep breath. Her eyes gleamed in the shadows.

"Your mother knows, so do all my people."

Sumitra listened in silence.

"I thought you would have guessed as well."

"What is it Madhavetta?"

He swallowed hard.

"I don't understand, Madhavetta."

He took out a beedi and put it in his mouth. The first match went out. Sheltering the flame of the next with trembling fingers, he managed to light it.

He did not dare look at her face. He gazed instead at the smoke curling out of the lamp and said, "About the wedding." He felt as relieved as if he had finished telling her a long story.

"Oh, that! I know about that."

Oh God! A cool breeze seemed to touch the intense Medam heat.

He saw torches at the gate. Devu walked in front, waving a palm leaf torch and her mother followed. Should he go to the tank before they came in? Confused, he looked at Sumitra. Sumitra stood leaning against the wall, partly hiding the calendar picture of Krishna behind her. Was she smiling? Why did she not say something?

"Edathi and Amma have come. Aren't you having a bath, Madhavetta?"

He walked into the darkness, his mouth full of the bitter taste of dissatisfaction. He blamed himself for not having spoken clearly. He had not even given her a chance to say that she liked the idea.

He thought about it again as he lay on the ledge that night, waiting for sleep to overtake him. How clumsy he had been! Sumitra knew and so did her mother. Whose permission did they have to wait for now?

Next day they had to cut down leaf-manure from the jnaval trees for the fields. All the trees in the village were being cut down and sold, and it was hard to find leaf-manure now. If they were not closely supervised, the cherumans would take away the leaves stealthily for their own vegetable patches. He decided to go home when they broke off for their noon kanji. Sumitra's goats were grazing near the illam compound. She came down the lane opposite him.

Her heavily starched mundu crackled as it brushed her ankles. She placed a foot on a rock that had rolled into the lane during the Thulam rains, ran her fingers over the thorns on the fence and said, "I was looking for you, Madhavetta."

He felt as if fishes were leaping inside him.

"I wanted to tell you something." She plucked a leaf from the fence, rubbed it between her fingers and said, smilling, "We don't have men in our family, that's why I thought I would tell you."

He whispered, tell me anything you want.

"I like you, Madhavetta.'

He smiled, trying to control the happiness that surged through him.

"You'll listen to me, won't you? You won't be upset?"

"Upset?" He laughed out loud. "Tell me what you want, Su-mitra."

"All of us want you to be part of our household."

He felt so light, he thought he would float away in the air like a wisp of cotton.

"I want you to, Madhavettan, I want you to . . . marry Edathi."

His right hand, which held the axe, trembled. He tried to keep steady as the ground spun beneath his feet. The breeze blowing through the bamboo thicket suddenly turned into a gale storming around his ears.

Only Sumitra's smiling face and her moist, parted lips remained clear in front of his eyes.

3

He was startled to hear hooting from all directions. He thought people were laughing at him, but then realized that they were children with oiled bodies playing on the sand before they had a bath. Women were coming down the path beyond the mapilla fisherman's house, probably from the southern side of the river. They walked along the banks, searching for a shallow spot, shouting at the children to behave themselves.

He finished his bath in a hurry—the guests must have begun to arrive and the bridegroom had no right to hide from them by the river. He went round by a marshy channel to avoid the women, cleaned his feet on the first bed of karuka grass he saw and climbed up from the river.

From the edge of the field he could see both the gates. The Embrandiri was coming from Vadakkethu. He must have been sent for to clean the shrine of the rakshasu and offer milk and water. Sumitra must have gone early in the morning to the temple to arrange it.

Sumitra had organized everything. As he walked on, thinking of all that had happened, he suddenly discovered a secret, a marvellous secret. It was not he who had given in, in a moment of weakness. Indeed, he had not actually consented at all. Sumitra had wanted this. And decided on it.

He had not dared to say anything to her in the lane. Wanting only to escape, he had run away and had realized only when he reached home that he had wanted to say a number of things.

Devu Edathi!

Sumitra did not know Devu Edathi. He thought of Devu standing in the dim light of the inner room at the illam, like a bad dream.

Do you want to hear, Sumitra? I saw, with my own eyes.

He thought of another night when he had not been able to sleep, when he had heard even the rustle of the dry banana leaves clearly. The darkness had been full of murmurs. The wind had grown stronger by morning. Cold had crawled out of the ground like a reptile and crept through him. Sleep had finally enveloped him like a fit of unconsciousness.

He had dreamed that he was drawing water for the areca nut palms from the tank. It seemed a bottomless tank, for even when he let out the entire rope, it still did not touch water. He decided to draw the bucket up but it was caught on something. Or rather, someone seemed to be trying to pull it down. He peered into the tank and saw a horrible shape surfacing in the water, clinging onto the bucket. Dripping wet hair covered its body. He slipped and fell in. The arms waiting for him below seemed to grow longer. As he came to the end of that interminable fall, he saw the creature's face, the long teeth protruding from a mass of wet hair. He almost collapsed. It was Devu's face!

He had tried his best to avoid Sumitra over the next few days, but he had not succeeded. She sought him out.

"I've told Amma."

"What?"

"That you're willing, Madhavetta."

"I . . . but." He had stood transfixed, his face black with anger. Sumtira came so close that she could touch him if she put out her hand.

"What are you thinking about Madhavetta?"

"I."

"Don't worry. I'm telling you, after all." Her eyes flashed. He wanted to stretch out his arms but they had suddenly grown heavy. She smiled and went past, her body almost brushing his, leaving him weak.

"So you've been having an elaborate bath today, Madhavan Nair." He made an effort to smile. People were seated on the mats spread on the verandah, having tea.

His sister brought him an unbleached mundu and a veshti with a thin gold border. "Parameswaran's father brought this for you to wear when you go to the bride's house."

He came out in his bridegroom's clothes. The younger of his sisters told him to light a wick to the household deity before he started.

The people crowded outside moved to make way for him. Krishnan Nair, who owned the teashop, teased him, "Why don't we cut across the garden? There's no need to go around by the fields, is there?"

Someone laughed. Sankunni said,

"It's only this one day that he has to take the trouble."

"Look who's here." His brother-in-law got up from his chair, "Do sit down."

Unni Namboodiri. Parameswaran came up to welcome him properly.

Unni Namboodiri stood scratching the scabs on his chest. He seemed reluctant to sit down. Sankunni pushed a grass mat towards him.

His brother-in-law sat down again and called out, "Madhava, what shall we give Unni Namboodiri? What about some bananas and a tender coconut?"

Parameswaran said, "Those days are over, aren't they, Unni Namboodiri?"

"Tea will be all right."

Madhavan went in and brought him tea and uppuma in a plantain leaf. "Please eat," he said, without looking at Unni Namboodiri's face.

They waited until it was dusk, chewing betel and smoking to pass the time. Their voices grew inaudible as he drifted into his own world. He no longer felt troubled. Courage flowed quietly back into him. He looked at Unni Namboodiri seated cross-legged on the ground sipping tea, and the knife-edge of enmity slipped back into its sheath.

There was nothing to be ashamed of. He was going to marry Devu of Vadakkethu. She was not good looking. But there was something else that no one knew. It wasn't Devu that mattered. He was going to be the master of the household where Sumitra lived.

He told himself that there was no need to be so timid before these people, who laughed and talked so loudly.

The teashop Nair's present wife had been his older brother's wife. The older brother had been poisoned and the younger one had gone to help the widow and her three small children. When she had had her fourth baby, he had accepted her openly as his wife. Surely, Madhavan Nair said to himself angrily, he did not have to be embarrassed before such a person.

As for Kuttappa Kurup, he probably thought himself handsome, in spite of having a face channelled and pitted with smallpox scars. Everyone knew why he had been appointed to supervise the Kandankulangara lands. There were people who had seen him turn back from his own door knowing that Chinnan Menon was inside. Oh yes, everyone knew these stories and laughed about them.

Padmanabhan's wife dragged a foot as she walked, like a buffalo with rheumatism. And Unni Namboodiri had brought home a frightful looking creature from a rich illam which owned elephants.

He suddenly realized that he had been staring at Unni Namboodiri all this time.

Padmu called from inside, "Deepam!"

"Make your obeisance to the lamp and we'll go. Hurry now."

They were all ready. He went down to the yard with them. His brother-in-law was busy giving everyone instructions.

He muttered disgustedly to himself, trying not to show he was upset. Here comes the bridegroom to the wedding pandal, his head held as high as the sky. The red heart of the earth thrills to his footsteps as he comes to wed Devu of Vadakkethu.

4

It looked as if it was going to rain during the day. The sleepy light would not open its eyes.

Madhavan looked at the courtyard, full of grey smoke, and thought of the night that had gone by. So he was a husband now and part of the Vadakkethu family.

When had he entered the poky little room, bathed in sweat? After the moment when they had set out for the bride's house, he had no clear idea of the sequence of events.

When had all the guests left? The house and compound were silent now. He heard footsteps in the outer hall and saw small oil lamps go to and fro.

"I'll hold a lamp for them. If they don't clean up at once, the cats and dogs will make a mess by morning." Sumitra's voice.

He stood by the window, looking through the bars into the darkness. It was very still and his shirt was soaked in sweat. He took it off and hung it on a nail, over the calendar of Krishna. He thought of Sumitra rushing around, busy with household chores.

The wedding rituals, the feast, being ushered into this room by Krishnan Nair and Nanu Nair—all had become hazy memories.

It had not been very dark when the bridegroom's party had reached the courtyard, and the lanterns had looked pale in the evening light. The rituals were over very quickly. There were just enough people to eat in two lots.

He heard Sumitra's mother's voice in the kitchen, "It's very late, girl. Don't you think we should try and get some sleep? We got up at cock-crow this morning."

He felt tired. He looked at the bed pushed against the wall, and the white sheet, longing to sit down. He took off the lid of the broken enamel cup and saw that it contained water. He swallowed a mouthful. Angrily, he remembered that he had left his beedis and matches somewhere outside. He was sure he could find them, but he felt reluctant to leave the poky little room.

An old woman croaked, "Imagine girls being so shy nowadays." She was one of the wedding guests. His heart beat fast when he heard murmurs at the door. He did not turn round. Were his legs trembling?

Footsteps. And more murmurs. The bolt grated with a mocking noise. He leaned his elbows on the ledge, cursing himself for having forgotten his beedis and continued to stare out into the dark.

He turned around slowly when he heard the tinkle of glass bangles and the sound of quick breathing. He could barely make out Devu's form in the shadows by the bed. When he had stood in front of the big oil lamp to tie the thali around her neck, all he had seen were the border of her red saree and the witlows on her toes. She had changed into a white mundu. She looked as if she was trying to shrink into the shadows.

He felt numb. She looked funny, he thought, cowering like a helpless insect. She moved from the shadows and placed a hand hesitantly on the bed. He looked at her contemptuously.

Ants swarmed over the ledge by the window. If he slept there, there would be a breeze at least after midnight. But it was impossible. It was full of ants and kerosene stains from the lamp.

The lights in the house went out one by one and mats were being unrolled. Someone snored. There was a clink of bangles and a yawn. Was that Sumitra?

He climbed into bed, ignoring Devu. He thought he would fall asleep at once, he was so tired, but sleep eluded him. He covered his eyes with his hands to shut out the light and did not open them even when he heard her moving around the room. The bolt on the inside of the door creaked. The room grew dark. He opened his eyes for a moment, then closed them again.

He pretended not to notice her creeping quietly into bed and moved closer to the wall.

When he next heard the sound of the door and opened his eyes, he was surprised to see that it was morning.

When had he fallen asleep?

He lay in bed for a while watching the grey light coming through the window. Then he went out. Karthu and the old woman were still asleep in the hall. He walked quietly to the front verandah. Crows pecked noisily at a stack of used banana leaves at the edge of the yard.

Sumitra had just come from her bath. She took a pinch of vibhuti from the hanging basket and asked, "Why did you get up so early?" She went in without waiting for an answer and came out again with his beedis and matchbox. Her mundu slipped a little as she put them down near him. Her wet footprints faded slowly as she walked away.

He squatted on the verandah and watched the noisy crows.

Sumitra came out again wearing crisp, dry clothes. She had brought him toothpowder and water in a gleaming bell-metal kindi.

"Will you have a glass of tea?"

He did not answer.

She brought him tea. "They'are plucking areca nuts at the illam, aren't they? I saw Kumaran and Kandunni go that side."

"Hm." He drank his tea and lit another beedi.

"There's something I need from Chalisseri. When you go next month."

"What is it?'

She said, "There's no hurry. My earrings are broken. I wanted to get them weighed and exchanged for another pair. Some other time, not today."

Her mother came out. "Why are you up so early?"

"They'll come to pluck areca nuts at the illam."

He saw Devu behind the door.

"Give me my veshti, Sumitra."

Devu said, "Tell him breakfast will be ready soon. He can eat."

Sumitra ignored her, went in and brought him a clean towel. "Here you are. I'll fold your veshti and put it away. Your shirt is dirty. I'll wash it out."

He stepped into the courtyard and hesitated, wondering what to say.

"It's Friday, so there won't be fresh fish. But come in time for dinner anyway," said Sumitra.

"It will be late when I get back from Chalissery."

"That doesn't matter. We won't lock the gate till you get back."

She came up to the gate with him. "Try to come early, the moon is on the wane."

He was sure of one thing now, that Devu had no place at all at Vadakkethu. Eagerness spread through him like the morning sunlight. He called out from the gate in a tone of authority,

"Sumitre!"

She was by the coconut palms, but she hurried down to him.

"Get whatever you need from Vappu's shop and ask them to put it in my account. I'll settle it later."

"Hm."

"Then." No, there was nothing more he wanted to say. He strode on confidently, thinking that she would look very pretty if she had gold studs in her ears.

Did Devu wear earrings? He could recall only her hairy arms and a face with jutting cheekbones.

No, Devu would never dare stand face-to-face before him.

PART FIVE

1

It was Friday. If Thangamani had written the day after she received his letter, the reply would have arrived today. Her letter usually came on the fifth day after he wrote.

Sreedevi Amma was taking a Chemistry class. He not only had to listen, he had to write down what she said in his notebook as well. She scolded them often and treated them as a mother would, but they respected her. In spite of the sloppy way in which she wore her saree, and her oily face, the class would fall silent when she stood on the dais.

The aura of a romance clung to her and all the students had heard of it. Maybe the compassion it awoke in them lay behind the concern and respect they showed her. She was the daughter of a highly placed official. She had fallen in love with her father's chauffeur. He was married and had children. She ran away from home to live with him. They now lived in a dirty little house in the workers' colony in the lime quarries. She had children by him. No one had met her husband. His first wife, who stayed somewhere quite distant, came at the beginning of every month to Sreedevi Amma to collect money for herself and her children.

Sethu always felt that her eyes held a deep sadness which she tried to hide. He had heard that all her sisters had married rich men. He detested the man, her husband, who had deserted his wife and three children. It hurt him to think of this princess who had sacrificed her kingdom for love. He could only guess at the depths of her sorrow.

Every Friday morning, Sethu woke up full of hope. It was the day Thangamani's letters usually arrived. Her big, rounded, childish handwriting seemed to be full of life. He read and re-read each letter and put it away under a sheet of paper spread at the bottom of his trunk, feeling that it added to a store of accumulated treasure.

The first time he wrote, he kept his emotions in check and composed a very ordinary letter. My dear Thangamani, I hope you are well.

He was disappointed when no reply came. As disappointment turned to anger, her letter arrived. A letter that could have been written to a father, an older brother, an uncle. She had added at the end that she had finished writing it five days ago, but had not been able to get hold of an envelope. When he wrote next, he sent her a self-addressed envelope.

I thought you had forgotten me, Thangam, when I did not hear from you.

I'll never forget you, Sethu Etta. It hurts when you say that.

Had she written that line because she was childishly upset? He analyzed it over and over again.

His next letter began, "My dearest Thangamani" and went on, I am so lonely. Only I know how much I suffer. I want to stay aloof from the noise and bustle in the college and hostel. On sleepless nights, the memory of you is my only pleasure , Thangam.

A love letter. He was afraid after he sent it. What if someone else opened and read it? What if it fell into her father's hands, and he sent it along with a letter of his own to Achan?

Would she understand, would she make out the tone of the very first love letter he had ever written?

After the special class on Saturday, he waited in the verandah for Francis the postman. The afternoon sun blazed outside, throwing flames on the tarred road. He recognized the self-addressed envelope at once. The words danced before his eyes and rivers of moonlight flowed through the noon sunshine.

"Amma asked, when I was reading your letter, whose it was. When I said it was yours Sethu Ettan, she asked me to keep it behind the mirror for her to read. But I did not put it there and luckily, she did not ask again."

If Sreedevi Amma finished her class ahead of time, he could go to the hostel, check the mail and join the first batch for lunch. But she always went on for a few minutes after the bell rang and no one dared to protest.

He persuaded two students who were already being served to move down and make place for him in the mess queue. He hurried to his room after lunch. There were no letters, only a card that had fallen under the table. Achan's, come by the day's mail. He would return on the morning of the ninth, by train. There had been unexpected expenses because of Madhava Ammama's wedding. He would be able to send money only after he got back. He hoped Sethu was well.

Oh yes, I am well. Very, very well!

Achan had not written before he went home. Maybe he had gone by bus. There was a bus from Pollachi to Thrissur.

It was Parameswara Ettan who had written to Sethu about Madhava Ammama's wedding. Sethu had given in his name for a study tour and had to pay forty rupees. Parameswara Ettan wrote that it was impossible that month since he had to send some money home. You must have heard, he wrote, that Madhava Ammama is going to marry Devu of Vadakkethu.

He had wished he could go for the wedding. He imagined Madhava Ammama and Devu standing close to each other. And Sumitra, running around organizing things. Would she have looked at him with contempt if he had turned up? "You'll come, Sethu, won't you? We can't afford a grand wedding."

He realized now why she had had a mocking look on her face that day.

The thought of the tears he had seen glistening on her face in the darkness of the bathing ghat often troubled him. It had been the only time he had seen her look weak and helpless.

He tried to convince himself that it was not his fault but God's. It should have been Thangamani he met first. Sumitra would never have entered his thoughts then. He would not have felt now like someone who had lost his way.

But the memory of her tear-stained face haunted him. Whose fault was it?

He decided that night that he would go and meet Achan's train in the morning.

He did not feel like reading. He looked through "The Garde-ner" and tried to find images for two of the lines:
I kissed her and said, you are blind even as the flowers are.
'You yourself know not how beautiful is your gift.'
No, he could not fit the likeness of the blind girl to a flower.

He got up earlier than usual the next morning. The train would arrive at nine thirty. There were passenger trains from the village at nine thirty and eleven thirty. Achan's card mentioned only the date. It must be the nine thirty train. Achan had not asked him to meet the train.

He ran into a group of friends returning from breakfast at Krishna Iyer's. "Hurry up," they said, "Swamy's oothappams are very good today."

"I'm going to the station."

"Oh?"

"My father will be on the morning train."

Balakrishnan said, "Look, I need to borrow ten rupees. Won't your father give you something?"

He smiled and crossed the road. Waiting at the crossroads for a bus, he thought, everyone looks forward to a visit from a guardian   a father or an uncle. It meant they would get pocket money. Some guardians took their wards shopping. The lucky one's friends would politely keep away from him. And, as a reward for good behaviour, they would be taken to the Madras Cafe that evening.

Daniel John in room number eleven had acquired a small battery operated radio set when his father came to see him. His father had noticed that there was no radio in the hostel. The students in the common room had stood up respectfully and explained that they had requested the warden for one. Daniel's father said he had one in the car and asked Daniel to fetch it.

"Thank you, Papa!"

"It's alright."

It was Nambiar who had told Sethu about this; he had been in the common room at the time.

Sethu had watched enviously as father and son took leave of each other. Daniel's father worked in a British firm in Coimbatore. Sethu did not know Daniel very well. Someone had told him that Daniel's father had arrived in a huge Pontiac.

Daniel's father was six feet tall, well-built, fair-skinned and bald. He smoked a pipe and wore white trousers and a white slack shirt. The cleanliness of the reddish heels above the polished black Punjabi chappals caught Sethu's eye. They were uncreased and a bright pink—baby feet.

Nambiar told him later that Daniel's father had said when he hugged him, "You smell of cigarettes."

"No!"

"Don't bluff." He had pointed to the empty cigarette packets on the bookshelf. "Probably you buy them to decorate your shelf." He had smiled and advised Daniel, "Stick to one brand and eat well."

The visit was the topic of the day in the hostel.

Sethu hovered around the verandah when Daniel's father was ready to leave. Father and son talked to each other like friends. As he got into the driving seat, he asked Daniel something which Sethu could not hear. Daniel laughed. The engine came to life.

"So long." Sethu watched wonderingly as they shook hands. As the car moved away, he noticed Krishnankutty leaning on the low wall, looking at it. Krishnankutty tried to smile but could not erase the scowl on his face. They looked at each other for a minute.

It was a mistake to have said he was going to meet his father. They would insist on knowing how much pocket money he had been given.

The bus was late. He heard someone say that the bus from Tirunellayi had broken down. They would have to wait another half an hour for the bus from Manapillikkavu. He tried to peer at the watch on the hand of a passer-by. Was it seven forty-five or eight forty-five? Had he counted wrong when the clock in the common room struck the hour? He had written to Parameswara Ettan and to Achan about a watch. Neither had responded.

He had heard that watches from Singapore were sold cheap, at eighty-five rupees each.

Krishnankutty had said that poverty was not a crime. But he realized how valuable eighty-five rupees could be as he prayed for a passer-by to hold his hand in such a way that his left wrist was visible. And when he walked out of the mess at night, his stomach revolting against the dried chapatis and the evil smelling radish sambar, he longed to have an anna and a half to spend on the bananas hanging before Ravuthar's shop.

The crowd at the bus stop increased. Women working in the tile factories hurried down the road speaking loudly in Malayalam tinged with Tamil inflections.

There was a stampede as the roar of the bus was heard. A number of trucks smelling sharply of beedis and tobacco went past. The bus came at last and he clambered on the footboard with four others, scared to death.

By the time he bought a platform ticket and crossed the overbridge, the train had come in. He rushed down the platform but did not see Achan. A porter told him that the train on the metre guage line was going to Pollachi. He must be in that, then. Pilgrims in ochre robes, carrying kavadis were crowding the doors. He found Achan in a compartment just behind the engine, sitting at the window with a newspaper. He was surrounded by a group of dark skinned Tamils and Chettichi women in bright red sarees, carrying brass water-pots.

Achan was engrossed in the newspaper. Sethu stood near the window uncertainly. From as far back as he could remember, Achan had seldom been at home. Sethu avoided him on his rare visits. He found it difficult to talk to him loudly, or call out "Acha" from afar.

Achan looked up suddenly. He folded his newspaper and asked, "Don't you have class today?"

He said, "No," although he did have classes.

Achan had not shaved before he set out. He stroked the grey stubble on his chin. His forehead creased and his eyes closed, he seemed immersed in thought. There were patches of fungus on his closely cropped head.

"When is your exam?"

"On December fifteenth."

"Um." They fell silent again.

His earliest memories of Achan were when he worked in the Nilgiris. Sethu used to wait eagerly for him to come home. He would stand next to him proudly as Achan sat in the easy chair with his embroidered red shawl around him. Achan smelled good as he walked by. Sethu had never tired of looking at Achan's glasses, Achan's chappals, Achan's shaving soap.

"When do you have to pay your dues?"

"Tomorrow."

"Um."

"Or by the twenty-fifth with a fine."

The boy selling tea repeatedly asked if they wanted some. Achan signalled no. As an afterthought, Achan asked, "Do you want tea?"

"No," he said, "I had tea before I came."

Achan mumbled, "So many unexpected expenses. I spent nearly sixty rupees on Madhavan's wedding. No one realizes that my income is not as good as it used to be."

Sethu pretended not to hear.

"I managed to educate one son and set him up in life. I should have retired by now. There was a time when I used to earn ninety rupees and send money to my mother and sisters as well as take care of my wife and children."

Were Achan's complaints directed at Parameswara Ettan?

A new group of passengers had come, bound for Palani, and were scrambling for seats.

He wanted to tell Achan that he never had money left over after paying his dues. But that would mean listening to Achan tell him how much he earned, how much he had to send to Amma and so on. He kept quiet.

He was relieved when the bell rang and the engine whistled.

Achan put his head out. "All right, then. Get along."

The sun was very hot. He waited near the market-place for the town bus, feeling irritated with himself. He should not have come.

He had only a rupee left. And he would have to change that as well, for the bus. Only a rupee for himself until his money came on the twenty-fifth.

He was drenched in sweat by the time he walked the two and a half miles to the hostel. Everyone had gone to class. The time on the tower clock was eleven. He did not want to go to class. He took off his shirt, changed his mundu, unrolled his mattress and lay down to read his library copy of *Leaves of Grass*.

He heard voices in the verandah and the sound of shoes. Balakrishnan and Daniel John were back from the first hour.

Balakrishnan came to the door. "You cut class?"

"I don't feel well. I have a headache."

They went away. Balakrishnan came back and said softly, "I wasn't joking. Give me ten rupees, Sethu."

"Why don't you ask someone like Daniel, who has money?"

"I don't want to. I don't know him all that well. Give me ten, Sethu. I'll return it to you when my money order comes."

"I don't have any money."

"You went to see your father, didn't you? What did he give you?"

Sethu kept his eyes on Whitman's verses and said, "He didn't come. He must have changed his plans."

"Bad luck." Sethu closed the door and lay down. And suddenly thought, surely there would be a letter from Thangamani.

His tired heart began to beat with anticipation. The postman was late.

Having something to wait for drove everything else out of his mind.

2

When he tried to recall Thangamani's house, what he remembered best were the glass windows. The images of the house and of its surroundings were vague.

There were new roads and shops. He remembered a bridge made of coconut tree trunks at the place where one turned off the road. He was a little anxious when he did not see it. He walked past the shops and asked a workman,

"Which way to Pushpoth?"

"Turn by the culvert into the field. It's directly east once you cross the field."

He retraced his steps, his eyes on the ground, feeling suspicious eyes darting around him like wasps. What did he want at Pushpoth, they asked. Going through the coconut grove into the field he saw a familiar clump of bamboos in the distance.

His uneasiness grew as he neared the house. True, he had waited months for this day. But only Thangamani had invited him. Did that give him the right to go there?

What if there were a lot of people when he arrived?

"Who are you? I don't know you."

"I." He imagined how he would introduce himself. How he would sit on the verandah, exchanging the cold formalities of small talk, have tea and leave. He blamed himself for not having thought of all this when he wrote to Thangamani that he would come.

He had packed three sets of clothes, a couple of books and borrowed a box camera. He tucked the leather bag under his arm, and opened the gate feeling helpless but determined to go ahead, come what may.

He tried to smile confidently and hide his nervousness. There was no one in the verandah. An old man was busy digging around the cucumber patch. His leather bag felt heavier and channels of sweat ran down his chest.

"Why are you standing there like that?" He was relieved to see Thangamani's mother come out, smiling.

He had seen her years ago but she did not seem to have changed much except that there was more grey in the hair over her ears.

He put his bag down and smiled, not quite sure what to say.

"Sit down, Sethu. The girl told me you would come, but I didn't really believe her."

"We had a students' meeting at Thrissur. A number of us had come." He made that up, reluctant to say that he had caught an early morning bus to come straight here.

Ten-year-old Unni ran in with a bandaged leg, wearing muddy shorts, his face stained with burns from cashew oil. He stopped warily by the pillar when he saw Sethu.

"Come along. Don't you know me?" He knew it was Unni who had been posting Thangamani's letters to him.

Unni came up confidently to Sethu, his body reeking of cashew fruits.

"It's Sethu," his mother said. "Remember, you've seen him at Valiamma's."

Unni nodded his head, sat down and began to twist the buckles on Sethu's bag. He ran his hands over it searchingly and his eyes lit up when he felt the edges of the camera.

Sethu had forgotten about Unni. He should have brought him something. When his mother went in, Sethu laid his hand on Unni's shoulder and asked, "Which class are you in?"

"Fifth."

He was sure that someone had come into the corridor. He stood up. Thangamani was at the door, smiling. He thought she had grown taller.

"So you were here, then?"

"Mm . . . I saw you from upstairs as you came over the fields."

Her voice sounded deeper. He saw her face flush, and her eyes dart fearfully at him.

"Did you get my letter?"

"Yes, the day before yesterday. I thought you would come in the afternoon. How many days' holidays do you have?"

"I have to be in college on Monday."

Unable to contain his impatience, Unni asked, "What is this, Sethu Etta?"

"It's a camera, I'll take a picture of you."

Unni took it from him and turned it over in his hand.

"Be careful. There's film in it, it might be wasted."

"Don't spoil it, Unni."

"What's wrong with you, Thangoppu? As if it will be spoilt if I touch it."

Thangamani's mother arrived with tea and jackfruit chips on a silver plate. She squatted on the floor to talk to him. She said she had almost forgotten what Sethu's mother looked like, it had been so long since they had met.

"I used to see Edathi Amma when she came over in the old days. Now she doesn't come. And I can never get away from here, I simply don't have the time."

Thangamani's mother used to live here with her mother, her older sisters and their children. Govinda Ammaman, Thangamani's father, had bought the house and compound when the family property was divided. Their mother now stayed with the eldest sister and sometimes came here to visit.

"I said we could divide the property after Amma's time, but no one would listen."

It was the eldest sister's husband who had first broached the subject of divisions. When there was a general protest, he had backed out. But then Govinda Ammaman took it up.

Sethu knew that Thangamani was in the corridor. His attention was concentrated on the faint movements he could make out behind the door. Her mother continued to talk about her husband's temper and his tantrums.

The land, she said, had been leased out to tenant-farmers and the two coconut groves were under the supervision of caretakers.

"He used to complain that he could not bear to spend even a few days amongst all the riff-raff here. And now look at me, alone with the children. He doesn't care to come even for two days in the year!"

He sent money every month. When she wrote that the blacksmith was selling his land, he had sent her money to pay an advance, and promised to have the documents registered on his next visit.

"But what's the use of money? He has no affection. When he comes, the first two days are peaceful, but on the third day there's a quarrel. He doesn't need a reason. I hear he's on bad terms with Sarada's husband."

Sarada, Thangamani's older sister, lived in Vishakapatnam. She was married to a man who worked for a shipping company.

Thangamani's mother mentioned the row Achan had had with Govinda Ammaman. "In the old days, your's was the first place he visited when he came on leave. You can never be sure when he's going to fall out with someone." Her voice began to tremble.

"Amma, isn't it time for your bath?" Thangamani called out, but she pretended not to hear. She talked about the oil-seller Paulose's son who had left the village looking for a job and finally arrived at Govinda Ammaman's place. Govinda Ammaman had found him a job in the mill. But he had been driven away in a month's time. He had come back to the village with scars all over his body. He had evidently been hit with a belt. The tales he brought back were the talk of the village.

"Sometimes, I think, why don't I go away with the two children when they have holidays."

Sethu watched dusk spread over the coconut grove and the field beyond.

"You'll want to have a bath, Sethu. Unni, take Sethu Ettan's bag upstairs."

Seated in the easy chair by the window at night, turning over the pages of an old magazine, he thought proudly that he was not a stranger here, but an esteemed guest. He listened to Thangamani move around in the next room. He could make out her footsteps distinctly.

She came up to the door to say something to Unni and he asked her reproachfully, "So you're terribly busy, are you?"

"What did you expect?"

"Have you eaten?"

"Um."

She had bathed and changed her skirt and blouse but the white half-sari with the blue flowers was the one she had worn earlier.

She brought him milk in a tumbler and stood for a moment between the armrests of the easy chair, her knees brushing his own. Sethu looked warily at Unni who knelt on the floor, chattering nonstop. Thangamani moved away, the edge of her long skirt touching his feet.

He heard doors being closed downstairs and the clatter of pots and pans. The old man who worked in the garden shook out his mat, coughing noisily.

Thangamani's mother came in, scolded Unni for being troublesome, and sat on the floor, her legs stretched out. Thangamani brought her the betel box and disappeared into the verandah. "Are you sleepy, Sethu? Spread the mattress for him, child."

"It's been spread already."

Unni unrolled a mattress for himself and lay down. He was asleep in a minute.

"Just the one boy and he's so disobedient. He's inherited his father's boorishness and temper. The only consolation is that he's not bad at studies."

"He's only a child. He'll be alright when he grows up." Sethu said, sounding grown-up and worldly.

They talked late into the night. Thangamani's mother was full of complaints against the husband who had given her a house, money, coconut groves, everything except affection. Last time he came, Sarada had been here with her husband and children and he had not spoken a word to Sarada's husband. After all, what harm had that man done?

"It's very late. You came just when I was longing to unburden myself, Sethu. After all, I have to tell someone these things."

It felt very hot when he blew the lamp out. He took off his vest. He heard them unroll mattresses in the next room. Thangamani talked softly to her mother. He reached out and opened the windows wide. The long shadows of the coconut palms made strange patterns in the faint moonlight.

He lay in the dark with his eyes open. Thangamani was only a few feet away, on the other side of the wall. Would she have fallen asleep? She said so much in her letters but was so quiet now.

He concentrated on a single thought and whispered to the darkness, Come.

Did he hear her snap her fingers on the other side of the wall? He cleared his throat to let her know he was not asleep, that he could not sleep.

As the darkness deepened, the clock in the corridor seemed to tick louder.

Amma would not like his having come to Pushpoth. Neither would Achan. As for Govinda Ammaman, he needed no real reason to start a quarrel. Even if people did what he wanted, he would be angry if they had not consulted him first, if he did not have a part in making the decision. Sethu thought that opposition could be a good thing to face. He would take Thangamani away from this house even if the whole world opposed him.

He did not know when he fell asleep. He woke up with a start and felt that someone was in the room. There was a soft tinkle of bangles. Thangamani!

It was fear rather than joy that took hold of him. He felt his heartbeats echoing loudly in the darkness. He sat up and glanced at Unni, fast asleep on the floor. He caught her hand and realized she was trembling. He was suddenly afraid of being caught like a criminal in a flood of light.

He said softly, "You didn't sleep?"

He held her close, unable to speak. Her thin wrists were now rounded. She was no longer the little girl he had held in his arms in Achan's house.

He thought, this is my temple, I am only a devotee here. He pressed his lips to her neck and cheeks, fragrant with the scent of sandalwood soap.

"Are you scared?"

"Why should I be?"

"What if Amma wakes up?"

"Hm." He could see her smile, even in the dark.

He wanted to say, "I've often thought at night about the time when you and I will be alone together. But now, it's enough that you're near me. I'm prepared to wait until you come into my room by right."

"When are you leaving?"

"Tomorrow."

Her voice was soft, but he could make out her anger and distress. "Why did you come, then? You needn't have come if you were in such a hurry."

"The day after then. But it's not enough, is it, if only you invite me?"

"Do you want Amma to invite you? She knows you write to me."

He stroked her shoulders.

She said, "We'll go to the beach tomorrow."

"Will your mother allow that?"

"We'll take Unni with us. I'll insist on going."

"It's so hot," he said, blowing on his chest. She wiped his forehead and neck with the edge if her half-sari.

"Your father won't approve of me." He thought of the lovers he had read about in poems and novels and said, "I don't have money. I have nothing. Rich young men will ask for you."

"And what if this is enough for me?"

"You'll regret it."

"Indeed?"

Unni turned in his sleep and muttered.

"Go to sleep now, Thangam." She said nothing, but her arms tightened around him. He was suddenly afraid. This was not Sumitra. This was Thangamani. No, he could not afford to be rash.

"Go to sleep Thangam. Your mother might wake up." He knew she would not understand, but still he said, "We must wait."

He led her to the door, and gently released her from his arms. He felt proud of himself when he came back and lay down.

Next evening, he dressed carefully to go to the beach. He wore the best shirt he had, powdered his face and moistened his thin moustache with his tongue. Satisfied, he took his camera and went out. Unni was in the courtyard. He guessed from her mother's look of displeature that Thangamani had an argument before she got permission to go. She made an effort to smile and said,

"Come back before it gets late," and muttered, "As if she's a child to go off like that."

He was astonished to see Thangamani in a sari. She had done her hair in two plaits with shining gilt paper roses tucked into them.

Sethu hesitated when he saw an old man come in through the gate.

Unni explained that he was his mother's older sister's husband. He used to be a village officer.

"Who's this?"

Sethu smiled respectfully. Thangamani's mother introduced Sethu.

Thangamani signalled with her eyes, let's go. She went out with Unni and Sethu followed, feeling embarrassed.

He was relieved when they reached the road. "Your uncle will tell everyone now."

Thangamani said softly, so that Unni would not hear, "Let him."

They went through the coconut groves and fields and came to the sea where it was cooler. He thought Thangamani's face, flushed from the sunshine, was the colour of faded four o' clock flowers. He hated the way the sturdy young boatmen who passed by them stared at her.

The seashore was deserted. Waves coiled around their feet like little snakes and slipped away.

"Come on." He went down to the water and held out his hand. The dark-skinned people who lived in the huts on the seashore were looking at them. He ignored them and took her hand.

Thangamani cried out excitedly when a huge wave tore away the sand under their feet.

They sat close to each other on the warm sand. Brushing the sand off the gold border of her saree, Thangamani said.

"Amma didn't like my coming with you. She gave in only because I insisted."

"Shall I take a picture of you?"

"No, I won't let you."

"We'll see."

"I never come out well in pictures."

"I don't care. It's for me to look at."

He first took a picture of Unni. All the rest were of Thangamani. He prayed that he had understood what Balakrishnan had taught him about the mechanism of the old box camera a couple of days ago.

"You must tear up the ones that don't come out all right."

"Sethu Etta, you must blow mine up and send it to me," said Unni.

The sea turned from deep blue to copper. Bright yellow and red clouds streaked the grey sky.

Unni wanted to go back, "Let's go, Sethu Etta!"

Sethu wanted to stay there, gazing at her faintly smiling eyes and the beads of sweat on her upper lip. He got up reluctantly. They walked through the dim twilight. As they neared the house, it saddened him to think that the few hours when he had been her protector were nearly over.

He spent another night listening for her footsteps. Holding her body that smelled of sandalwood soap close to him and talking softly to her of the future, he told himself, "I am a god now."

He saw her reddened eyes as he said goodbye in the morning, and pain spread through him like a black cloud.

"Tell your mother I asked after her. And come whenever you're free, Sethu."

His eyes ached when he tried to smile. He turned back at the edge of the field and saw the flash of a blue skirt among the bamboo thickets.

3

Sethu had planned to go straight back to college and not go home on his way back. He had two and a half rupees with him and he could take a direct bus to town with it. But the bus which should have arrived at eleven thirty had not come even at noon. A vendor who sold booklets of folk songs and wooden clogs put down his tray of wares near Sethu and sat down to rest. It was from him that Sethu learnt the bus had broken down. The next one would come only at three. The bus to his village arrived as he waited, uncertain what to do. Tired of having been on his feet since morning, he decided to get in, if only to sit down.

Amma asked, as soon as he got home, "Where are you coming from, at this time of day?"

The tone of her voice warned him not to tell a lie. "Parameswaran came to Palghat looking for you and said you were not there."

"When did he go?"

"The day before yesterday."

Sethu thought for a moment, then said, "I had to go to Thrissur for a meeting. After that I went to a friend's house with him." Should he mention the boy's name, his family name, his father's occupation? And describe the house? No, Amma wouldn't be interested. Very casually, he added, "My friend lives close to Pushpoth, so I dropped in on the way back."

He did not look at Amma's face as he spoke. He thought she would stop frowning and ask him about Pushpoth. But all she did was to open her betel box and stare at it unconcernedly.

Sethu had not had lunch. Hunger spread through him suddenly like a flame.

He went upstairs, took off his shirt and vest and lay on the ledge, fuming. What would Amma have thought? It was the first time Parameswarettan had visited him. What an occasion he had chosen.

He took the camera out of his bag and fiddled with it. Padmu brought a glass of coffee and left it on the window sill. The glass felt sticky. It had probably not been washed properly. Specks of coffee floated in a liquid the colour of dirty water. He swallowed a mouthful. It had the filthy flavour of palmyra jaggery.

He heard Cheriamma ask Amma, "Who's that upstairs?"

"Sethu."

"Does he have holidays now?" Amma did not answer. He pushed opened the crumbling door of the makeshift bathroom, threw away the contents of the glass and left it on the ledge.

He did not feel like going out. He thought he would lie down. He tried to fix the images of the last two nights clearly in his mind and felt a pleasant laziness run through him.

At dusk he went down and walked in the yard. A lamp had been lighted and left on the steps. The flame flickered and died because there no oil. Madhava Ammama came in with a teak leaf packet and gave it to Padmu, "Take this in through the outside verandah."

Fish was never taken directly into the kitchen. Madhava Ammama sat down on the verandah, took out a beedi and asked,

"When did you come?"

"This evening."

Amma came out just as Madhava Ammama got up to leave. "Are you leaving?"

Madhava Ammama waited.

"Shall I serve dinner?"

"No."

"They sent for you from the illam a couple of times. Have you been there?"

Madhava Ammama did not answer.

"That poor young Kunhathol dragged herself to the fence, big stomach and all, to call you."

"So what can I do about that? I can't force Govindan to give them the paddy in his granary, can I? I'm not a paid employee. They have a sturdy young man there to look after their affairs, anyway."

"But we all know that Unni Namboodiri is quite useless."

Madhava Ammama did not say anything to that.

"I got them some petty cash twice from the areca nut transactions. I can't go asking for any again."

"But she is near her term. There'll be a curse on us if she starves."

"Give them charity then, if you're so concerned."

Amma gave her younger brother a long look and went in. Madhava Ammama left.

Amma muttered to herself, "The insensitive brute!"

Sethu realized that the opening in the fence between their house and Vadakkethu had been closed again.

He would have liked to see Sumitra. He wondered how the newly married Devu was. He would have to call her Ammayi now.

Cheriamma began talking to the old cherumi woman who had brought a bundle of drumstick leaves in a very low voice. Sethu realized that there had been a quarrel four days after the wedding.

"You tell us now, do we have to worship her, I and my sister, just because she's married to our brother? We cannot forget the past." Evidently, Padmu had called her "Devu Edathi" by mistake.

"It's like we have a mother-in-law!"

The river was full now, so the water would be muddy. There were no sounds from the illam tank. There was probably no one there. He asked for a towel. He was given one that had been washed and flung in a corner while wet, and it smelled dank. When he got to the illam tank, there was a someone in it. He sat down on a stone in the coconut grove. He could hear the indistinct voices of people going home from the market through the fields.

"Who is that?"

"It's me." Sethu stood up.

"When did you come, Sethu?" It was Unni Namboodiri.

"This evening. I was waiting for the tank to be free."

Unni Namboodiri squatted down next to him. "Have you finished your studies, then?"

"No, I've got another year. I have to write my BA examinations."

Someone came up from the tank murmuring prayers.

Sethu said, "The tank is free now." Unni Namboodiri walked with him.

Sethu was relucant to get into the water, so he started to wash out his towel. Unni Namboodiri squatted on a step above.

"You weren't here, Sethu, were you, when my mother died?"

"Valia Kunhathol died? I didn't know."

"Yes, in Thulam. I wasn't here. I was at the Amakkavu temple. They sent for me."

Sethu suddenly realized that he had not heard Unni Namboodiri's usual laugh. He could not make out Unni Namboodiri's face as he sat hunched up, stroking his spiky hair, but he felt he had changed.

"Why don't you become a doctor, Sethu?" Why had Unni Namboodiri thought that a good idea?

"It's very expensive. People like me can't afford it."

"Doctors earn a lot. For my wife's confinement. . . ." Unni Namboodiri's anterjanam had been in labour for four whole days. They had had to send three times in succession for the doctor, who lived all of six miles away.

"He's a Variar, the doctor, from Shukapuram. He asked me, do you want the child or the mother. The child was still born. And that Variar had to treat her for a long time."

Unni Namboodiri lit a beedi. Sethu saw that he looked like an old man.

Sethu had a quick dip. The water was very cold. Busy wiping his hair dry, he did not hear what Unni Namboodiri said.

"What?"

"What kind of job can you get with a BA?"

"I'll have to look around."

"What kind of salary, anyway?"

Sethu smiled at Unni Namboodiri's ignorance. "It depends on one's luck."

Unni Namboodiri grunted, then laughed his familiar foolish laugh. "You're lucky, all of you." He had a bath, came out of the water and said, "My torch is spoilt; the batteries have run down."

It was very dark in the coconut grove, so they returned by way of the illam. Sethu felt a sudden surge of compassion for Unni Namboodiri as they stood together in the courtyard and he used the old formula of respect, "Adiyan, is leaving tomorrow."

Unni Namboodiri scratched his head. "I believe the newspapers say that the tenant-farmers can take all the lands for themselves. Did you read it, Sethu?"

Sethu was embarrassed. "They can't take over completely. The landlords will have smaller incomes. Only the landlords with a lot of land will be affected."

"I asked the lawyer. He said it was no use going to court. What can we do if the government is on Govindan's side? I didn't know this was what Independence meant!"

Sethu waited quietly for a minute. "Adiyan must leave."

He thought of the dead Kunhathol as he walked through the dark. He could still remember her tired eyes lighting up as she stood in the shadows behind the door, listening to the gramophone play kathakali songs, her long earlobes swinging as she shook her head. What had she died of ? He had forgotten to ask Unni Namboodiri.

He overheard Amma and Cheriamma discuss the troubles at the illam. Madhava Ammama went there now only on the days when the areca nuts were plucked. He had paid an advance for the purchase of the Kandankulangara seedling nursery. He would have five hundred rupees' worth of tapioca to sell. Vadakkethu was going to be tiled. Cheriamma had heard about it from someone. When Amma came to know, she had exploded.

"Let him build their palace for them. The wretches used to live on others' leavings. Phoo!"

While Sethu ate, Cheriamma asked curiously, "Amma said you'd been to Pushpoth?"

"Um."

"What's up with them?"

He said, without looking up from his plate, "They're all right."

"Does Govindan Nair send them any money?"

"Maybe he does. I didn't ask."

"Is the eldest girl there?"

"She's in Vishakapatnam."

"There's one younger—what's her name now? She must have grown up."

The younger one whose name you can't remember. Ah, it's from her name that a whirlwind will burst in this house.

"I think she's in the tenth."

"And the youngest is a boy, the same age as my Padmu."

Sethu said, to change the subject, "I didn't know Kunhathol died until Unni Namboodiri told me."

"Poor thing, she went quickly without too much suffering. She was lucky."

At night, he spread his mattress on the ledge in the verandah. The night before, he had slept on a double mattress in the room with the glass windows.

The sky he could see now through the areca nut palms was not beautiful. He could hardly believe in the past two nights, the nights that had murmured so softly to him. Maybe they were a dream. But no, Thangam had lain here, in the circle of his arms. He could still feel her breath, faintly warm. Here, in his arms.

He decided to leave by the nine thirty train next morning. Amma was in the kitchen, slicing raw bananas into a winnowing tray.

"I'm going. I want to catch the nine thirty train."

"Um."

"Can you give me five rupees?"

Amma raised her head to look at him. Then she threw the knife down, wiped her banana-stained hands on her dirty mundu and went inside. She brought him three filthy one rupee notes. "This is all I have."

He took them and went out, bending his head so that it did not knock against the door. Amma said,

"We don't have money in deposits or a treasure to educate you. Remember the old man is working hard for you in some strange place."

He was furious. He asked angrily, "And what can I do about that?"

"If you go wandering around the countryside when you should be studying, you'll be a fit companion for your brother, I'm sure."

He fought down his anger and sadness. His mother's harsh words lingered in his mind like specks of dust. He had scored the highest mark in every examination in high school, although no one had asked this of him. At every annual function in school, he had gone up to the stage to receive his prizes. No one at home had cared about them. No one ever checked whether he had paid his fees or hostel dues on time, whether he had enough money to travel up and down.

The day after he reached college, he managed to see Krishnankutty alone. They went out for a walk. He had secrets to tell Krishnankutty now. But when they settled down in a corner of the maidan, in the shadow of the fort, he felt confused.

His joy was tinged with pain. He was in love. The world was against him. It was difficult to start describing it, but once he started, he had a lot to say.

"Who is against it?" asked Krishnankutty.

"My mother doesn't like it. My father doesn't know, but he will not like it either."

"And your brother?"

"He'll be against it as well."

"What about her people?"

"Her father is sure to object."

The imaginary pictures grew sharper as he talked. His love affair was being discussed by everyone in the family. He was now ready for anything. Her hard-hearted father might try to marry her to someone else. He felt inspired, delighted, by all these illusionary obstacles.

Krishnankutty listened attentively, gazing into the distance. "Tell me frankly," he said. "Are you serious? Or is this a passing fancy?"

Sethu's eyes were full of appeal. You too, Krishnankutty?

"Don't be upset. I've seen a lot of people your age confuse the two."

"Do you know, Krishnankutty, how many days it is since I slept soundly? I can't even concentrate on my studies."

Krishnankutty stood up. "Do you have faith in this girl?"

"Of course, a hundred per cent. But if she is forced."

Krishnankutty would not allow him to go on. "No, I don't want to listen. There's nothing for you to worry about."

It distressed him to think that he had not succeeded in arousing Krishnankutty's sympathy. They walked in silence. As they neared the hostel, Krishnankutty said.

"Let me tell you something Sethu. I never went in search of love. You can only imagine what my life was like. I needed someone to have faith in. I finally found her, this girl. I liked her." He stopped, as an acquaintance greeted them. When they were alone again, he went on, "You are a poet and everything you look at is tinted by the imagination. After all, it is often the image of the maidservant next door, a mother of three, seated on the pounding stone and combing out her hair, that inspires most of you to write words like `you are a dream in blue stone'."

Sethu kept quiet. At least the ruffian had admitted that he was a poet. That was a relief.

A week later, the letters arrived together, Nalini Edathi's and Achan's. He read Nalini Edathi's first.

"Ravi told me that you had come to Pushpoth. It made all of us very sad that you came so nearby and did not visit us. I know you'll come to Pushpoth again. Don't forget it was I who introduced you." Nalini Edathi's complaint did not distress him. It made him happy that she had guessed the reason for his going to Pushpoth. Let the whole world know, he thought.

Achan had written about the examination fees. He had repeated Amma's advice, "Don't go wandering around when you should be studying." He re-read the letter and was glad to acknowledge an enemy.

Achan had always been a stranger to him. The relationship between them was confined to the sixty rupees he sent Sethu every month and the accompanying letter recounting his problems.

When Achan came home once, he had shown him the prizes he had won for general proficiency and general knowledge with great pride. Achan had turned over the leaves of the prize books, put them on the arm of the chair and remarked, "How badly they bind books nowadays."

Although they had never said a kind word to him, they were quick enough to find fault with him now.

"Whose letter is it?" Krishnankutty asked.

"My father's."

"Any news?"

He did not answer. He stared at Krishnankutty. You don't believe me, do you? Wait and see. The battle has begun!

4

There was a house near the Aralikkara temple that Sethu had always admired as a high school student. It belonged to Chandrasekharan Master, who dragged a wasted foot as he walked. The house was on the banks of a small canal and big rocks lay behind it. Children who came with their mothers to the temple played on the rocks. Rows of plants with yellow flowers grew on the fence. The garden was not big, but it was pretty, with the tiled house set in the midst of areca nut palms laden with flowers and nuts, lovely and tender as young women. Whenever Sethu thought about a family of his own, it was the image of this house that came to his mind.

Sethu remembered with relief that he would soon finish his studies and be independent. Then he could have a house like that.

In the month of Edavam, the areca nut palms in its garden swayed in the wind like women with long hair. In Chingam, shadows lurked shyly between patches of moonlight. In Thulam, when the canal overflowed with the rains, you could sit on the verandah and watch the water bubble over the beds of karuka grass, listen to the bells from the temple, people talking near the temple tank.

"Thangamani, we must find a name for our house."

"You tell me."

"No, you must."

"Shall I? Kavita!"

When he sent the examination fees, Achan wrote, the question of my extension is still under discussion. Most probably, I will have to retire by the thirty-first of March.

Sethu's reading had been confined to poetry books from the library and Thangamani's letters. He became terribly nervous as the examinations drew near. He had not made notes. He did not have textbooks for Rural Economics and Public Finance. If he could manage a first class in the first or second part, he would at least get a job as a tutor in a college.

Thangamani wrote that her examinations would begin on March tenth. She was writing a government examination as well. In his reply, he wished her success, and wrote that he was going to work very hard over the next few days. It is your fault, Thangam, that I cannot concentrate. You disturb me when I read and when I try to sleep. I shall punish you severely for this when we meet next.

It made him happy to think of her smiling and squirming with pleasure when she read that.

He ended the letter, "Dearest one, won't you pray for me?"

As soon as the exams were over, the atmosphere in the hostel changed. Senior students had to say their goodbyes. Even those who normally kept aloof joined the others. It was hard to take leave of all the people he had met here. He felt he would never find such good friends again. Juniors whom he hardly knew wanted him to write messages and childish words of wisdom on the coloured pages of their autograph books. He wrote down addresses and gave his own to many friends.

When he came back from writing the last paper, someone said, "Balakrishnan is looking for you." He went to Balakrishnan's room.

Balakrishnan said nonchalantly, "I just waited for half an hour. These fools don't let you out before that. I'll make an attempt to do the exam in September."

"Why were you looking for me?"

"I've fixed up something for the evening. Don't go out."

"What is it?"

"I'll tell you in time. Don't tell Krishnankutty. He'll make a fuss."

Krishnankutty was busy stacking his books at the bottom of his trunk.

"Packing?"

"How have you done? Will you get a first?"

"I don't know. I'll pass."

"A third is no use at all. You can do a BT or find someone to recommend you for a job, that's all. Won't your father be able to get you a job on the estate?"

"He's going to retire soon."

"But he's sure to have contacts. If you're not going to study further, it's best to get into some white man's company."

Sethu did not say anything. When Krishnankutty went on his usual walk in the evening, he stayed back. Most of the students had gone out to celebrate. He found Aravindan and Daniel John in Balakrishnan's room. Balakrishnan closed the windows, bolted the door and took out a handful of small bottles from the cupboard, like the ones sold by medical salesmen in trains. There were five of them, with pretty labels. Sethu read—banana essence, strawberry essence, tomato essence.

"Not to worry, it's liquor."

"But there's a prohibition on." The first thought that occurred to Sethu was that it would be breaking the law.

"Prohibition doesn't apply to these, they're sold in all the shops. They're the best of their kind."

Daniel described the special qualities of many kinds of alcohol. There were frequent parties at his house. After two or three rounds, his father would invite him, "Pull up a chair and have a small."

Balakrishnan said, "Toddy is best for the body."

"Come to my place. I'll give you the best toddy."

Balakrishnan opened one of the essence bottles, poured out some and topped the glass with water from the mud water pot. He held out the glass to Daniel.

Daniel savoured a mouthful and said, "Fine smell. Not bad at all."

There was just one glass. Aravindan drank, filled the glass again and extended it to Sethu.

"Please, no. I've never touched it till now."

"Touch it now then."

Aravindan told him, "One sip of this and then two puffs of a cigarette."

Sethu hesitated, "No."

Balakrishnan said, "I wasn't interested in such things at all. A friend in my place insisted that we have a drink the very day they declared prohibition. Who is the government, he said, to decide what we should drink."

"But it's not good to make a habit of it."

Sethu looked at the pale yellow liquid which had the smell of lemon grass and said, "Give it to me."

But Balakrishnan snatched the glass, emptied it in a gulp and lit a cigarette. Sethu observed that no one seemed surprised.

"I'm against prohibition. The law cannot make Mahatma Gandhis of us."

Aravindan's eyes seemed to have grown smaller. The glass exchanged hands once more.

Balakrishnan seemed to be suddenly inspired. "My friend says, will the government feed you if you are starving? Will they undertake to give you a job when you finish your studies? They and their laws!"

Sethu felt distanced from them. He leaned his elbows on the quilt spread over the coir cot and listened. When Balakrishnan opened the last bottle of essence, poured the liquid into an ounce glass, mixed it with water and held it out, Sethu accepted it. It did not taste too bad. He drank half and gave Balakrishnan the glass.

"I've had enough. You drink the rest."

He took a cigarette from Daniel's packet. What a relief, he felt all right. He got up. "See you then."

Balakrishnan came out with him and whispered that Ramakrishnan the watchman had arranged for them to go to a place in Kalpathy that night. It would cost five rupees.

"Coming?"

"No."

"She's a brahmin, and young."

"I'm not coming."

He opened the window in his room, unrolled his mattress and lay down. What if his head began to spin? Krishnankutty came back. Sethu was surprised his head felt perfectly clear.

What would Thangamani think of him ? Her examination would be over now. Would she get through? If she scored high marks, she would insist on going to college. Sethu did not like the idea of her leaving the protective circle of home. He imagined how the boys would pursue her on bicycles, how they would watch as she came out of the ladies' hostel with her friends.

"What are you thinking about?"

He smiled. "Actually, I was praying."

"To pass?'

"No, that my girlfriend may not pass."

Krishnankutty stared uncomprehendingly. He explained. If she passes, she will go to college. What if she changes after four years in the city?

Krishnankutty laughed and declaimed, "Selfishness, is not thy name Sethu?"

The next day they said their goodbyes. When he went to Balakrishnan's room to get his address, he whispered to Sethu, "You should have come. It was very safe. That rascal Ramakrishnan could have told us earlier."

Krishnankutty and Sethu left together next morning. Their friends helped them load their luggage into a horse-drawn cart. Students who had finished their theory papers were still waiting to complete their practicals. Everyone looked gloomy as they shook hands, even those who were normally rough and insensitive.

He dropped Krishnankutty at the bus stand and asked, "When will I see you again?"

"Sometime. Maybe very soon, maybe after many years. Maybe we will never meet at all. These things are not certain."

"Oh come on, you're only forty miles away. We can always meet. I'll write."

Krishnankutty smiled. "I haven't met people who live four furlongs away for years."

Sethu did not know what to say.

"Good luck!"

"I do not believe in luck, so I will not wish you the same."

Krishnankutty groped in his pocket for change to give the jutka driver. Sethu said, 'I'll pay."

"No, we'll share. You need only give him eight annas now." Sethu watched angrily as he counted out the coins. They had shared a room for three years and told each other all their secrets. Did he have to render accounts for eight annas now?

As if reading his thoughts, Krishnankutty said, "I believe in affection. Let us not be indebted to each other. Eight annas is a debt, even between us."

Sethu stood uncertainly, not sure what to say. Krishnankutty laid a hand on his shoulder and said, "Go along now, don't miss your train."

The emaciated carthorse walked slowly over the road, on which the tar had begun to melt in the heat. Whipmarks lay like threads of blood on its back. The whip cracked threateningly and Sethu could see the black, wounded flesh quiver as it whistled through the air. With a courage born of helplessness, the horse refused to speed up and ambled along slowly, dragging its hooves.

5

He got down from the train at three thirty. Since he had written earlier to Amma, Thami the cheruman boy was at the station. He had the same big teeth and spiky hair and had grown bigger.

It was Thami's father who had carried his trunk to the station that rainy night four years ago. Sethu had heard that the old

man no longer worked. He had become an oracle for the cherumans.

The river was an endless stretch of sand. There were stagnant
pools of muddy water where the water's flow had been checked.
Even with his sandals on, he could feel the heat of the sand. Thami
walked unconcernedly over the burning sand carrying the tin
trunk filled with books and clothes and the rolled-up mattress
on top of it.

Achan was seated on the easy chair in the verandah. Sethu
had always come back home with a sense of uneasiness. But this
time he felt confident. I have become a man now, I am going to
begin my life.

As he helped Thami put down the luggage, Achan got up from
his chair, spat into the courtyard and said, "Didn't you write
that your examinations would be over the day before yesterday?"
Achan's tone implied, why did you stay on for an extra day?

"Yes, they were over."

The first person he saw when he went in was Cheriamma.
"When did Achan come, Cheriamma?"

"Yesterday. He came on here after visiting his house. He doesn't
have to go back to work."

They seemed to be happy that he had retired. They knew he
had put by enough money. They could tile the roof now. Amma
had always wanted a bit of land near the river so that they would
have enough paddy through the year if the crops did not fail.

"Why should he stay in strange places and live a hard life?
He's too old for that now." Sethu knew that what Amma really
hoped for as she said this was a tiled roof and a bit of land near
the river.

Sethu sat down on the window sill in the kitchen and said, "I
haven't given Thami anything."

"Um, I'll give him something."

Amma poured the tea she had made for Achan into two glasses
and held out one to Sethu.

"Padmu, take this to the verandah."

She moved the aluminium vessel to the corner, put the shabby
old tins of tea and sugar on the shelf and sat at the kitchen door,
scratching her arms. "Um, and isn't it gold, real gold, that he's
brought home when he retired. I just pray that I don't say too
much."

Amma evidently found it difficult to control her anger. "He's come after being fed and entertained by his sisters. I knew, even then."

Sethu provoked her. "He might have money in the bank. How would you know?"

Amma imitated Achan's tone and expression. "Why would I need wealth? I have two sons after all."

Cheriamma contributed a profound statement. "Fulfilment is a matter of destiny!" She had an example to illustrate this. Madhava Ammama did not have a job, but he could live on the tapioca and nenthram bananas that he grew. He had given Vadakkethu a tiled roof and their garden was full of newly planted saplings.

Achan's shirt and veshti hung in the upstairs room and the old leather case was on the ledge. Sethu tried to open it, but it was locked. It was then that he saw the half empty bottle under the cot. The inverted glass next to it smelt of alcohol.

He hurried down when he heard Achan come up the stairs, coughing. He stood aside on the stairs for him to go by. Achan paused and asked, not meeting his eyes.

"When will your results be out?"

"In two months."

The thought uppermost in his mind was that he no longer had a place where he could be undisturbed. He walked up and down the yard, feeling disgusted. Achan had come down again. Lying in his easy chair, he kept wiping his face with his towel and spitting into the yard.

"As if it's so easy to pay for a boy these days until he finishes his BA. So many rich people around, but how many of them educate their children? I didn't do all this in the hope that the children will be useful to me. I don't want them to feel that way."

The next time he spat, the spittle fell on the verandah. Sethu watched him, full of irritation and disgust.

Whom did Achan want to accuse? Him? Amma? The world?

"I had enough, educating one of them. If I'd used that money to buy a coconut grove, I would have been sure of a hundred rupees a month now."

"And your nephews and nieces would enjoy all of it. Why blame us," said Amma, who had just come to the verandah. Achan fell silent. He cleared his throat, blew his nose, got up, threw down his slippers from the rafters noisily and went out.

Sethu thought of the debts that Krishnankutty had talked about. He had kept accounts for all the money Achan had sent him. He told himself that he had to go through them. Father must have already exhausted his capital. An image of the moneylender Sait doing the rounds to collect his interest flashed through Sethu's mind.

He had boasted about his father to a lot of his friends. He thought uneasily of all those to whom he had given his address.

What if Daniel turned up here!

Hullo, meet my father.

This is my mother.

He moved into the southern room and called out to Padmu for a lamp. Amma said, "You've finished your exams, haven't you? It won't hurt you not to read for one day. It's not even three days since I bought a bottle of kerosene oil, and there's not a drop left."

Sethu lay flat in the dark on the creaky wooden ledge and muttered, "Home, sweet home!"

PART SIX

He waits as the ferryboat creeps slowly over the river from the farther shore.

The thought suddenly occurs to him that the boat has always been on the farther shore every time he started on a journey. And whenever he got down from the train in the hot afternoon sunshine and came to the farther shore, the boat would be rocking gently on its moorings on this side.

Is it only here that this happens?

Does this happen only to me?

As he waits for the eastbound train, the porter says, the westbound train is due to cross here. He listens attentively for the bell. Good, it is the eastbound train that has been blocked. Bag on shoulder, he prepares to elbow his way in, only to see the train come in on the second line! He has to wait resentfully until the westbound train arrives, spits out a crowd of people, takes in another crowd and finally moves off.

My boat is always on the farther shore, and my train on the second line!

As he sits in the bus, hot and thirsty, waiting for the closed railroad crossing to open, it is the gate on the farther side that opens first. Exhausted, he waits for rows and rows of vehicles to pass. He tells himself, it is because I am in this bus that it so happened.

1

There were sounds of a quarrel one evening at Vadakkethu.

Amma said, "Wretches, they're at it again. There's no rest or peace for the neighbours."

It took Sethu some time to realize that it was a squabble. Devu's voice rose to a wail and Ammayi began to scream. Sumitra kept her voice down. After that he heard Madhava Ammama shout, "I'll kick out the whole lot of you."

The screams became sobs. Cheriamma stood at the northern door, listening and giving Amma a running commentary.

When all was quiet, Amma said contemptuously, "They're as bad as the cherumans. Only he would bother to look after them."

Sethu was afraid to go out. Everyone would ask, "Haven't you found a job yet?"

"I'm looking for one."

"In what field?"

He would answer, the Railways or the Customs, to escape further questions.

Everyday, he would stand at the door of the post office, craning his neck to find out whether any of the envelopes that the postman had stamped were official. He tried to look casual, careful not to show that he hoped the next name to be called would be his. Then he would leave pretending he had just dropped in while passing by. His face and forehead beaded with sweat, he would pray that no one would notice him. And as he walked home, keeping in the shade of the screwpine bushes, someone would ask,

"So Sethumadhavan, you haven't found a job yet?"

People had their own ideas about jobs. Most people were happy to hear that he was trying to get a job in the railways. It meant good money. If he became the station master at Tirur or Thanur, he could make a hundred rupees a day effortlessly. In the bigger stations, it was better to work in the goods or parcel section. He did not have to receive money directly. Bribes paid by those who came to book their goods were shared by all the employees. The villagers were full of stories of people who had made money in railway jobs.

He had been able to put people off until the results came.

He finally stopped going to the post office. If there was something for him, the delivery man would bring it next morning. A stream of letters came from his friends as soon as he got home, but had soon dwindled. Congratulatory messages had arrived as soon as the results were announced. Those who had passed wrote to him about their future plans.

The congratulations had not moved him. He had a second class in the first and second parts and a third in the subsidiary subjects.

Krishnankutty had passed but had only a third. There were no letters from him. Sethu thought of writing to him many times, but put it off. He would write to him, he thought, after he found a job.

Thangamani's letters came regularly. He needed four annas a week to reply to her. He had made a habit of sending her a self-addressed envelope, so he could not break it now. He would ask Amma for a rupee or two to send his application forms. He had to walk six miles to meet a gazetted officer or a doctor in a government hospital, who would attest the copies of his certificates. Amma usually gave him the money for his applications without any questions. Except once, when she asked.

"Wasn't it just the other day that you said you were going for a certificate?"

"That was another one."

She looked disgruntled, but did not dare protest since it concerned his career.

He saw Thangamani once after the results came out, when he went to see Achan about a job. Amma asked, "Is it for a post on the estate?"

"Mm."

Amma had no money to give him for the journey, so she sent Padmu to the illam. They had none either. The young Kunhathol herself had to borrow small sums from the women who came to the ghat to bathe.

Cheriamma suggested sending Padmu to Andoor Meenakshi Amma's house. Her guess that they were sure to have money since the mud pots they made were selling at better prices proved right.

Sethu had been worried that Amma would ask him to delay his going by a couple of days. He had already written to

Thangamani that he was going to see Achan and she would be expecting him.

When he reached Achan's house, Thangamani and Unni had already arrived that morning.

He knew that Nalini Edathi and Achan's sisters were watching him closely. So he kept away from Thangamani. In the evening, seated near the kuvalam tree, talking to Unni, he saw her near the pounding shed.

He tried to keep track of her as she moved around the house. A lucky chance suddenly came his way.

Valia Oppu grumbled, "I wonder whether there's oil in the lamp upstairs. It's not been cleaned for days. I suppose you have your usual headache, Nalini. Don't provoke me into saying something I shouldn't—Thangam, go and get me the lamp."

He said to Ravi, "I forgot, There's something I want to show you." Unni wanted to go up with him, so he asked him to get him the newspaper from Achan's room and went quickly into the house. He was lucky, no one was about. Valia Oppu was in the verandah, scolding Nalini Edathi. "You and your headaches! Who wants to see your gloomy face?"

He went up quietly and waited. The stairs creaked. Thangamani. She ran into his arms like a baby bird seeking shelter.

"Did you get my letter?"

"Yes, this morning. I started at once."

"I have to leave tomorrow."

"Won't you come home?"

"Not this time, Thangam."

"I've been waiting for so many days. You don't care for me, do you?" She sulked like a child. He thought her eyes were wet.

"It's because I can't come. Please understand, Thangam."

He stroked her shoulder and said, trying to make his voice sound sad, "Why give people a reason to talk? I'm ready for whatever they say about me, but if they talk about you." He gazed steadily at an invisible point beyond her, hoping that tears would come to his eyes.

They heard footsteps outside and quickly drew apart. It was Nalini Edathi.

He felt intensely irritated. She had come up as quietly as a cat.

"I have a headache. I'll lie down for a while." She brushed past Sethu and went into the room. He hurried downstairs without talking to Thangamani. He had only himself to blame. He should have taken care.

As he went into the courtyard wiping his forehead, Ravi asked, "Where is it, Sethu Etta?"

"What?"

He suddenly remembered the lie he had told Ravi. "I wanted to show you a photograph. But I think I've forgotten to bring it."

Achan called out, "Have you had a bath, Sethumadhavan?"

"Yes."

"You can sleep here."

In Achan's room. He did not say anything to that. Achan came down and began to pace up and down the courtyard. Sethu waited, leaning against the cement pillar, hoping he would say something.

"What happened to the job in Madras?"

"They haven't replied."

"Um."

He thought the topic was closed when Achan asked, "What job is it?"

"A tutor's post in the office of the Education Department of the Director of Public Instruction. If I get it and work for two years, I can do my MA privately."

"There are so many other good departments. Why don't you apply to them?"

Resentment flared up in him. When he had wanted to subscribe to an English newspaper, they had not allowed him. They had told him that Parameswaran would look at the newspapers and tell him if there was anything suitable. So he had had to wait every evening by the fields and waylay Krishnan Master of the Elementary School in order to have a look at his three-day-old paper for job vacancies.

After a while, he hinted to Achan, "Anyway there's no point these days in just sending an application. You need to know someone with influence."

If only he could get a clerk's job on a white man's estate. They started with a salary of at least a hundred and fifty. Surely Achan could write to someone he knew?

He had dinner with Achan. He kept his eyes on his leaf whenever Nalini Edathi passed by them.

After dinner, he sat by himself at the end of the verandah. Nalani Edathi came up to him. "Why are you sitting in the dark?"

"Just like that."

"Shall I bring the lamp this side?"

"No."

She sat down on the floor, below the open window. He knew she wanted to talk to him. He got up and said, "I think I'll go to bed early today."

"Why, aren't you feeling well?"

"I have a headache."

Nalini Edathi smiled. "I have a headache all the time. Amma says it's just my imagination. Cheriamma thinks it's an excuse to shirk housework."

Edathi Amma's room was empty, but they had spread his mattress in the outer room, on the floor, beside Achan's cot. Was it because Achan had told them to do so? Or had they made the decision because Thangamani was in the house?

Unni and Ravi slept on the front verandah. They invited him to join them.

A lamp had been lit at dusk before the picture of Krishna in Achan's room, and the odour of the burnt-out wick still clung to the room, mingling with a faint smell of alcohol.

Achan's cot creaked every time Sethu was about to fall asleep. He woke up with a start. Achan coughed constantly and called out, "Amme, Guruvayurappa!" or "Ah, my Gods!" Did Achan usually pray in his sleep?

In the morning, Sethu stuffed his clothes into his bag and said, "I'm leaving."

"Why are you in such a hurry? You can go tomorrow," said Achan, but his tone implied that he did not really care.

"There might be some information in the post."

Achan did not insist. He gave Sethu five one rupee notes and said, "I'll be there next week."

Nalini Edathi and his father's sisters asked him to wait and have breakfast before he left. He offered all sorts of excuses. He had to catch the nine thirty bus. He had to collect two certificates on the way and send them immediately by registered post.

He had tea and left as if in protest. As he walked through the lane he saw Thangamani beneath the papaya tree near the pounding shed.

2

Achan came home after a week. He asked, as usual, "What happened to your application?"

Which one? There had been so many.

"Nothing so far."

Appu Nair of Kunnathuparambil brought a bit of news. Narayanan Nair, the High Court Judge, was home on vacation. He was a kind person and had recommended many people to good positions. Appu Nair's older brother managed Narayanan Nair's affairs and would speak to the Judge on Sethu's behalf.

The Judge was his student when Achan had been a schoolmaster. Sethu had often heard Achan say so.

Appu Nair said, "Come home early one morning and go with Ettan. He'll do whatever is necessary."

Appu Nair and Achan talked about the Judge's good fortune, his generosity, his food habits. Sethu went up the hill and saw the train come over the bridge with the red mail box on it. The mail was late. Surely there would be something for him today, he hoped, as he watched the delivery agent Kuttinarayanan pass by each day.

He had sent applications to all the firms whose addresses he knew. He knew the formula by heart now and could write without thinking. "Having come to understand that there are a few vacancies in your company, I beg to. . . ."

Some of them, generally the British companies, sent printed regret cards. Only they had the kindness to put an end to the agony of waiting.

He walked through the jnaval grove to the rocks above. The stretches in the distance which had once been covered with grass were now marked out into sweet potato fields. A few isolated cattle grazed on the hillside, over which the last rays of the setting sun still lingered, making it impossible for darkness to take over. He came down the hill and began to walk home. By the jnaval trees, he met Sumitra.

"When did you get back from your father's?"

Sumitra looked darker in the dim light. Her blouse seemed too large for her.

"On Friday. Where are you going, Sumitra?"

"I went to Mani's. Her chit had matured. I have a half share."

He noticed black shadows under her eyes.

"I never see you these days, Sethu."

He did not reply. To change the subject, he asked, "What was the noise about?"

"It goes on all the time. It's just that you haven't heard it before, Sethu."

"Who is she quarrelling with?"

"I try my best to be patient. What can I do if Edathi is determined to start a fight? When she goes too far, I say something as well."

"What does Edathi have against you?"

"How would I know?"

Sethu kept quiet. She asked, "Don't you go to collect the post now?"

"Why should I?"

"I just asked, that's all. I often see you go. But even if I stand at the gate, you take no notice of me." She tried to speak casually but Sethu could make out the distress in her voice.

"I didn't see you, Sumitra."

"You wouldn't."

Darkness had settled in the bamboo thickets and the jnaval leaves.

"When will you get a job, Sethu?"

"I'm trying for one."

"Boys can always go away somewhere, they're so lucky." She walked ahead and asked, without turning around, "Shall I come with you, Sethu, when you get a job and go away?"

He could not see her face. Was she teasing him?

"Don't be silly."

"I'm serious. If you feel ashamed of me, you can always tell people that you took me along from the village to cook and clean for you."

He was disappointed with himself, because he could not laugh loudly and pretend it was a joke.

They walked in the dark, close to each other, without touching. Sethu stopped at the turning to his house. Sumitra was so near him. He caught the unpleasant odour of her sweat and of her hair that had been gathered into a knot before it had dried properly.

He thought with astonishment that Sumitra had once been the flame that blazed in his blood, his nerves, the pores of his skin. Now, standing next to her, he felt no excitement, nor did his heartbeats quicken.

He patted her shoulder as if to reassure her.

"I'll have to go."

She gripped the fingers of his left hand. "When will I see you again?"

"I'll see you."

"When?"

"I must find the time, child."

She would not release his hand. He walked with her, feeling uneasy. They went through the broken fence, and he made no attempt to free his hand. The old teak tree, shorn of its leaves, looked like the skeleton of a rakshasa. He took his hand away from her grip, put an arm around her waist and touched her cheek gently.

"It's dark Sumitra. Go home now."

Sumitra smiled. "I always knew that that was all you cared."

He could not bear to think that she had begun to understand him. He pulled her to him roughly, "What did you say, what?"

He murmured all kinds of meaningless words, not even sure she heard him.

When he pulled her down on the moist earth covered with dry leaves, she did not protest.

Raindrops that still clung to the rakshasa's skeleton from the morning's shower dripped on them. He was filled with cruelty, not excitement.

"Sethu, wait, there are thorns." He paid no attention.

A sudden wind ran wildly through the leaves, making strange noises.

He leaned against the worm-eaten trunk of the teak tree and said goodbye to her. He thought she would go away quietly into the darkness.

She rubbed her elbows, came close to him and peered, as if trying to make out his face in the dark.

"Why did you you come back so soon from your father's?"

"Just like that."

"You didn't go to Pushpoth?"

"Um."

"Of course you did."

"Um?"

"You think no one knows?

"Knows what?'

He was full of happiness. So Sumitra knew. She could not accuse him now of having deceived her. He felt as if he had been absolved from all blame.

"Do you do these things to Thangamani?"

"Don't talk like that!" He raised his hand as though to hit her. "It's very late, Sumitra. Now go along."

He hurried away without waiting for her. It took him some time to find the opening in the fence, in the dark.

He saw Achan in the courtyard and quickly went round by the south, pretending he had just come from the illam tank. Achan said,

"You had better get up early tomorrow. We can come back before it gets too hot."

"Where are we going?"

"Across the river, to see Menon. I don't want anyone to blame me for not doing my best."

He heard Achan's voice from the darkness in the southern room. "It's not enough that I educated him, now I have to find him a job as well. He expects me to do everything for him. Boys should be able to handle their own affairs. And be smart. No one hands out a job for the asking."

Sethu said to Amma, "Let Achan go by himself. I'm not going."

Amma drew herself up, ready to do battle. "Why waste good things on a dog? Shut yourself in your room with your silly books and squeeze out your pimples to pass the time."

Sethu pushed open the door angrily and went in.

3

Achan asked at the gate, "Have you taken all your certificates?"

"No, should I?"

Achan muttered something indistinctly. He said, "I'll go and get them."

He had already turned when Achan checked him, "Don't go back now."

Then Achan said rather sadly, resentfully, "You turned back anyway. Go and get them now."

He hurried up the steps, went in and took the envelope with the certificates out of the tin trunk. He told himself firmly that it was just a silly superstition that you should not turn back once you had set out on a mission. A foolish old saying. But when he remembered that it concerned his own career, he was afraid. He consoled himself— as if everyone in the world lived by such beliefs!

Patches of blue showed here and there on Achan's over-starched shirt. His long veshti with the black border kept slipping off his shoulder and he had to stop every ten yards to put it back. He walked very fast, the edge of his mundu and his umbrella clutched in his hand.

When Sethu had gone to bed, he had decided he would not go to meet anyone about a job, even if it were the governor himself. But his courage had gradually dwindled. What if he had arrived at fortune's door? The Judge's recommendation might open the way to new worlds. It would be foolish to be obstinate. There was nothing to lose. What if he regretted it later? He finally decided to go and meet the Judge.

As they crossed from the field onto the road, they met Madhava Ammama. He moved aside and asked Achan respectfully, "Where to?"

"Across the river."

Sethu thought Madhava Ammama looked a little more well-groomed. He wore a double mundu and a new vest obviously bought in the town, not the kind the local tailor sold. It had white silk seams at the sleeves and neck.

The river was quiet after the floods in Thulam. The ferryboat was on the farther shore. As they waited, people asked, "Where to, father and son?"

Sethu was embarrassed when Achan explained at length that they were going to see Judge Menon about a job. Why did he want to tell everyone this ? Nor did he stop there. He went on to tell them how he had taught Menon long ago.

Achan had worked in many places during the last thirty years. But he had remained a villager in his speech and attitudes.

The post master said he had been to the Judge's house before he became a High Court Judge. "He's so well off. They say he's built a mansion in Madras, a splendid place. There's nothing he can't do for you."

A man sitting on the culvert took up from that point. "You cannot accuse him of not helping the villagers. It was he who found our Sankunni's son Chathukutty a position. He's an ameen in the Ottappalam court now." Sethu had seen the old man in he vicinity of the post office, but did not know his name.

Anyway, Achan had laid the matter of his job open for the villagers to discuss.

One of them might ask what the envelope in his hand contained. If he told them, many of them would want to look at the certificates. Not one of them would understand what the certificates meant, but they would discuss the quality of the paper, the colours, the typed letters. He quickly slipped the envelope inside his shirt.

The ferryboat arrived and they crossed over. People waiting on the other side asked, "Where to, father and son?"

Unfortunately, there was no donkey. There should have been a father, a son and a donkey.

The river bed, used to cultivate vegetables in summer, was full of holes now filled with muddy water from the Thulam rains. The old pathways were covered with dirt. Sethu slowed down as they reached the field which had been ploughed for the summer crop. Achan was way ahead.

They went past the building in which Cheriachan used to have a shop. It looked the same except that the provisions occupied only half the space. The other half was a teashop. He saw a mappila with a rounded beard seated in front of the provisions. They passed the weavers' huts, came to the lane and crossed a number of unmarked compounds without walls or fences before they reached the temple. Achan took off his slippers, stood on the first stone step of the temple, tied his veshti around his waist, joined his palms and closed his eyes.

They could not see the temple from the dilapidated steps. A huge banyan tree obscured their view.

Sethu wondered, should he pray? He closed his eyes for a second. Bhagavathi, take care of me. That was enough. Faith was in the mind, the mind would prostrate itself.

Achan made sure he was behind and went on. They saw the big tiled gatehouse at the edge of the field after they had walked a mile. Achan turned and said, "That's the house."

People were clustered together in the courtyard. The sun had begun to get hot. Nambisan came out of the house, a tulasi flower tucked behind his ear, a big sandalwood paste mark on his forehead and a leaf cup in his hand. Achan asked, "Is he in?"

"Yes."

Huge crotons stood in pots on both sides of the pathway. Sethu felt that the eyes of everyone waiting in the cemented courtyard were on the newcomers. He suddenly felt afraid as they climbed into the verandah. The grey-haired man with spectacles stretched out on the easy chair in the room just beyond the verandah must be Judge Menon. The room was filled with people. Sethu kept behind Achan.

Achan stood at the door and joined his palms to make an obeisance. The boatsong he had learnt in the fourth class suddenly came to mind. "Clasping to his breast his fellow-disciple whose breast smelled of sweat." The lines from Ramapurathu Variar's poem on Kuchelan that Krishnan Master used to recite.

But this was not Achan's fellow-disciple, this was his student. Sethu waited impatiently for the Judge to get up, come and take Achan's hand and lead him inside. Maybe Judge Menon had not seen Achan properly. But Achan was standing right at the door, he could not have missed seeing him. Maybe he had not recognized him. Sethu moved towards the end of the verandah.

Achan continued to stand there hopefully with his palms joined. Then he slowly came back to Sethu. Sethu gazed at the garden. The people waiting outside must be watching him and Achan. He did not dare turn and look. What if there were other young men here who had come for a recommendation?

Steps led from the verandah to the eastern courtyard. The kitchen would be somewhere there, thought Sethu. He recognised the person who had just come out, the man with a stoop, wearing a knee-length towel. It was the manager, Govindan Nair. Achan saw him at last and went towards him, looking relieved.

Govindan Nair pushed a copper pot towards the door and came up to Achan. Sethu watched resentfully while they talked. Imagine asking this old, stooping servant for a recommendation. He made an effort to smile as they came up to him.

Govindan Nair asked Achan to sit on the bench in the verandah. Achan hesitated, but sat down when the other man insisted.

Govindan Nair spoke in a low voice, "People have been

streaming in since morning. It's only natural, since he comes only once in a way. I'll go and tell him." He scolded Sethu affectionately, "Why can't you sit down for a bit."

Sethu refused. He could avoid facing the people in the verandah if he stood near the bench. Some of them inched their way to this corner, had a look at them and went back.

A litter of puppies covered with dirt fought playfully with each other near the pit into which used banana leaves were thrown. They had just begun to open their eyes. A skinny mongrel lay near them with its eyes closed.

Sethu's vest was soaked in sweat. He took out the envelope with the certificates. It was wet. He opened the envelope carefully. The University certificate was dry, but the ink had spread on the conduct certificate his professor had given him.

The first time he had read the certificate, he had been ecstatic. He had gone to the professor's house late one evening to say goodbye. The professor was an asthmatic and always spoke in a soft voice which hurt Sethu. Master's younger daughter had brought him Ovaltine. Sethu had asked for a certificate. The professor had put on his glasses and asked his daughter for his letter pad. He had taken half an hour to write the certificate. When Sethu had returned to his room and read it, he had felt weak with delight. Brilliant, imaginative, a man of initiative and drive—he had been generous with words. He had not even forgotten to praise the style and expressiveness of the poems Sethu had written for the college magazine.

He had shown the certificate secretly to friends, and had felt very proud when he sent a true copy of it along with his applications. This is me!

He realized now that no one would have read it. It would have taken its place amongst the papers swept up by those who cleaned the managers' rooms and offices in big establishments.

Govindan Nair hurried out of the kitchen with two glasses of tea and put them down near Achan. "Here, have some tea. Five minutes more. Madhava Menon is with him, the lawyer from Ottappalam. As soon as he goes."

Sethu took the glass reluctantly and the tea spilled. He emptied it quickly and cleaned the pool of tea on the bench with the bottom of the glass.

The puppies had stopped playing and begun to suck the mongrel's flat teats as she lay on her side, her mouth open.

People went in and out. An old woman in a rowka came out and threw the strands of hair she had wound around her fingers into the yard. They waited, expecting Govindan Nair to come out any minute.

"What's the time?" asked Achan and Sethu realized it was the first time Achan had spoken to him directly since they left home that morning.

He was tempted to answer, I don't have a watch. Instead, he looked out at the sun and said, "It must be eleven."

As a student, he had never had enough money. He had always thought that he had shouldered a great burden and had nursed a resentment towards everyone because of it. He now realized that those were really days of happiness. As long as he had been a student, he had been able to hold his head high and give an answer when asked what he was doing.

"What are you doing?"

"My BA."

He thought of many things while they waited for the manager to appear. Of the speeches he had learned by heart for the High School Debating Society. The students of today are the citizens of tomorrow. Our future engineers, physicians and political leaders will take shape from this young generation.

Who had written all this for him?

Applause. To which he had listened, thrilled, at the school anniversary function.

The audience filled the space between the two sheds. The invitees were always in the front row. His heart beat rapidly as he listened to the headmaster read out the list of prizewinners from the temporary stage put up next to the verandah of the main hall.

Sixth Form. First Prize for General Proficiency, Sethumadhavan.

As he made his way through the cordoned path between the crowd of boys and girls, the students of Sixth A began to clap. And the others took it on until it spread into a steady rhythm like the beating of waves.

He returned and looked through his prize books, still listening to the list being called out.

General Knowledge, First: Sethumadhavan, Sixth A.

He received his prize and joined his palms before the President and the audience. The headmaster said, "Don't go back."

Versification, First Prize.

His friends cheered wildly as he climbed onto the stage once more. The applause echoed.

Pisharoty Master had collected students to start a handwritten magazine and said to them, "Sethumadhavan has a bright future."

He waited for the bright future to unfold.

All his college mates used to remark that Sethu was the only student who was not frightened by examinations. They could barely score thirty-five even if they pored over their books, while all Sethu needed was to turn over the pages.

You have a bright future.

Why don't you try for the IAS?

Govindan Nair was here again. "Come on, if we wait for everyone to leave, we'll waste your time and mine."

Father laid his umbrella on the bench, took off his slippers, straightened his veshti and followed Govindan Nair. Sethu tried not to betray his anxiety and embarrassment. There were three people in the big room besides the Judge. Sethu saw the Judge at close quarters for the first time. He wore a white half-sleeved shirt and had a towel over his shoulder. His lifeless eyes peered out from behind thick glasses.

"Yes?" He straightened up and looked at Govindan Nair and Achan in turn.

Achan stood with joined palms.

Govindan Nair introduced them. "They're my neighbours from across the river."

Sethu stood with his head bent.

Govindan Nair added, "He taught for some time in the Athirattakodu school."

Achan started to say, "I was your. . . ." Before he could finish, the Judge took off his glasses, rubbed his eyes and said, "What is it?"

"This is my son. He's done his BA. He hasn't found a job yet."

"Can't you do teachers' training?"

Sethu realized that the judge was addressing him. He did not answer. He made an effort to smile and look respectful.

"That's the best thing to do. Then you can get a job in Kerala."

Achan said, "It doesn't matter where he works. I have already retired." Sethu wondered whether he would begin to talk about his problems.

"It's not like old days. It's difficult to find jobs outside Kerala now."

"His marks are good. We've brought his certificates." Achan held out his hand for the envelope.

The judge wiped his face with the towel and smiled. "There's no use my looking at them. I don't have the authority to give him a job. And recommendations are not allowed."

Govindan Nair had already skirted the easy chair respectfully and gone in.

"All right, then, I'll keep it in mind."

He turned to the stout, bald man on his left and asked, "Then what was the immediate provocation?"

Sethu prayed that Achan would have the good sense to leave now, before the Judge asked them to leave. Thankfully, Achan joined his palms again to take leave.

Sethu was drenched in sweat when they came out. The faint breeze from the banana grove sent the blood rushing back to his face.

Achan put on his slippers and took his umbrella. Sethu did not look at his face. Govindan Nair came out from the kitchen with an air of satisfaction on his face.

"What, you're leaving?"

"Yes, we must go."

"No, no, it's time for lunch. Lunch is ready here by eleven. Please eat. No one will mind."

Achan ignored this invitation and said goodbye to Govindan Nair.

"Did you tell him everything?"

"Um."

"What does he think?"

Achan said indifferently. "He said he would consider it."

"That's enough then. That's all he usually says. But he always keeps his word. He's very fond of everyone who belongs to the village. I'll remind him again before he leaves tomorrow."

Sethu smiled at Govindan Nair and followed Achan.

The sun was blazing. Achan stopped near the temple once more
and took off his slippers to go up the steps. Sethu walked on
without waiting for him.

4

He had heard much about this town sixty miles away from home,
but it was the first time he was here. There had been students
from this place in college with him. He tried to remember who
they were and looked at the faces of those who passed by without
much hope.

There was a light drizzle. Stagnant pools of rain water from
yesterday's showers lay stagnant in the potholes on the road. He
moved aside to make way for vehicles carrying passengers who
had arrived on the train. A passing horse cart splashed muddy
water in all directions, but luckily it missed him. By the time the
people who had been spattered began to scold the driver, the cart
had already gone quite a distance.

He saw the board of a hotel just beyond the culvert. It said, Jubilee
Hotel, Boarding and Lodging. It looked a modest place, so he went
in. Yes, there was a room. The rent was two and a half rupees.

The room was a cubicle with asbestos partitions, hardly bigger
than a box. The hotel boy spread a blue cloth over the dirty, oil-
stained mattress. There was only one small window opening onto
the tiled roof. He pushed it open. The shabby brown roofs of the
city houses stretched as far as the eye could reach.

He had to appear for an interview next day. He had been asked
to report at the Collectorate at nine.

How many times had he done this!

He had heard that more than a hundred candidates would be
selected, so he was hopeful. The minimum qualification they had
asked for was SSLC, so there would not be many applicants with
a BA. They would pay a stipend of fifty rupees during the six
month training period. After that he would get a salary of a
hundred and five rupees. The interview card said that those who
were selected had to leave at once for the farm. They had even
enclosed a cyclostyled list of the things that had to be taken along.

A bucket, a broom, two pairs of khadar shorts, two khadi shirts, a bedroll, a big plate and a small one.

He had begun to regret the postage he had to spend each time he sent an application.

He had felt nervous and confused when the interview card came. If he got the job and did not accept it, there would be a scene. How could he refuse a government job!

He imagined visitors asking his parents about him.

"Where is Sethu now?"

"Where is the place? He told me its name."

"How far did he study?"

"He did his BA."

"What job is he doing?"

Achan might say, he's in the National Extension Scheme. Amma would not know, so she would say, "He's a rural service worker or something like that."

He had prayed with great fervour before an interview for a tutor's post in a college. His going to Madras had been quite an event in the village.

He had given charity to all the beggars at the station, thinking, may the force of their prayers support me.

He had written to his acquaintances in Madras, even to Daniel, who was doing his MSc in Christian College. Until the train reached the Central Station, he was nervous. He saw Daniel waiting for him with a sense of relief. Daniel had arranged for him to stay in the hostel as a guest and had taken leave from work next day. He knew every nook and corner of the city. He took Sethu to the DPI's office in a taxi, wished him luck and promised to be back in two hours.

There were more Telugu and Tamil candidates than Malayalis. The Director was a Malayali. There were candidates in full suits, in full shirts and gabardine trousers and shining ties. Some of them spoke English with an American accent. Sethu was too timid to talk to any of them. How many of them, he wondered, would have got a first? Although he had only a second, he had the consolation that he had scored fifty-seven per cent.

It was the first time he had worn trousers. He had bought a pair of cotton trousers the day before from Moore Market for seven-and-a-half rupees. And chappals for six rupees. He felt naked. What if his fly was open? His skin felt raw where the strap of the new chappals chafed against it. He looked enviously at the young men waiting under the trees and told himself that it was not important to wear a suit and a tie. A good director would be contemptuous of things like that. He would know that what a teacher needed were knowledge and simplicity, that only ignorant people dressed up fashionably.

The names were called out in alphabetical order.

His interview was at eleven. He opened the spring door nervously and his voice trembled when he said good morning.

They signalled to him to sit down.

Was this Menon, the Director? He reminded Sethu of Kurup the sorcerer from Kalladikothu, who used to come to his house often when he was a child.

He had been told that it was bad manners to place his elbows on the table. His chair had no arms and he felt his hands grow heavier since he had to keep them hanging down its sides. The light green paper lying on the table was his application.

"Certificates."

He held out the envelope.

What would they ask? Marlowe? Milton? Donne? He hoped it would be one of the modern poets.

The first question was, "How did you miss your First Class?"

He had not expected it at all. He could not answer. There had been no reason. He realized he had to say something.

"I don't know."

In the column marked talents and preferences, he had written that he wrote poetry.

"You write poetry?"

"Yes, Sir."

"About what?"

His palms felt moist. He could not speak.

"Tell me briefly about your latest poem."

God, if only he could think of a poem.

Ah, giver of happiness, when you come with the blue pleats of your skirt unfurled, my heart plays the music of flutes.

The serpents of grief hear, and gather around me.

No, he could not explain all that in English. He said, without looking up,

"The last one I did was a translation of a Tagore poem."

The Director pushed the certificates towards him and said, "That is all. You can go."

His head spun as he came out. They had not even glanced at the conduct certificate that his professor had written with such care.

He hurried down without looking at the candidates still awaiting their turn. Daniel was at the gate. He held out a cigarette and asked,

"How was it?"

"Not bad."

He lit the cigarette and felt his taut nerves relax. They wandered round the city and went to a Hindi film at night. They had dinner in a dimly lit restaurant where soft music played. Daniel told him about his new girlfriend. She had come to his hostel for dinner once with her cousin who was at Queen Mary's College. After that, they had met in church. They had talked to each other on the telephone a few times and now they met every Sunday. Many people had tried to bring him down to earth, but had not succeeded.

Bring him down to earth? Daniel's term was new to him.

He had a sense of relief when he said goodbye to Daniel and his friends and boarded the crowded Mangalore Mail, even though he knew he had to go back to the days of endless waiting for the postman.

And now here he was, with another interview ahead of him.

At least in Madras, Daniel had been with him for company. Here, he knew no one. He kept to the sides of the crowded streets, feeling a little scared. He was a total stranger here. The Collectorate, where he had to appear for the interview, was just a furlong away from where he stayed.

In the evening, he went to the beach. A long line of cars was parked near the footpath, under the casuarina trees. The wet stretch of sand was deserted. The wind blowing over the roaring waves was laden with drops of moisture. Was it at this spot that da Gama's yachts had glimpsed the shore? He had no desire to explore the city.

He had to ask his way twice to the hotel. The narrow room was dark, moist and smelly. He heard soda bottles being opened beyond the thin asbestos partition, and voices rising steadily in volume.

"Come on, try it, it's good."

"Um, um." That was a woman.

"Just gulp it down."

"I'll feel nauseous."

"Rubbish."

Raindrops splattered the tiled roof. The window banged shut in the wind, and then flew open again.

The rain grew heavier. As it rose to a roar, the sounds in the next room died down.

He thought of Sumitra and suddenly longed to see her. He saw her very rarely now. They quarrelled all the time at Vadakkethu. Sumitra and Devu, Sumitra and her mother, Madhava Ammama and Devu.

Madhava Ammama hardly ever came home these days. Sethu heard that there had been proposals of marriage for Sumitra. One of them had nearly materialized. The horoscopes matched. The boy's family liked the girl. But Madhava Ammama visited their house in Muduthala, came back and said it was not a suitable match.

The reason he gave was that the boy's mother and sister worked as servants for a rich family. Amma heard this and asked, "And what were the Vadakkethu women doing at the illam? Were they visiting?"

"That was in the old days. They're Madhavan Nair's wife's family now."

Amma and Cheriamma whispered in the kitchen, "He probably doesn't like the idea of another man living there." The whispers gradually became inaudible.

Sethu lay awake wondering why he could not concentrate on Thangamani. He had had a letter from her quite some time ago and knew she would be upset that he had not replied.

What could he write? That he had not achieved anything? That he would never enter a class in a city college as an eager tutor? That he would never write his MA privately, or become a lecturer. Nor would he write a thesis, be awarded an MLitt and have his picture in the papers.

5

All the candidates were gathered in the upstairs verandah of the Collectorate. Most of them wore khadar shirts. Sethu wondered whether some of them who had come earlier in borrowed gabardine suits to the DPI's office had turned up here in khadar shirts and mundus.

A fair, good-looking man came and asked him, "Aren't you Sethumadhavan?"

"Yes."

"I've seen you in Palghat, I used to come to the hostel with Aravindan."

Aravindan had been Sethu's classmate. Gopi was his relative.

"What is Aravindan doing now?"

"He wrote his exams in September and again in March, but didn't get through."

Gopi had done his SSLC and then worked in various places, in a cooperative store, a petrol bunk and a handloom society. They had all been leave vacancies.

"The Head Clerk told me that not many graduates have applied. So you stand a good chance."

Gopi knew everything about the job. A Grade One employee was paid a hundred twenty rupees. In the Higher Division Clerk scale, you had a chance of being promoted as a Secondary Education Officer or a Block Development Officer since fifty per cent of the recruitments were from the department.

Gopi moved from group to group. The crowd kept increasing. How many were there? Three hundred? Four hundred?

Gopi was very nervous. What would they ask at the interview?

Sethu stood at the end of the verandah. He could see the washermen washing clothes in the open maidan and policeman practising exercises in the courtyard of the building beyond.

Gopi wove his way through the crowd, took Sethu's hand and led him to a deserted corner. He whispered, "They will question us on the Five Year Plan."

"Who told you?"

"Never mind that. But I don't know a damn thing about this Five Year Plan. What is it?"

"I haven't studied it either."

"What is the difference between the first and the second Five Year Plan?

"I don't know."

"My God, we're finished."

Gopi questioned candidates who he thought were intelligent.

Sethu watched the multicoloured clothes flapping on the lines like festival flags and thought to himself, who cares, let them ask whatever they want.

Gopi came back beaming. "I've got it."

"Um?"

"Industry is the most important factor of the first Five Year Plan. The second one emphasises agriculture, cottage industries and the electrification of villages."

"Really?"

"What if they ask about the National Extension Scheme? Isn't it meant to accelerate village development?"

"Maybe."

"Go on, tell me what to say if they ask."

Sethu was irritated. Gopi seemed to imply that he wanted to keep information to himself.

"Come on now, tell me. I won't tell anyone else."

"If the National Extension Scheme is implemented, there will be electricity in all the villages, parks for the children, good roads, jobs for everyone—in short, our country will become a heaven. Milk and honey will flow through it. You can tell them that."

Gopi wondered whether Sethu was joking. No, he looked serious.

"We have a National Employment Scheme in our village. A handful of women rush about in a jeep. But of course I'll tell them what you said if they ask." Gopi began to repeat what Sethu had said.

They had begun to call people in. Gopi tried to find out from those who had finished what questions they had been asked. Gopi was called before him. He came back smiling.

"It's over!"

"What did they ask?"

"It was all in Malayalam. They asked how India's economic status can be improved. I reeled off a quotation from Gandhi. The only way the poor of India can progress is through agriculture. Agriculture that uses all types of manure. I think it's the Revenue District Officer who is conducting the interview."

They called Sethu's name at last. How long had he waited for this door to open! From between the stacks of yellowed paper that surrounded the table, tired grey eyes peered out at him as if from inside a well.

He had a feeling that all of them looked alike, bored and angry at once. Sethu did not feel as nervous as he had been in the Director's office.

"So you're a graduate?"

"Yes."

"Why did you apply for this job?"

Do you want to know? Because I could not find anything else. Because I had come to the end of my tether. Because I thought that if I get this job, I will earn at least fifty rupees. Because I wanted to escape questions about my attempts to find a job. Because I wanted to run away from my family.

"Come on, answer me!"

"I." He debated for a minute. "I wish to serve in the villages. I believe that the greatest service I can render to the nation is to work in undeveloped villages. Factors like starvation, unemployment, superstition. . . ."

Whose voice was this? He was back in the Debating Society in school. Did they want to hear more?

"I believe it is the duty of every educated person to lift our brothers in the villages out of the darkness in which they are sunk."

Their tired eyes focused slowly on him. He paused for a moment, wondering whether to go on. The officer said,

"All right. We will let you know."

He hurried out quickly, but Gopi caught up with him in the street.

"Wait, I'll come too. How was it? You must have done well."

"Yes, I did." Sethu smiled. They went back to the Jubilee Hotel.

It would be a real Gandhian life, said Gopi. No tea or coffee, no cigarettes. Prayers in the morning, then field work. Would they be asked to clean shit?

"I don't know."

"I heard that we might have to."

Gopi said, "I don't mind herding cattle, or digging, or drinking panakam instead of coffee or tea. But if they ask me to clean shit?"

"You have to do it then. Mahatma Gandhi said so, didn't he?"

Gopi's face, which had been bright and happy, suddenly darkened. He lowered his eyes and fell silent.

6

A list of train timings had been cut out from the newspaper and stuck near the counter. Sethu thought he would go to the station fifteen minutes ahead. He arranged for a rickshaw to take his luggage. He bought his ticket and went in only to learn from the chalked mark on the black announcement board that the number two mail was running sixty minutes late.

The platform was terribly crowded. There seemed to be more people waiting to receive incoming passengers than those travelling on the train. He asked the porter to put his luggage down by the bookstall. The old man walked contentedly away with the four annas he paid him. He felt he should have given him another four annas. Perhaps he had not really seen the coin that Sethu had placed in his shrivelled palm?

Porters were usually a dissatisfied lot. It was the first time Sethu had seen one who had not protested or complained. Maybe this fellow had never heard about the porters and jutka drivers in Olavakkode!

Two pretty girls in short dresses stood at the bookstall, leafing through the English magazines. They spoke in a convent-trained English accent. Their middle-aged guardian waited patiently some distance away, a folded ten rupee note held in his hand.

"You buy that. I'll buy a Denise Robins," said the one who looked the older of the two.

"Do you have *A Wounded Heart*?" She spoke Malayalam with the air of one committing a crime.

"Hurry up, girls," said the man, loosening his tie.

"One minute, Daddy!"

"Do you have *Lovers' Fate*? No, I've read this."

The salesman laid out all the Denise Robins novels he had, *A Flaming Heart, A Lonely Girl, The Ill-Fated Affair.* She did not want any of them.

"Any new book by Hermina Black?"

Sethu craned his neck to peer at the titles on the dusty spines of the paperbacks arranged behind the bookseller.

Someone tapped his shoulder. Gopi.

"What a fellow. I've been looking everywhere for you. I even wondered whether you had gone by bus." Gopi took a newspaper from the counter and browsed through it, pretending he was going to read it.

It was Gopi who had brought the news to the hotel the day before that the list of selected candidates had been put up at the Collectorate, and that Sethu's name was there.

Sethu had not been surprised. Only rejects from elsewhere had turned up here, after all.

Gopi was enthusiastic. "There are only forty on this list. The peon said there would be a second list. But I can't bear to think of their training programme. Damn! Do you think we can buy a bucket and broom after we get there?"

Sethu did not reply.

"Don't you think we can wait till we get there?"

"I suppose so."

"We'll buy khadar for the uniforms here, it's cheaper. We'll travel together."

"We'll see."

"Why are you lying down?"

He pressed his hands to his temples, closed his eyes and said, "I have a headache, I'll lie down for a while."

Gopi went away. Sethu wondered whether he should sleep for a while. All kinds of things seemed to be crawling over the pillow, which was as stiff as wood, and polished with oil and sweat too.

He got up, changed his mundu, put on a shirt and went out. The concrete road blazed in the sun.

My name is there, among all the lucky ones that have been chosen. The name that time had waited to enter on fortune's list! He wanted to laugh as well as cry. Here he was, with a day of celebration before him!

He hesitated in the Collectorate compound for a long time before going up to the verandah. Were any of the applicants around? He had come for the interview as if it was a casual matter. He made sure no one was about and went upto the notice board. Yes, his name was there for once, on the typed list!

He walked until it was dusk and he was hungry, then went into a Muslim hotel. There were no vacant tables downstairs, in the common dining area. He felt reluctant to sit at a table with strangers. The manager noticed him and said, "There's room upstairs."

There were small cubicles upstairs with partitions of coloured glass. The hall was deserted. Fans turned above the cubicles. The fat little waiter opened an empty cubicle and switched on the fan. The room was meant for four. The waiter wiped the table and waited for his order.

"What will you have?"

"What is there?"

Soda bottles were being opened noisily in the next room. The smell of liquor and slurred voices floated in from beyond the shoulder-high partition.

The boy removed the dirty handkerchief wound around his head, tied it on his neck and rattled off the names of various dishes. He was fleshy and blue-eyed. If he had worn clean clothes, he could have been taken for an Embrandiri boy. He reminded Sethu of Balan who used to hang around with the football players in College, whose nickname had been "Plymouth."

This was a day for celebration. Two cigarettes, then biriyani. He made a quick calculation—he had seventy rupees in all, including what he had borrowed from Madhava Ammama. Khader shirts, shorts, a bucket, a plate.

The boy asked with a meaningful smile, "Nothing else?"

"What do you have?"

"Country stuff."

The head waiter opened the half-door and asked, "Haven't you taken the order yet, Abu?"

The boy asked, "Soda, or iced water?"

"Iced water."

The boy brought him two cigarettes and a box of matches on a plastic plate. Sethu realized what he had meant when the big glass arrived and the stench of country arrack rose to his nostrils.

Taken aback, he said, "This?"

"It's only a quarter bottle." The boy would not leave. All right then, if that was what he wanted! His throat and palate burned with the first mouthful. Flames raced inside him.

He said, without looking up, "Bring the food."

The boy brought the biriyani and asked, "How was it?"

He emptied the glass of water in the wash basin, and pushed the glass towards Sethu, "Let me have a drop as well."

Sethu poured out half a glass gladly, it meant he had that much less to swallow. The boy drank it down in one gulp, wiped his chin and tossed his head.

Sethu asked, "Don't you have Prohibition here?"

The boy's blue eyes gleamed. His face was flushed. "The Inspectors are in the next room. They've already finished three bottles." He lowered his voice, "Didn't you come here with the lawyer the other day?"

Sethu did not answer. He picked up the onion slices soaked in vinegar from his plate and ate them. He held his breath, grimaced, drained the glass and felt better. He had not really tasted the disgusting odour. The boy went out and he began to eat. A fire blazed inside him and sweat broke out on his forehead. The first few mouthfuls nauseated him. His head felt heavier and his legs were unsteady. He washed his hands at the basin, wiped them on his hair and lit the second cigarette.

The boy brought the bill. Two-and-a-half rupees. He looked again to make sure. Yes, two-and-a-half rupees.

"A rupee extra for the other thing. It's not included in the bill."

Sethu placed five rupees in the saucer. The boy stood smirking, his elbows planted on the table. Sethu said angrily, "Get me the change."

He left a four anna tip and left. The neon lamps had come on and the city smiled at him. The streets had grown crowded. He kept to the side of the street, feeling unsteady. He wanted to get back quickly to his room and write to Achan, to Amma, to Parameswara Ettan. By the grace of your blessings, I shall now begin to eat the salt of the sarkar!

But when he opened the whitewashed asbestos door of his room, all he wanted was to pitch into bed. He thought about the letters. He had to write to Thangamani as well. It could wait until he reached the training centre.

He woke up only when Gopi knocked on the door.

Gopi finished reading the paper, hovered around the ladies' waiting room for a while and came back. "Let's go to the other side. Our group is there."

Sethu was still thinking of the night that had gone by. He had dreamed that he had a quarrel with someone. He could not remember the face.

The other side of the platform was crowded with boys bound for the training centre, seated on their bundles and boxes. There was a mountain of luggage—buckets, brooms, bedrolls of different types, boxes.

"Where's your box and mattress?"

"Near the bookstall."

"Let's bring it over here." Gopi brought the steel trunk and bedroll himself.

"The Mail is going to be crowded."

"There won't be room for all of us in a single carriage. We'll get in wherever there's space."

Gopi knew everyone and introduced them one by one to Sethu.

Nedungadi from Tirunavaya asked, "Aren't you a graduate? Why didn't you do a BT? You would have a higher pay scale."

Sankarankutty from Parappanangadi said, "I can't bear teaching. I could have got into the TTC if I tried. But it's such a bore."

Venkataswamy from Kozhijambara thought that a secondary school teacher's job near home would have been better than this. He had tried to get one for two years. You needed very good marks to be on the Government list. Otherwise you had to have a recommendation. And if you wanted a job in the training school run by the management, you had to pay.

A young man in a coarse khadar shirt said, "You can always get into a basic school."

"Indeed," said Nedungadi, moving from a mound of bedrolls to Sethu's trunk. "The basic school takes five hundred rupees as well. But they don't call it a bribe, they have some other name for it. My Valiamma's daughter paid to get into Minister Sankara Menon's son's school."

Sethu smiled, "You could call it a sambhavana, a gift for rebuilding the nation."

"No, no, sambhavana is in Malayalam. The Sarvodaya people would never use the word. They think people won't understand if you call cottage industries 'kutil vyavasayam'. They insist on calling it 'gramodyog'. What do they say for 'basic,' Master Ramakrishnan?

Sethu took a liking to Nedungadi, with his narrow eyes and a sandal paste mark from his morning bath still fresh on his forehead.

Ramakrishnan of the khader shirt said indifferently, "Nayi talim," and moved down the platform in order to spit and blow his nose.

Gopi muttered, "He's a Sarvodaya fanatic. They say his father is a Jeevandani."

"Well, what more can one give than one's life?"

"One could always do nothing. Or be lazy and go to sleep. Or commit a fraud."

Ramakrishnan came back ready for an argument. "I studied in a basic school. And I'm proud of it. This new fashion of turning out people who aren't fit for any sort of job. . . ."

Gopi interrupted, "Look my friend, what's the name of that drink in which they put coriander?"

Nedungadi knew. "It's called jappee. Mahatma Gandhi's special jappee."

"Ah, yes, jappee. Will Sarvodaya be destroyed if one drinks tea instead?"

Ramakrishnan would not give in. It was a drink suited to Indians. Many great men had praised it. Gandhi, Vinobha Bhave, Shankar Rao Deo, Kelappaji.

"Do you want to listen to a joke?" That was Nedungadi. "My village was a donated one. A lot of the villagers are jeevandanis. One of them, Kuttisankaran, after being a jeevandani for two years, sells arrack now. He's doing quite well. His house has been tiled and he has enough money. But that's not what I wanted to say. Shankar Rao Deo came to our place to receive the donation. Have you seen him?"

Controlling his irritation, Ramakrishnan said, "Yes, I know him. He visited us at home. My father knew him in Wardha.

"I'll tell you for the benefit of those who don't know. He wears only a mundu, no shirt. He shaves once in three months. He was supposed to stay with a man who had returned from Singapore, who had a latrine with a septic tank. Sarvodayas are forbidden to use them. He controlled himself for three days, and on the fourth, a pit was dug for him in the compound."

When all of them began to protest, Ramakrishnan changed his tone and laughed foolishly, "You'll find out when the training begins. You can play at being rich landlords until then."

"We'll see. There are quite a few of us, after all."

Many had doubts and fears about life in the training centre.

"It's only for six months, after that we'll be independent."

Venkataswamy was full of sympathy, "It's a pity graduates have to stoop to manual labour of the lowest type."

Gopi consoled Sethu, "We're the second batch, remember? Graduates stand a good chance of being promoted."

Thomas of Kunnamkulam invited Sethu for a cup of tea but he declined. "Come on, the train has not yet been blocked."

Venkatachalam and Nedungadi went along with them as well, and so did Ramakrishnan. Gopi teased him, "We'll see whether they'll give us jappee."

The train came finally after an hour and three quarters. The platform was suddenly crowded with people. Porters in dirty blue shirts with red turbans on their heads came out of their dens and surrounded the luggage like vultures.

An old porter came limping towards them. His blue shirt had faded to grey and his turban to ochre. It was difficult to believe that his lips had once been red. Scratching his face, where grey stubble grew in the furrows in his creased skin, he bared his decayed teeth in a smile and asked, "Shall I take your luggage in, mudalali?"

Before Sethu could answer, Gopi said, "No, there are enough of us."

Sethu felt sorry for the old man who waited for some time, his mouth still open in a pitiful smile, then limped slowly away into the crowd.

The train was more crowded than usual, and their group had to spread themselves over three compartments. Sethu found himself with Gopi, Ramakrishnan and Thomas.

"Where's Nedungadi?"

"In the last compartment."

There was hardly any space to sit. Gopi elbowed his way into a seat which he shared with Sethu.

So this was the beginning of his journey to his place of work. Sethu was not happy. An uneasiness like a black rain cloud that kept changing its shape moved through him. He rebuked himself. Six months. If you can manage on fifty rupees a month for six months, you'll have a career and be independent!

Gopi found one more person who was going to the training centre. He was tall and dark, with curly hair and glasses and the scar of a burn on his left cheek. Gopi kept asking him questions and he finally folded the copy of *The Hindu* that he was reading, took off his glasses, wiped them and sat up.

Gopi said, "Unni Narayanan is a graduate as well. You don't know each other, do you?"

Unni Narayanan asked, "Which college?"

Sethu told him.

He said, "I came there in fifty-one."

"I was there then."

Unni Narayanan had come for the Inter-collegiate Debate from Thrissur. That year someone from Thevara had won the first prize and Unni Narayanan had won the second. The following year he had won the trophy at Ernakulam.

Sethu asked, "Which year did you finish?"

He had been a year senior to Sethu.

"You haven't worked anywhere?"

"I tried, but nothing came through." The young man who had won trophies for his College in debating competitions fell silent. Then he said, "Actually, I've been thinking. They say two to three years' experience is essential for every job. But if no one gives you a job how can you have experience?" Unni Narayanan's eyes glinted behind his glasses.

"The only other way is to be born a lower caste, as a pulaya or a pariah. Unfortunately, I'm not one. Or you have to be a girl, a fairly good-looking one."

He asked, "Do you know Antony? He left our College and joined yours."

"The footballer?"

"Yes. We were classmates. He lived next door to me. He took three years to do his Inter and then came over to your college." Sethu had seen him. Someone had pointed him out admiringly when he was chosen as a University player.

Antony's photograph had been next to the poem he had published in the college magazine. He had been wearing a blazer with the name of the University on it and a dotted silk scarf around his neck.

"He is with Mafatlal now. All you need is to be good at sports, and you can earn a salary of seven hundred rupees. He will get an increment after the next season in Calcutta. His brother told me that all the clubs are fighting over who is to have him."

"Didn't he go abroad?"

He had played in the Indian team at Bangkok and came back a star.

Unni Narayanan seemed to grow more and more irritated when he described how Antony had risen high because he played football. Then he told Sethu about another one of his classmates who had barely managed to graduate. He was the Assistant Manager now in a white man's rubber estate. He had a salary of seven hundred rupees and four months' salary as bonus. And a jeep.

Sethu consoled Unni Narayanan, "It's just a matter of luck."

"Luck indeed! I know him well. He's an arch fool. He cannot write a single sentence in English without making mistakes. He fawned on his examiners and bribed them to get thirty-five per cent. His father worked in Singapore and his mother was a society lady. They wined and dined the General Manager of the estate and prevailed on the Labour Minister to recommend his name. What more did he need? It wouldn't have mattered if he was illiterate."

Sethu gazed at the backwaters, choked with scum.

"Didn't you try to do your BT?"

"It's not easy. I tried to work as an untrained teacher. Have you heard of Unni Krishnan Nair who is in charge of appointments at the District Board Office?"

"No."

"He won't relent even if the President recommends someone. He is the type who would have faced a firing squad in the white man's regime. Teachers who want a transfer have to go and meet him at home. If they are male, he accepts money. If I could have worked in a high school for some time, I could have done my BT. But how can one get in with people like him running things?"

There was a sudden silence in the compartment. Sethu remembered that there were other passengers as well. Unni Narayanan must have realized it too, for he opened his paper again. Sethu looked at the coconut groves and the fields rushing by.

Here I come, here I come, here I come.

The train gathered speed. He listened to the steady rhythm of the iron wheels, to the song they played on the rail track. He felt words take shape from the music. Here we come, to awaken the villages that are filled with darkness!

Thangamani must be asleep upstairs now, after lunch, on the clean floor in her house, her hair spread over the red cement.

He had to write to her. I dreamed of you, my darling, on my journey to freedom.

The train hooted with delight and broke into song once more,

Here we come, here we come!

7

The well-known farm waited for them somewhere across the river and between the hills. His very first place of work. He felt happy when he saw the familiar line of the Western Ghats in the distance. Looking at them from atop the hill on the west of his house, from the railway track, from the downstairs verandah of the hostel, their indistinct shapes had always seemed to him like the boundaries of his life.

The train arrived at four. Gopi arranged for the luggage to be loaded on a handcart. The spirits of the tired young travellers suddenly rose as they walked in a procession behind the cart. It began to drizzle when they reached the bus stand. They took shelter under the sloping roofs of the little box-like shops on the roadside.

Sethu bought a half packet of cigarettes so that the owner of the shop on whose verandah he had sought shelter would not be displeased. He held out the packet to Unni Narayanan, who refused. He had never smoked, he considered it a luxury that he could not think about until he began to make money himself.

Unni Narayanan reminded Sethu of Krishnankutty, except that he had a kind expression, while Krishnankutty had always looked stern.

As he lit his cigarette from the wick hung on the bamboo pillar, he wondered whether Krishnankutty ever thought of him.

Gopi had found out that there were buses going every hour to their destination, the farm, and that one was due now. It started from the city and more than half the seats were vacant. There was a scramble for seats. It saddened and disgusted Sethu to watch his companions, who had all travelled together and who were bound for the same place, suddenly fighting with each other.

This is how we battle for standing space on the footboards. We hurt and kick each other so as not to be left behind.

Unni Narayanan had been thrown back. When he finally reached the door to salvation, the conductor said expressionlessly. "There are no seats left."

Those who had managed to get in shouted to Gopi for their luggage.

Gopi had loaded all the luggage and was practically drenched in the rain. When the door closed, he shouted an obscenity. Sethu said consolingly, "We'll go on the next bus."

Gopi, Unni Narayanan, Sethu and two others whose names they did not know were left behind. Sethu lit another cigarette and decided to wait on the shop verandah. But Gopi would not accept defeat. He argued with the conductor until he was given permission to stand in the bus. The others got in as well. They would have to hang on and balance themselves for thirty miles.

As the bus wound though the narrow streets, the town looked smaller than he had imagined. Most of the football players in college had been from here. Sethu peered out, bending his head, as they came to the railroad bridge.

The river, which had broken free from the hills, suddenly lay quiet here before the fearful sea.

Nedungadi moved aside and gave Sethu a little space to sit down.

The hills spread out from the farther shore. The uneven path, full of ruts, circled the barren hills. The wet path gleamed like a channel of sweat running down a cherumi girl's chest.

Large compounds lay beyond the village. Then came the cashew groves. There was the scent of moisture and old leaves in the air. Scraps of sunlight were lost in the patches of shade covered with dry leaves.

The dark shadows of the Western Ghats grew thicker and heavier between the clumps of the trees and over the bare hills. Shreds of cloud below dissolved into fine wisps of mist in the band of blue-black behind the range of hills.

They covered the distance rapidly. The bus stopped. All eyes turned to the gate. Here was the gate to the new life they had been waiting for.

Varika varika sahajare!
Veeraram yuvakkale!
Come, come my brothers,
Brave young men!

Sethu could not remember who had started to hum the famous marching song of the Communist Party.

Gopi became their leader again and rushed up to unload the luggage.

There was a huge board showing the name of the farm on the concrete pillars at the beginning of the red clay path and below it, a small one with the name of the training centre fixed to a wooden post.

Remember, right foot forward.

Everyone fell silent as they entered the gate. They put down the luggage on the verandah of the first building they saw. A few of them went in search of the office.

Chilli creepers climbed over the huge trees. Rows of yellow notice boards detailed statistics.

Those who had gone to look for the office returned, "All of us have to go to the quarters."

"Who said so?"

"Did you see the Director?"

"Where are the quarters?"

"Over there!" No one knew exactly where they were. They saw a man in a khaki shirt and turban come towards them, dangling a big bunch of iron keys. They were happy once more. Here was someone to show them where they had to go.

Sethu found it difficult to walk carrying his tin trunk and bedroll. They went through a papaya garden and a grove planted with coconut seedlings. The quarters were at the end of the path.

A long building with a tiled roof. The rough cement floor was marked in squares.

Khaki shirt turned. He said, "Four in each room."

Sethu went to the third room. It smelt of whitewash and varnish. When he opened the big window, the room was filled with white light. Unni Narayanan, Gopi, Venkataswamy and Nedungadi were all in the same room. When he heard there was place elsewhere, Venkataswamy left.

Sethu was hungry and very tired. None of them had had lunch. Sethu pushed his bedroll against the wall and sat on it.

As they assessed the room, the man in the khaki shirt came back. Unni Narayanan took the lock and key from him. Sethu called out to him as he left, but he did not hear.

"Hey!"

The peon turned, looking displeased.

"Don't you have chairs or tables or furniture of any kind?"

"No. The rules don't permit them."

Gopi went up to the door. "No beds either?"

"The order says you have to bring mattresses."

"We've got them. But what about cots? Do we have to spread the mattresses on this cement floor?"

The peon looked unmoved. "Those are the rules. You can talk to him yourself."

Gopi muttered, "Has Mahatma Gandhi said that even people with rheumatism cannot sleep on cots?"

There was a well nearby, and bathrooms. The Gandhian latrines were a furlong away. The dining room was visible from the verandah. The hall where classes would be held was next to the tall office building.

Gopi and Unni Narayanan went for a walk around the farm and Nedungadi for a bath. Sethu unrolled his mattress and lay down. His forehead felt hot and his head ached. The boys from the next room dropped in, but went away when he said he had a headache.

It grew dark very quickly and was unpleasantly cold. Someone turned on the light in the verandah and a ray of light came in.

The others came back and said, "We have to assemble at seven."

"What's the time now?"

"Ten to seven." They began to change and get ready to go.

"Aren't you going to change?"

Sethu got up and said, "I feel so tired, I just want to cover myself and go to sleep." Outside, the cold wind pricked like needles.

They fought for front seats on the mat spread in the hall. Sethu sat near the door. When the wind blew in raindrops, he shivered.

The dais was empty. There were framed pictures of national leaders on the wall with khadar garlands decorating them. Seven o'clock. As the waiting prolonged itself, there were angry mutterings that soon grew to a roar.

The round dial of the clock that hung next to the coloured picture of Gandhiji standing with folded hands showed seven thirty. Shoes grated on the verandah outside. Everyone got up. By the light of the bright bulb that swung over the dais, they saw a man in dark green khadar trousers and a brown bush-shirt. The Hitler moustache under his flat nose added to his ugliness.

"Sit down." Everyone sat down.

The man on the dais reminded Sethu of a cartoon he had seen in an advertisement.

He began in Malayalam. "From today, you are government servants."

Sethu placed his hand on his chest. Did he have fever? He shivered; it could have been the cold.

The responsibilities of a government servant, the amount of money the government would spend on this training scheme, the kind of discipline expected during the training period. Sethu tried to pay attention. He found the rough North Malabar accent amusing. His attention wandered. The rebuilding of the nation, Mahatmaji, the future of India, and finally, instructions.

They had to report to the field at seven thirty and there would be field work till noon. They were free after that and could go to the town to buy what they wanted. They had to be back before eight.

Sethu was famished. He regretted not having bought a plate when they reached the dining hall. There were others like him, however. One of the servants went out and brought big teak leaves.

They were given chapatis and steaming hot green gram dal. A young instructor announced, "Prayers first. Everyone has to take part."

He put back the dal.

> Om sa ha nav avatu
> saha nau bhunaktu
> saha veeryam karavavahai.

> May he protect us both
> May he be pleased with us both
> May we work together with vigour

He pretended to move his lips along with them while they intoned the invocation to the Kathopanishad.

Om Santhi! Santhi!

Sethu came back to his room, lay down and covered himself with a used mundu. He thought he would fall asleep at once. But he did not. Everyone was writing letters home. He pulled his tin trunk towards him, sat cross-legged and began to write. To Amma, Parameswara Ettan, Achan.

He knew he should write to Krishnankutty, Balakrishnan and Daniel. But what could he write? Dear friends, let me convey to you the happy news that I have arrived here in order to serve our villages.

He imagined Padmu stumbling through his letter, reading it to Amma. Cheriamma would arrive just as she finished. "Is it from Sethu? Read it again, girl!" And she would comment, "At least he's earning a living now."

Amma would be quiet, undemonstrative as usual, praying silently as she always did. She would say, "I must send four annas to the temple on Friday to have a flower offering, done on his star."

Achan would not talk about him at all. Parameswarettan might speak to Edathi Amma about him.

Everyone spread out their mattress. Sethu did not feel so cold now. He felt pleasantly lazy and his headache had gone.

It was very dark outside and nothing was visible through the indistinct outlines of the bushes. The western wind roared outside the closed windows.

"Shall I put out the light?"

"Wait." Sethu pulled out the magazine he had bought on the way and sat back against the wall to read.

Gopi warned him, "Lights out at nine, that's the rule."

Sethu pretended not to hear. He had just one cigarette left. He rolled it between his palms to warm it, then lit it.

He had not written to Thangamani. How would he begin? Maybe you are annoyed with me. I write this in the solitude of the night, far away on the hills, listening to the music of the darkness and the whirlwind.

Someone knocked on the door.

He said, "Come in," thinking it was one of his companions from next door.

He did not make out the person who came in at once. He looked closer at the bespectacled face with a muffler wound around it, the long-sleeved sweater, the tucked-up mundu. The Director!

Sethu threw his cigarette down and stood up.

"What is your name?"

"Sethumadhavan."

The others woke up and scrambled up hastily to their feet.

"Lights off at nine o'clock. That is the rule."

"I did not know, Sir."

"You are a government servant. Ignorance of the rule is no excuse."

Sethu kept quiet.

"Which school did you study in?" Sethu told him.

"Hm. Smoking is not allowed in the campus. You know that?"

"But this is my room, Sir. In the room. . . ."

The small thick moustache beneath the flattened nose quivered. He moved towards the door, turned and asked, "What did you say your name was?"

"Sethumadhavan."

The others crowded around him when the Director left, including their neighbours from next door.

"I told you, didn't I, to turn off the light?"

Sethu was irritated. "Get lost. What is this, Napoleon's military camp? Even there, you'd have rules like this only in wartime."

The others went away. He switched off the light and lay down, but could not sleep. He felt very uneasy. The cold of the cement floor crept in worm-like through the thin quilt.

He woke up startled just as he was about to fall asleep. A jackal howled somewhere. The wind had died down. Only the coconut palms rustled softly.

Someone shook him awake. The sky was so dark, he could not believe it was daylight.

"It's seven fifteen. Get up."

"Seven fifteen?"

He sat up, rubbed his eyes, looked out through the window and asked,

"Couldn't you have called me earlier?"

"I did, a hundred times."

As they left, they said to him, "Get ready quickly. We'll be in the mess."

He brushed his teeth, washed his face and changed hurriedly. The mess was deserted when he got there. He did not wait for coffee. Where did they have to report for field work? The servants in the mess did not know. Confused, he looked around, not knowing where to go, then ran to the office. The peon told him the way.

He cursed himself as he walked quickly. Why did he always find himself alone?

He was relieved when he caught up with them a couple of furlongs away.

The Director was there, as well as the Instructor who had led the prayers the day before. The Director stopped speaking as Sethu came up.

Sethu walked with his head bent towards the students. He heard the Director's voice, "Look here."

Surely he was not talking to him?

"I say, look here."

Sethu stopped, and realized that all eyes were on him.

"You can go." The Director turned to the instructor and said, "Mark him absent."

Sethu wanted to say something. I'm sorry, sir. From tomorrow. The words eluded him.

He walked away, his head bent. His eyes hurt, but anger drowned the pain. Three minutes! He had been only three minutes late. He had glanced at the watch of the last person in the row.

His friends came back at eleven to find him still in bed.

"Did you have coffee?"

"Yes."

No one mentioned the morning's incident. Many of them wanted to go to the city.

The peon came half an hour later. "Sethumadhavan is wanted in the office."

Sethu got up. Gopi whispered, "Don't answer back. It will be better if you apologize."

Sethu was amused. "It's a court martial, isn't it? They'll sentence me to death."

A car drove into the portico as he reached the office. A fair-skinned, fat young man got out and went in swinging his keys.

The peon said, "Wait till he leaves." He added, although Sethu had not asked, "He's Kunhappootty Mudalali's son."

He waited, leaning against the pillar in the verandah. Ten minutes, fifteen. When the young man came out, the Director was with him. Sethu moved aside. He was sure the Director had seen him. The Director got into the car with the young man and said to the peon, taking no notice of Sethu,

"Kunhikanna, I'm going to the quarters."

His friends came to find out what had happened. The peon said consolingly, "He'll be back soon."

Noon. Sethu asked the peon, "Where are the quarters?"

"He'll be back now."

"Call me when he comes. I'll be in my room."

The peon came in half an hour.

The Director did not look up when Sethu entered. He went up to the table and said softly, "Sir!"

"You know you are a Government servant?"

"Yes, Sir."

He stubbed out his cigarette in the ashtray and leaned forward. Sethu caught a faint whiff of liquor.

"If people like you cannot obey the rules here, you would have done better to stay at home."

Sethu trembled. "How did I go against. . . ."

"You know you are a Government servant?"

God, how many times?

"Who gave people like you degrees?"

Sethu could not contain himself. "Your old man!"

Sethu felt his arms grow stronger. The tall, thin figure before him trembled. After a moment's silence, the Director shouted,

"Get out!"

"I'd decided to go without your telling me."

"I said, get out!"

Sethu felt the blood race to his head as he went out. His eyes were blinded.

There were many people in the verandah. Their faces looked indistinct, but he was aware that they accompanied him to his room. He put his hands on Unni Narayanan's shoulder and Gopi's. "Help me. I want to leave at once."

He did not hear what they said. Someone packed his things. They walked with him silently in a sorrowful procession. No one spoke even at the bus stop. He attempted to smile as he put out his head and waved at them from the window.

"Goodbye!"

He closed his eyes as their faces moved away from his line of vision.

"Goodbye!"

Part Seven

The river has grown dry. He stands for a minute on the sandy bank, which looks different every time he sees it. There are no more streams of running water. He thinks, I am here again after so many years, on the banks of a river of time which flows endlessly.

Where is the broken-down Bhagavathy temple in which the cowherd boys used to play games with stones? He can still imagine it clearly, the worn wooden engravings, the mouldy tiles, the yali lying with its nose buried in the sand.

Rows of the boat-shaped instruments used to draw water move over the vegetable patches that have encroached on half the river. The tiled roof that could be seen as soon as one climbed the bridge is no longer there, nor the path bordered by tamarind trees covered thickly with creepers. On the banks of the river that waits for the Edavam monsoon, the roots of trees waiting for death grope in the emptiness like skeletal fingers.

The question he wants to avoid asking himself keeps teasing him: is it only I who have changed?

I have come back finally to the shores of this drained river of time.

He searches the faces of the people who pass him on the narrow path hopefully, waiting with mingled fear and delight for a memory to surface and for a smile to light up their shrivelled faces. But they lower their voices when they see him, a stranger, and raise them again only when they escape from the pall of silence that envelops him. He rushes anxiously towards the next group of human voices.

As he walks, panting and sweating over what seems like an interminable stretch of sand, the man carrying his tin trunk comes abreast of him. "They've started to build the bridge, Mudalali. Next time you come, you can take the car across the river."

He pays no attention and the man calls out again, "Mudalali."

"How many years is it since you last came, Mudalali?"

The rains have washed over this stretch of sand thousands of times since I last came.

1

He got up when the musical chime of the calling bell sounded twice. The summons was for him. The bell chimed once for Menon; twice for him.

He pushed open the flush door of the air-conditioned room. The Mudalali was seated with his legs on the window sill and an elbow planted on the table behind him, reading a letter. He took his legs down, swung around, and put the letter in his pocket.

"Is the cash balance right?"

"Yes."

"What about the thousand I took the day before?"

"I've put it in the suspense account."

He listened attentively: bills, letters of credit, overdrafts, accountable, unaccountable. As he turned to leave, the Mudalali called him back.

"Writer!"

He thought, I no longer have a name. The peon Menon called him Writer. Everyone else knew him as Srinivasan Mudalali's Writer.

The Mudalali was lost in thought. Running his fingers through his grey hair, he seemed to be trying to remember something he had forgotten. A faint smile spread over the face pitted with smallpox scars. His red eyes glittered with a suggestion of madness when he smiled.

"And how is the house, Writer?"

"It's fine."

"Where do you eat?"

"In a hotel."

"I'll send a boy from the warehouse to work for you."

His smile was a blend of gratitude and respect, as if to say, You are very kind.

He went back to his seat and sorted out the letters which had to be answered. He had a terrible headache. His eyes would not focus on the paper. Another late night was taking its toll.

He had been with Rajettan the night before till midnight, in a room of the third-rate hotel in which he usually stayed. He had first met Rajettan, the car broker, when he had come to see the Mudalali. Everyone called him Rajettan. Rajettan began to invite Sethu to his room each time they met somewhere. Sethu liked talking to him. He knew a lot more than car dealers normally know. He was interested in subjects like Eisenhower and Kruschev and Sputniks.

Rajettan had sent for Raman, a short, stout man with a face scarred by knife wounds.

"What do you have for us?"

He said to Sethu, "He's known as Acid Raman. He was in jail for three months. He came out the day before yesterday."

"We have first rate stuff, Rajetta."

"I don't want any. Give me a half bottle of the lowdown one."

The man turned, moved aside his mundu and took out a big bottle from the pocket of his shorts. "Take a full bottle, Rajetta. Then you don't need to keep calling for me."

Rajettan stopped talking about world leaders by ten. "Do you know Pappammal?"

"No."

"What do you know then, you BA fellow?"

He would grow familiar after half a bottle. Later, he would apologize.

Pappammal belonged to Coimbatore. Her permanent address now was "Delhi Hotel." Which meant that Pappammal kept her clothes, her mirror and her powder in a bundle in a small space under the outer staircase of the Delhi Hotel. A letter sent to that address would reach her. She had sent money orders regularly over the last fifteen years to her son Marimuthu, who studied in Coimbatore. Rajettan wrote the address for her.

When Sethu had finally got down from a rickshaw at midnight at the gate of the new residence his Mudalali had given him, he had felt as if floods were heaving through his stomach. He had held on to the pillar in the verandah, swaying, the bitterness of vomit clinging to his mouth.

"Menon, can you get me a lime?"

A young man in khaki shorts and a checked shirt came up the steps and asked Menon in Malayalam whether the Mudalali was in. Sethu was surprised. The visitor was a white man. Menon ushered him in respectfully, came back and said,

"That's Wilson Mudalali."

"Is he a sahib?"

"His father was. They have a huge coffee plantation in Wynaad."

The lime juice was refreshing. The sahib came out and said light-heartedly to Menon, "Spare a thought for me, Menon."

The Mudalali emerged from the office. "Are there any cheques to be signed?"

"No."

The garage doors grated on the cement tracks with an unpleasant sound. The jeep started. Sethu always recognised the Mudalali's jeep by the sound it made when the gears were changed at the turn in the road.

Menon looked out of the window, "It's the Mudalali who's driving today."

Menon spent most of his free time standing at the windows. The road was visible from the northern window, and the courtyard of the Mudalali's house from the southern one. Menon knew everyone who came to see the Mudalali, their profession and the make of their cars.

"There's Rarichan Mudalali's Impala. It's a later model than Hajiar's but the Mudalali's Benz costs more."

The office was at the edge of the compound, above the garage. If Sethu lay back in his chair, he could see the tops of the gulmohur trees in the yard. Once the noon mail had come and he had replied all the letters, he was free. He would lie back in his chair and watch the parrots quarrel on the branches of the trees or listen to Menon gossip.

Menon had been the first to greet him when he came here. With the sandalwood mark on his forehead and the two protruding teeth that made him look as if he was always smiling, he had looked a harmless person. So Sethu had made friends with him quickly. Karunakaran Writer, who had been pensioned from the PWD, had been in charge of the office. As thin and dried up as a slate pencil, he never smiled. The dull shortsighted eyes behind the glasses seemed full of unbearable sorrow.

One day Sethu had asked, "Are you feeling ill?" but he had not answered.

It was Menon who had found Sethu a place in the lodge by the smelly canal on the outskirts of the city. Menon moved freely between the office and the Mudalali's house. He looked older than he really was. Rajettan had told Sethu how Menon had gradually acquired control over the Mudalali. Sethu found it difficult to believe.

Rajettan said, "The Mudalali gave him a thousand rupees for his eldest daughter's marriage, you know."

Sethu did not let on to Menon what he knew about this gift. Rajettan had counselled him that it would be useful to be friendly with Menon.

The accountant, Nambiar, usually came at one o'clock. He worked part-time in many places. His Income Tax accounts were flawless. He had taken over from Karunakaran Writer. The Writer had been too clever. When he had sent a cheque for two thousand three hundred rupees to the Sea Breeze Hotel to cover a week's bills, he had scolded the hotel employee who brought the bills. The hotel owner had reported this to the Mudalali. When the Mudalali questioned him, the Writer had advised him like an old friend. Next day, the Writer did not come for work. Menon had related all this to Sethu.

"Did the Mudalali find fault with him then?"

"Oh no. All he said was, 'I'm not drinking the money your old man earned.' That's all."

Menon went out for lunch. Sethu got up, moved the curtain at the window and looked out. He had heard that the Mudalali's bungalow had been built during the period of the timber auction in Coorg. The rounded pillars in front were of gleaming rosewood that had stood the test of time. There were Venetian blinds at both the windows. A spotted tiger skin lay over the easy chair in the front verandah. A sleek Siamese cat dozed under the gulmohur tree.

He saw the old servant woman's shabby mundu and scaly feet behind the half-drawn Venetian blinds. And then pink feet in red slippers sinking into the red carpet in the hall. A yellow satin underskirt swirled under the gold border of an off-white saree.

His heart began to beat very fast when she came out to the southern end of the verandah, near the potted plants. Her movements were like those of a dancer performing before an invisible audience.

Mrs Lalitha Srinivasan!

Unknown to her, he watched her whenever Menon went out, with fear in his heart and a secret delight.

He could see her clearly now that she was no longer hidden by the Venetian blinds. The black blouse with the gold flowers embroidered on it tightened every time she neatened the unruly strands of her unoiled hair.

She looked prettier now than in the picture he had seen of her yesterday in a magazine, standing with a group of Rotarian wives wielding brooms during the clean-the-city week.

A bright red Standard drove into the portico. Because of the pillars he could see only the khaki-clad legs. He moved to the next window. It was Wilson Mudalali. He pulled out a handkerchief from his pocket and wiped his reddened neck. Sethu could not hear what he said. All he could see were the red chappals at the edge of the carpet.

Sethu went back to his chair as soon as Wilson Mudalali came out. There were no parrots today on the gulmohur.

He heard Menon clear his throat outside and the stench of beedis came up from the stairwell. Menon never smoked in front of Sethu.

Menon asked, as soon as he came in, "Aren't you going for lunch, Writer?"

He was famished, but a bitter taste still lingered in his mouth. "Can you send someone for a cup of coffee and a banana?"

Menon went to the window. "Has the Mudalali returned?"

"No."

"I saw the car from Breeze parked here. Who was it?"

"Wilson Mudalali!"

"Hm. Wilson Mudalali loves to have a good time. Do you know how much money he spends when he comes up from the estate for a couple of days?"

Sethu hastily reminded him about the coffee, unwilling to listen to Wilson Mudalali's history. "If I could have my coffee. I'd like to leave as soon as Nambiar comes. I don't feel very well."

The telephone rang in the office. Sethu answered it. It was the Income Tax Officer. He had tried to reach the Mudalali at the club, the mill, at Sea Breeze. Where was he? "Is that Writer?"

He paused for a moment and said, "Yes."

"I need a car for an hour."

The Fiat was in the workshop. The Benz was used only for long trips. But he remembered the Mudalali's instructions. The caller's name was high on the list of people to be kept in good humour. So he said respectfully, "I'll send one."

The driver Appu was not in the garage. He usually dozed there when he was free or sat on the kitchen verandah talking to the maidservants.

Bougainvillea grew in profusion over the gate of the bungalow. The red Standard was still parked in the portico. He hesitated on the verandah and ran his fingers over the tiger skin on the easy chair. The drawing room was empty. He came out again and rang the bell.

He listened carefully, but there was no sound or movement. He wondered whether to go back and send Menon.

He heard Wilson Mudalali's voice, "I'll telephone."

"When?" A woman's voice.

Wilson Mudalali and Mrs Srinivasan emerged in front of him, parting the pagoda patterned curtains. He moved aside without looking at them.

The red car drove away. She waited near the curtains.

"The Income Tax Officer wants a car."

"So?" Her voice sounded harsh.

"I can't find the driver."

"Do you want me to drive it then?"

He felt only contempt for her, no irritation. Trying not to show his feelings, he turned back into the courtyard.

She called out, "Writer!"

He wanted to say, "I have a name," but her voice was gentle. She came out. She had changed into a black saree embroidered with gold and a gold blouse.

"The driver is not available. Please arrange for a private taxi."

Her full rounded face, lightly covered with pimples, was no longer angry and begged his forgiveness mutely.

"If the driver does not come in the evening, the car will have to be sent to the convent for the children as well."

The accountant Nambiar was in the office when he got back.

Just as he was about to leave in the evening, Menon said, "She's sent for you."

"Who?"

"The lady."

"She wants to see me?" He thought Menon was joking.

"She wants you to go there when you are free."

She came out as soon as he reached the verandah. "Come in." She invited him to sit down in the drawing room. He sat on the sofa opposite the huge mirror framed in elephant tusks.

She sat on the divan, pulled up her sari which was slipping down and swung her legs. He quickly withdrew his eyes, feeling it was wrong to stare.

"Aren't you a graduate, Writer?"

"Yes."

"I have to make a speech at the Baby Show next week. I can give you the points; will you write the speech for me? I can't manage Malayalam."

"Yes, I can do it."

"Not too many difficult words. My Malayalam is very poor. Or I'll write it in English and you can translate."

"All right."

He got up.

"Are you in a hurry? Have a cup of coffee?"

"No."

The children came in noisily. Red ties, dark blue dresses.

"Mummy, Sushma says."

"Go in now." Both the little fair-skinned girls ran in clutching their aluminum school boxes. The older one even had a mole on her right cheek like her mother. The dark little boy with the skinny face and dull eyes clung to his mother.

She got up. "Once they are back, there is utter confusion. We'll discuss it tomorrow."

She pushed back the hair on her forehead, smiled and asked, "What did you say your name was?"

"I didn't say. Sethu."

He smiled to himself and went out.

2

In the evenings, the streets were more crowded. The sound of people and vehicles drowned the stench from the gutters.

He went through the narrow lanes of the Anglo-Indian quarter and came to the street where pot-bellied Multani money-lenders sat cross-legged behind low tables. He had been walking for hours and longed to sit down.

Entering the street where provision lorries and trolleys lay in disorderly rows, he looked at the tiled shops on either side of the dusty road, thinking of the transactions running into lakhs of rupees that took place in them. Piles of rubbish lay on the edges of the road and the air resounded constantly with the obscenities of the cart drivers. He skirted a lorry unloading heavy bales of palm leaves, jumped over the yoke of a stationary bullock cart and came face-to-face with a young man coming out of one of the shops. He had a towel over his shoulder and a zipped bag under his arm.

Sethu could not believe his eyes. Swamy. Wasn't it Swamy?

Sethu hurried on, but could not help looking back. The other person was staring at him as well.

Swamy came up to him. "Weren't you at Palghat?"

Sethu had a deep sense of hurt. They had shared the same room for a whole year.

"Don't you remember me, Swamy?"

"Hullo, room-mate!"

They shook hands and made sounds of mutual delight. Sethu tried to remember forgotten formulae.

Swamy said, "I didn't make you out."

I don't blame you. Most people would not make me out, room-mate. I don't recognize myself!

"You've put on weight, Swamy."

Swamy smiled. He used to be as thin as a broomstick. He used to wear half-sleeved mull shirts and the tip of his tongue used to show between his lips even when he was not talking. He looked well-settled now, and prosperous.

They moved towards a lamp-post.

"What are you doing, Sethu?"

"I work in a firm."

He asked Swamy about himself in order to avoid being questioned. Swamy had stopped his studies after he finished his Intermediate and joined his father's business. His father had died two years ago and now he ran the business himself.

"Are you married, Sethu?"

He laughed foolishly. He had become an expert at this. "No, no."
Swamy said, with an apologetic air, "I have a one-year-old
child. I did not know your address to send you a wedding
invitation."

He did not tell Swamy, I have no proper address. A coffee estate
in Wynaad, Hajiyar's petrol bunk, a gambling den at a carnival—
he drifted like foam on a wave.

"Which way?"

"Nowhere in particular."

"I've parked the car beyond the market. Come, I'll drop you."

"No, I'll walk with you till there."

Swamy asked, "Care for coffee?"

"No." He wondered whether Swamy still kept accounts on what
he spent for charity.

The black Fiat was parked just outside the arched gate of the
market. Swamy started the engine and asked, "Can I drop you
somewhere? I have to see Viswanatha Iyer, the wholesale tea dealer.
He's my wife's uncle."

"It's all right. I have to go somewhere nearby."

"See you then. I'll write."

The Fiat made its way confidently through the undisciplined
crowds on the road. Swamy must have felt as relieved as Sethu
when they parted. They would not meet again, or write. They
had put an end to an old bond forged six years ago with a polite
exchange of words. When they met next time, they could pretend
not to recognize each other.

He no longer wrote to anyone, nor did he receive any letters.
Three months after he joined Srinivasan Mudalali's office, he had
a letter from Parameswarettan. It had been soon after he ran into
the mapilla, Aseesukutty, who worked in a teashop next to the
provision store in his village. Maybe he had carelessly mentioned
Srinivasan Mudalali's name to Aseesukutty, that must have been
how Parameswara Ettan found out his address.

When Menon brought the post in and left it on the table, he
always felt anxious. He would pray that there would be nothing
for him. He had not opened the last latter which had come with
Thangamani's handwriting on it. But he wrote a reply. "I am
going away and do not know when I will be back. I was a good
person once, the person you loved. All the doors of escape are
open before you and you are free to decide." The words sounded
meaningless when he re-read them, so he tore the letter up.

He stopped near the Gandhi statue in front of the Town Hall. Where now? He turned west, towards the sea, wanting to sit down somewhere by himself.

Young men sat on the stone benches next to the footpath, under the casuarina trees. He kept to the side of the road. Beyond the lamp-post, in front of the locked building belonging to a British firm, the crowd was thinner. Water had collected in pools after high tide. He watched the children dragging shreds of netting through the muddy water in order to trap fish.

Scooters and cars went slowly along the road. A speedboat raced over the water. The vague outlines of cargo ships were visible on the open sea beyond. A bearded madman, with a piece of sacking over him, leaned against the walls of the building opposite and called out to invisible powers.

Sethu realized that he had to eat somewhere and get home fast. Food had become a problem after he had moved to the house the Mudalali had found for him so far from the town.

When Nambiar had found him the house, the post office clerk who had shared his room in the lodge near the stinking canal had been surprised.

"Do you have to pay the rent yourself?"

"I don't know."

"I'm sure the rent is sixty, maybe even seventy rupees."

So the Mudalali had found him a house that fetched a rent of sixty rupees. And he had thought that kindness was only a myth! He could not believe that someone who lived in a house with high walls covered with glass peices, with Gurkhas and Alsatian dogs at the gate, knew the meaning of kindness. He had never read of kind-hearted Mudalalis.

"If I rent it out," the Mudalali had explained. "I'll never get it back when I want. I'm going to demolish and rebuild it when I'm less busy."

"Forgive me for having misjudged you, Mudalali," he said to himself.

Each time he wrote out cheques for the Mudalali's monthly bills, had them signed and sent them through Menon to be paid he had been shocked at how insignificant a commodity money could be. Hotel bills, club bills—the figures ran into thousands. The cigarettes alone came to two hundred rupees a month. Even though he knew that the Mudalali's bank balance multiplied by tens of thousands every time a truck took a log of rosewood to the Cochin harbour, he still felt astonished.

If only his forefathers had thought to plant a few trees on the empty hillsides, he had said once to Menon, instead of breeding bulls and fighting legal cases!

The little boys who had been fishing ran away. When the dirt settled, the blackish water shone like a mirror, and he could see the reflection of his face.

Every morning, he would look at his own face in the little folding mirror and think, the last two years have changed my features. The black dark of the nights when hunger had wiped out sleep had gathered into shadows under his eyes. His teeth were stained a dirty yellow. The frames of his glasses had become loose.

He felt that he could no longer smile, that his face looked more distorted when he tried to do so.

On sleepless nights, he thought of the dark room where he had experienced the odour of death. It was the day he had left the training camp. He had rented a room for a rupee and a half on top of an old dilapidated building and sat in it, thinking about death, while it drizzled outside.

Smoke blowing in from the kitchen downstairs clung to the room. The unpleasant smell of wet smoke, worm-eaten wood and crumbling walls had reminded him of a dead body. He took up a pen and paper. Whom should he write to first? Whom could he console? His fingers trembled as he held the pen.

The lights went out suddenly and the city was plunged in darkness. He leaned his head on the table and waited for the lights to come back. One of the servants who passed by had said they would not be back because a tree had fallen on a transformer and damaged it.

He put away his pen and went out. Brisk trade was being done in the shops in the bazaar by the light of candles and petromax lamps. He clung to the darkness like a shadow and walked on, beyond the seashore and the railroad bridge, towards the military camp. He sank down on the wet grass. A newspaper headline danced before his eyes. Dead body found in hotel room!

Red flames shone in open fireplaces near the culvert and the stench of burning rubber wafted on the wind. He heard low voices. Someone seemed to be coming towards him.

"Sh, sh."

He walked faster. Full of fear, his heart beating fast, he fled, thinking, I love life! I want to escape!

He heard footsteps behind him.

"You're going away?" It was a woman's voice. He hurried to the edge of the maidan to find out how to reach the road. She came up to him, her protruding teeth gleaming in the dark.

"Give us a beedi."

He gave her a cigarette. When he lit a match, he saw her round, pockmarked face and projecting teeth clearly. The red glow of the cigarette between her teeth reminded him of a fire spitting demon.

"Give me money for a tea, Mudalali."

He wanted to laugh. Mudalali, indeed!

He found a five rupee note in his pocket. She examined it unbelievingly while he walked on, laughing aloud.

"Don't you want me, Mudalali?"

He did not look back. He spent the rest of the night in the room that smelled of death, lying prone on the dirty mat and laughing to himself.

He had ten rupees left. In the morning, after he settled his accounts, he would have seven and a half rupees with which to start a new life!

"Writer."

Moopan, who had two boats of his own and held a contract to load and unload timber for the Mudalali, got down from his cycle.

"What are you doing by yourself, Writer?"

"Nothing. Where are you going, Moopan?"

Moopan invited him for a cup of tea and described the difficulties of building a house. He was going to invite everyone for the house-warming; the writer must come.

"Whatever people say about the Mudalali, he's a person who cares. He's helped me a lot." Moopan remarked that everyone who had joined the Mudalali had prospered.

"You're lucky, Writer. The Mudalali trusts you."

Moopan asked, as he left, "Is there anything I can do for you?"

"No, Moopan."

Fat Gujarati women dragged their chappals noisily over the cement path. The sea gleamed under the black sky like an open container filled with kohl. The lights on the cargo boats grew brighter.

Life began to flow through the black arteries of the city at night. Thousands of little sounds merged into an indistinct symphony. Prostitutes who had been asleep all day crowded around the municipal tap to get ready for their work. Brokers hung bits of sacking outside the shuttered shops to establish their place of business and waited, smoking.

Sethu walked slowly through the bustling crowds, feeling contented. He could wander among these people, crowded as densely as worms in an abscess and be sure no one would recognize him!

He had begun to love this city, with its overflowing gutters, its pockets of darkness, its foaming streams of people.

When he reached home, someone was waiting on the steps.

"Who is that?"

"Mm." It was probably the servant boy the Mudalali had said he would send. No, it was Menon, the peon from the office. Menon came up to him respectfully, "You're late, Writer."

"What is it, Menon?"

"Nothing."

Sethu noticed that the front door was open.

"Has the servant boy come?"

"What?" Menon was quick to prevent him entering. He said softly, "Sh. The Mudalali is inside." Sethu was surprised. Why was the Mudalali here?

"There's someone with him."

The Mudalali called out, "Who is that, Menon?"

"It's the writer."

There were no chairs on the verandah. All Sethu wanted was to sit down somewhere. The Mudalali invited him, "Come in, Writer."

Menon gave him a meaningful smile. The Mudalali was at the door of the bedroom, wearing only a mundu and smoking a cigarette.

"Come right in, Writer."

The room was filled with cigarette smoke and the smell of liquor. A young girl leaned against the wall. She wore a knee length white skirt and a green blouse.

The Mudalali sat down on the cot. "Sit down, Writer."

Sethu took the glass of brandy he held out.

"My friend. She's a nice girl, isn't she, Writer? What's your name, child? I've forgotten it again."

The girl shrank into the shadow of the saree hanging on the clothesline.

"Sarojini."

"Writer, this girl will stay here for two days. The servant boy will be here tomorrow morning. He will bring her food. Look here girl, this is our Writer. Now come and sit here. What a shy thing you are!"

The Mudalali screwed up his reddened eyes and said, "No one will suspect anything here. Tell the servant she's your relative."

Sethu kept quiet.

"Why are you playing with your glass? Come on, the Mudalali and the writer will drink together. What do you say, girl?"

The girl stood silently in the shadow, her head bent.

"Writer, tell Menon to let me know when the car comes."

Sweat broke out on Sethu's forehead as he left the empty glass on the table and went out. Where was Menon? Would he have to go to the gate and look for him? Ah, there he was, with a fresh cigarette at his lips. His breath smelt of alcohol. Menon seemed to be celebrating.

"You met her, then?" Sethu did not answer.

Menon offered him a cigarette. The unpleasant taste in his mouth lessened as he blew on it.

"You're lucky, Writer. It was I who thought of this place when she refused to go to a hotel."

He sat down on the floor and listened to Menon laugh and chatter, trying to fight down his anger. So that was what the Mudalali had wanted, when this little house surrounded by high walls fell vacant, a tenant who would not arouse anyone's suspicions. No one would wonder why the Mudalali's car was at the writer's gate. And Menon would hang around like a faithful watchdog.

Sethu suddenly wondered what Mrs Lalitha Srinivasan would be doing now. He remembered her seated on the sofa in her living room, her flushed and glowing face, her light-coloured eyes, her dishevelled hair. The radiance of her smile was still alive in him.

He felt light-headed. Here I am, waiting on the verandah of my own house for my bed to be empty. He felt no distress, only self-reproach and mockery.

"Writer!"

"Shut up!"

Menon was startled. "Writer!"

"Don't speak. If you do." He checked himself. When he saw fear spread over Menon's face, he smiled to himself.

Waves of heat began to course through his bloodstream.

3

The cry he heard in the distance turned into the roar of a train. He looked out of the window. Dismembered bodies, still alive, writhed in chains on the path next to the railroad track. He saw eyes blazing in the emaciated face of a little boy who was trying to break free of the chain piercing his leg. The roar grew and diminished.

Someone seemed to be shaking him awake. He sat up. The bright yellow light of the dusty bulb on the verandah went through his eyes like needles.

Still haunted by the distorted shapes he had seen, he asked, "Mm?"

"Go in and lie down, Writer, I'll come in the morning." Menon was leaving.

Sethu saw an old man curled up on a mat in the verandah. Where had he seen him before? Yes, he had been at the gate when Sethu came back.

"Close the door and go to sleep, Writer. The Mudalali has left." The smoky haze of sleep cleared for a second. So he was not alone in the house. He went in and switched off the verandah light. The corridor was dark. A yellow patch of light lay in the bedroom.

He found the room as disorderly as a third class waiting room just cleared of passengers. Greasy yellow bits of paper, morsels of bone, and empty soda bottles lay everywhere. The girl lying on his bed, fast asleep with her face turned to the wall, looked like a child.

He brushed grains of yellow rice off a chair and sat down. A bottle encased in fine silver wire, a quarter full, lay on the ground with an unopened packet of biriyani near it. He gazed at the yellowish-red liquid in the bottle and at the picture of the crown and grapes. Then he poured out a glassful of water from the earthenware pot on the floor and drank a mouthful.

What was her name? She had told the Mudalali when he asked. "Sarojini." She did not answer.

"Sarojini."

"Um."

"Get up."

She moved closer to the wall. He raised his voice. "Sarojini!"

She sat up and rubbed her eyes. She wore an underskirt that had turned a faded yellow with repeated washing, and a blouse with red dots. She looked tired and a little frightened.

He thought of the image of a prostitute that he had cherished, culled from books and hearsay—moist, intoxicating eyes, a passionate presence that made one uneasy, naked surfaces.

She seemed vaguely familiar as she sat on the edge of the cot, looking at the floor. She brought to mind the country girls he knew who would walk through the village lanes carrying baskets of straw and bottles of oil.

"Have you eaten?"

"Um."

"Are you sleepy?"

She covered her mouth to hide a yawn, rubbed her eyes with the back of her hand and shook her head as if to say no.

"Where do you live?" She gave him the name of a village about seven miles away from the town.

He opened the packet of biriyani, but did not feel hungry enough to eat.

"Have you been to school?"

"Um."

"Till which class?"

"I failed in the seventh and didn't go any more."

"You have a family?"

She did not answer. He repeated the question. She said, "Yes."

She could not have been more than fifteen or sixteen. It could not have been very long since a man had first used her. He wondered who had brought her to this town.

He had been insatiably curious about prostitutes. As a child, he had often overheard people talk in low voices about a woman who lived on the northern bank of the river who knew how to lure men. In his last year at the elementary school, he had asked Vaidyan Govindan's son, Ramankutty, to point her out to him. He had to part with two of his pebbles and a snuffbox with a broken lid before Ramankutty would consent. They walked through the lanes, full of fear, and Ramankutty said, "Look!"

He saw her clearly, sitting with her legs stretched out in the verandah of her small house, combing her hair. Her red nose ring glittered. It was one of the great events of his life, seeing this woman who stood at the ate every evening like the yakshi under the coconut palm, waiting to ensnare men.

But it distressed him to look at this child, playing with the black rubber bangles on her wrists, thin as papaya stalks. He got up and laid his hand on her sweat-stained shoulder. She attempted a smile, hardly that of a prostitute.

"Get up." Somehow, he felt disgusted.

He threw his quilt down and said, "Go and lie down some-where."

The unspoken question in her eyes irritated him. "I'm not being kind. Go and lie down."

He thought to himself, I've seen your face everywhere, in the taxis parked behind big hotels, in isolated travellers' bungalows, in dark lanes, in the marshes near the railway track. Nothing about you astonishes me!

He straightened the wrinkled sheet, turned over the pillow, which smelt of oil and cheap scent, lay down and covered his eyes with his hands.

"Turn off the light."

He saw her spread the quilt in the corridor. Seconds later, he heard footsteps and the clink of empty soda bottles. She was in the room. Was she trying to steal something from the pocket of the shirt he had hung on the wall? He turned quietly to look. There was nothing valuable in the room.

She went away and he heard the front door being opened. The old bolts creaked in spite of the care she took to be quiet. Maybe she was going away. Convinced that she had stolen something and was trying to run away with the old man who lay outside keeping watch, he got up. Her cheap silk saree still hung on the line. He followed her softly and heard her voice at the door.

"Achan, how can you sleep like this!"

The old man grunted and sucked his lips.

"Get up, Achan, come on." She shook him awake.

"What is it?" He was still half-asleep.

"Here, eat this."

He saw the old man open the leaf packet she gave him and eat greedily by the faint light of the municipal lamp beyond the wall. He hiccuped, stopped eating for a minute and asked,

"Did you eat something?"

"Um."

"When did the Mudalali say we can go?"

"He didn't say."

"Can you get me some water to drink?"

"Where can I get water?" Her voice was suddenly rough. "Don't create a racket. He's asleep."

Sethu went back to bed. He heard her close the door carefully and come back to the corridor.

He wanted to cry. He no longer thought of her lying so close by, just beyond the door, ready to give herself to him. Instead, he pictured her family, lying asleep on a torn mat in a little hut in her village. The younger ones would ask their mother,

"Where's Edathi, Amme?"

"She's gone with Achan."

"Why didn't Achan take us?"

"Shut up and go to sleep."

The mother would console herself thinking that now she could at least face her creditors.

The girl would go back after a few days and her mother would wash the nine rupee silk saree and put it away carefully. When she took the rolled gold chain off her daughter's neck and tucked it into the niche above the picture of Krishna, would she ask, "Where did you go?"

When the old man took a newspaper packet from his waist, coughing and grunting as he squatted on the floor, and handed the notes to his wife, would she ask, where did you take her? Who was it?

They would sleep contentedly that night, all huddled up together on the three mats, the father, the mother and the seven children.

Sethu heard a train hoot. He was not sure when he fell asleep. He woke up to the sound of water being drawn from the well. The quilt had been neatly folded and the mat was rolled up against the corridor wall. There was no one outside. He walked through the courtyard and came upon the man. He was not as old as Sethu had thought, he could not be more than fifty. The man waited uncertainly, scratching the grey stubble on his chin.

"Get a vessel from inside and buy tea for all of us."

He smoked a beedi while he waited for the tea, which the man brought him in a freshly washed glass.

Sethu went in to get a towel. She was in his room, in her saree, combing her hair in front of the mirror hung on the window. Ants crawled over the greasy bits of paper on the floor.

"Clean all this up."

She called out as he left, "Don't you have talcum powder?"

She looked uneasily at his angry face. He walked to the well without answering her.

He wanted to get away quickly. He washed his face, dressed hurriedly and combed his hair. She had had a bath and her hair, spread out to dry, trailed over the sheet on the bed. The glittering red silk saree did not suit her. He thought she would look pretty in a mundu, with a sandal paste mark on her forehead, and a mandaram flower wound into the tips of her hair.

Menon came in as Sethu left.

"Why are you off so early?"

"I have to meet someone."

Menon had something more to say, but he did not wait to hear it.

4

The beginning of another unpleasant day.

There was a time when he used to feel relieved when it was evening. Once he reached his den, he felt he could escape at least for a few hours. But now he had become a stranger in his own house.

Eleven o'clock. He stood at the window looking at the gulmohur trees. The Mudalali came in with one of his friends. Sethu took him some cheques which he signed without looking up. Sethu thought of how ready the man had been to share his most secret experiences with him the night before.

The Mudalali spoke only of office matters. Sethu's fear that he would talk about the house had been unfounded.

After Menon left, Sethu went back to the window. There was no one on the verandah. Disappointed that he could not see her, he was about to go back to his seat when the Benz rolled into the portico. Her butter-coloured saree with the broad red border matched the tone of her skin perfectly. She caught the pallu as it slipped and drew it over her shoulder. He went back to his seat as she entered the house.

There were two cars parked at his gate when he got back that evening. The number plates looked familiar, but he could not quite remember whose they were.

Why was he so afraid to come back to his own house? The old man sat outside, stroking the stubble on his face, looking bored.

"Who is in the house?"

The answer was indistinct.

A chauffeur came in carrying a canvas bag, in which bottles clinked.

"Do you have a beedi?"

Sethu spat into the yard and walked out without answering. Someone clapped and waved out to him at the petrol pump. "Writer!"

Rajettan stood next to an old Ford, waving his arms vigorously and arguing with a group of people. As Sethu approached, Rajettan said, "Look here, I have to go with the writer now. Don't waste my time, Pillai. Come on, close the deal, quickly."

Rajettan said to him, "You go on, I'll be with you soon." Rajettan caught up with him in a few minutes.

"Thank God, that's over. I've been at it three days and my throat is parched. I made a profit of a hundred and fifty rupees. May God help the buyer!"

They went to Rajettan's room, asking Acid Raman to keep watch outside.

"Whose car is KLC 8181, Rajetta?"

"Why?"

"Nothing, I just asked, that's all."

"It's the one Choyikutty sold to the DYSP. There's some patchwork on the body but the engine is in good condition." Rajettan knew the inside and outside of every car in the city.

Sethu could not keep his mind on what Rajettan was saying.

"What's the matter with you?"

"Nothing."

He emptied the second glass and went to the window.

"What do you want?"

He did not answer.

"What is it, Writer?"

"Don't call me Writer. That's the first thing I want. Then."

"Then?" Rajettan handed him the third glass. "What else?"

"I want a car. I want to drive up to Srinivasan Mudalali's house in my own car."

Sethu checked himself when Rajettan began to laugh. He went back to his chair and tried to put his scattered thoughts in order.

I stand on the terrace and play the fiddle like Nero as all the buildings around me burn.

He burst out laughing. What I want is. . . .

Rajettan's speech grew slurred. He put his head on the table and went to sleep. Sethu went out into the deserted street. The lights burned dimly and it had begun to drizzle. He walked home dragging his unsteady feet. The cars were no longer there. He leaned his hands on the moss-covered wall and threw up. As he spat out the bile and recovered his breath, someone called,

"Sethu Etta."

He turned, and made out who it was as he came nearer. Unni!

"Sethu Etta."

Sethu leaned his head on the wall and retched again. Unni laid his hand on his shoulder.

"Unni!" Unni stroked his back and he wept. He staggered towards the house holding on to Unni and asked, "Why did you come, Unni, why?"

"Thankoppu asked me to come."

Sethu sank down on the verandah. Unni had grown so much. How quickly children grew!

"I arrived at five thirty. They gave me your address at the office. I found my way here somehow."

There was no one on the verandah. He pushed the door open and stumbled in, nearly tripping over the old man, who muttered something in his sleep.

"Unni!" He went out again and saw Unni still standing outside, hesitating.

"Couldn't you have written that you were coming? I would have been expecting you then."

"Thankoppu wrote."

Her letter must have been among the ones he had thrown unread into the wastepaper basket.

Unni opened his bag and handed him a letter. He took it without looking at Unni.

"Don't you have class today?"

"It's Saturday."

What could he talk about? The little boy in shorts with cashew fruit stains on them was a young man now. He shrank before Unni's probing eyes.

"Come, let's go. You can't stay here." Holding on to Unni for support, he walked to the lodge on the main road, next to the Muslim hotel. The fat man at the counter with the checked towel wound around his head kept staring at Unni. Sethu wanted to kill him, though he could hardly hold himself upright.

He glared vengefully at the man while taking the key, as if to say, "Come on, if you want to die, come on!"

He fell asleep at once, feeling that he was slipping into a pit of darkness. He tried to hold on to the roots of consciousness, but kept sliding back into a bottomless abyss.

He woke up with the sun in his eyes. It took him a minute to remember where he was. The dark night detached itself from a dream.

Where was Unni? He asked the boy with the light grey eyes who was sweeping the verandah, "Did you see the person who was in the room with me?"

"The fair boy? He took his bag and went away early morning," answered the servant with a leer on his face. Sethu longed to slap him and felt ashamed of his cowardice. He could not hold himself up even in front of this silly boy.

He had a splitting headache. The house was empty and the corridor full of muddy footprints. Thangamani's letter lay on the floor. He bent down and picked it up with trembling hands. Fragments of glass were scattered over the floor and the air was laden with the smell of liquor. He lay down on his mattress, stained with the grime of countless dark nights and wept.

5

The letter was wet and smudged and tear stains had changed the shape of the words. She had asked, what did I do that was wrong?

It was my fault, Thangamani.

Once, his mind had been filled with thoughts of her. A sliver of moonlight gleaming through the shadows of the coconut palms, a faint fragrance of flowers wafting in on the breeze, a childish face glimpsed in a crowd—they all brought back memories of her. He had not cared that no one approved; it had only made him more obstinate. He had wanted to climb to the top of the world and shout, "You are mine, no one can keep me away from you."

He used to feel that he would explode with anger when he heard people discuss her marriage. When had that anger turned into a secret prayer? A prayer that she would soon be married, that he would stand somewhere where she could not see him and watch her go around the lamps in the pandal. He had hoped that he could go to her new home as a visitor, suppressing his own pain within himself.

He found it difficult to believe now that he had imagined all this. He spent days composing unwritten replies to her. Finally he decided to leave the city, go back and beg her forgiveness.

He would write, I am coming back to you at last. You will realize how wrong you were, to believe that human beings can live by their dreams. Do not curse me when you discover this.

Sunday. He detested Sundays, when the city was as still and sluggish as a snake shedding its skin.

It made him happy to think he could go to the office next day, settle accounts and leave. Who did he have to say goodbye to? To Rajettan. And the Mudalali. Should he go to the bungalow and see the Mudalali's wife? He had not written the speech in Malayalam after all. She had not asked for it. He decided he would go and see her once more.

He shaved, had a bath and changed. The sun had gone down. To console himself, he thought of the letter to Thangamani. He would write tonight, and make up for the long silence.

The shops were closed but the main roads were still crowded. Hawkers had established themselves outside the closed shutters of the shops, to sell calendars, peacock oil and siddha drugs. Groups of people were clustered around quack astrologers with parrots, and palmists.

The beach was deserted, maybe because it was wet after the rain and the sea had an angry look. He walked over the wet sand towards the sea. The waves dragged the sand from under his feet and he thought of how Thangamani had laughed that day, long ago.

It seemed to be raining at sea. Everything looked indistinct. The western sky was a blur of many colours, like a homam ground after the rituals, when the sacred drawings had been rubbed out.

He realized how long he had been walking only when the lamps were lit. Small oil lamps blossomed like little red buds in the thatched huts. He found his way back to a footpath, and came upon the Mudalali's Benz near the children's park. The children stood near the ice cream cart. The older girl looked grown up in a salwar-kameez. A ring flashed at the door of the car and its lightning gleam sent an answering glow through him. He turned, walked casually along the seashore and pretended to have come upon the car by accident. He stopped, looking surprised and respectful.

"Hullo!"

He smiled. The children had finished their ice cream and were counting the seconds it took for the decorative lamps to come on one by one.

"The Mudalali is not with you?"

"He's in Coorg." She opened the door fully and said, "Even if he had been here, do you think he would have bothered to take his family out to the beach? You should know his habits by now, Writer." She laughed, as if she did not want him to feel that she was finding fault with her husband.

"No activities today?" he asked.

She laughed again. "I'm fed up with social service. I'm trying to find a way to escape from it now."

"It's the first time I've seen you at the beach. Do you come often?"

"I hate it. Such a crowd, and the noise! The children insisted. I've been in bed all morning with a headache."

The children ran up noisily. She scolded them and sent them away. He realized how beautiful the English language sounded when she spoke in it.

"I like to park somewhere here and watch the sea when it rains. There's not so much noise then and less of a crowd."

She opened the door, got out, and stood looking silently at the overcast sky. The wind ruffled her hair.

"I like empty spaces. When we were in Jaipur, I used to take the car out without telling my father and visit the lakes and fortresses for which the city is known. I love to be by a lake or on a hillside by myself. Alone in the wilderness. My father would have been angry if he knew. Nobody understands that solitude gives you peace of mind." She looked unhappy and spoke rapidly to hide the trembling of her voice. She seemed to have lost all her confidence.

"Life is miserable here. Nothing to see, nowhere to go. And there's no one you can trust." She checked herself and went on, "Don't take it seriously. Do you want to hear something funny? A young girl came to me saying she was starving and I employed her in the house. She would not be more than fifteen, sixteen. I dismissed her this morning. See, you can't trust anybody." She emphasized the last word.

He kept quiet.

"Do you have a lot of friends?"

"No, I don't have any friends."

She sat on the cement parapet and talked about the north Indian towns where she had spent her childhood, about holiday resorts and people.

"Why don't you sit down?"

He sat down, a little away from her.

"Do you live alone?"

The question was unexpected. "Yes."

"How do you spend your time, then, say on Sundays like this?"

He smiled. "I read, or go for walks."

She told him she loved books, that she used to read a lot when she was in the convent at Cannanore and then at Queen Mary's in Madras. She had no time for anything now.

"Some people have an aversion to reading. Look at my husband. He does not even read a newspaper. I persuaded him to take me to a film during our honeymoon."

"People who are in big business don't have time for anything."

Her face suddenly hardened like stone. Then she calmed down and said,

"Yes, yes."

He paid no attention to what she was saying. Seated there against the background of the dark sky, her words seemed to break free of meaning and turn into music. The roar of traffic in front of them and the boom of the waves flowed into the distance.

"I wanted to go abroad, and I asked my father to try for a job in the foreign service, but he did not like the idea."

She asked him, "Why did you accept this job?"

He wondered uneasily whether he should tell her. He had been drifting around the city until he found a job as a part-time cashier in the hotel where he had met the Mudalali. The Mudalali had arranged for him to go as a witness in a fraudulent case. The proprietor of the hotel had vouched for the writer and the telephone operator as witnesses.

"Your name?"

"Sethumadhavan."

"Are you educated?"

"I am a BA."

"Your occupation?"

"Hotel clerk."

"Where were you on the sixteenth at dusk?"

"In the room next to the counter."

The case was dismissed. However, the Mudalali was impressed with the witness. He had described what he saw through the window exactly as the lawyer had instructed. He had seen the accused trying to prevent the Mudalali getting into the car. He had heard him use obscene words. Fearing that the accused might attack Srinivasan Mudalali, he and the PBX operator had rushed up.

The Mudalali had offered him fifty rupees. Instead of accepting it, he had said softly, "I need a job."

Trying to put the moments in the witness box out of his mind, he said, "I am leaving tomorrow."

"Where are you going?"

"Somewhere. I wanted to come and tell you before I left. I want to find another job, another city."

The children sounded the horn of the car. She got up. "Time went by so quickly."

She got into the car. "Which way are you going?"

"Nowhere in particular. I usually walk around a long time and then go home."

"I wish I could roam about like you. Come, I'll drop you."

"No. I. . . ."

"Oh, come on."

The little boy was in front and the girls at the back. He hesitated even when she switched on the engine.

"Get in. Little one, open the door."

The boy, who was playing with the plastic dog hanging over the dashboard, opened the door unwillingly and moved as close as he could to his mother.

The girls lowered their voices to a whisper. She braked at the gate of her house and sounded the horn. The old cook came out. The girls got out and slammed the doors.

"Get down, little one." Sethu got out first and took the child's hand. He shook it free and ran up the cement path to the house.

She asked the cook, "Has she left?"

"No, she said she would wait until the Mudalali got back."

Her voice trembled with anger. "Didn't I tell you to throw her out?"

The old man stood quietly, his eyes on the ground. She muttered something to herself.

"Get in."

"I'll walk home."

"Get in. I want to see that house. My property, I'm told. One day I may live there. Give me the key when you leave. I want to repair it and make it comfortable."

He started to open the back door but she reached out and opened the front one. She took the road skirting the beach, and speeded up, laughing. "Let me give you a ride in the Benz, Writer. This is your send-off party. You're leaving tomorrow, aren't you? I will see you off."

He shrank into his seat, feeling he had no right to be there. By the time they reached the town, the streets which had been crowded in the evening were deserted. Through the corner of his eye, he watched her delicate hands move effortlessly over the steering wheel.

They turned off the main road. She asked, "So how was the last party?"

"Which party?"

"Your party. Why is it you invite only the Mudalali for your parties?"

He was taken aback.

"Who were there?"

"I don't know."

"You are the caretaker. You should know." She added, "I get to know everything, even if it's later. Everything. There's nothing I don't know."

The streets seemed unusually dark. Perhaps some of the municipal lamps had gone out. He gave her directions. The house was in total darkness. He pointed it out to her. She seemed not to have heard, absorbed as she was in an invisible point on the steering wheel.

"Do you want to see the house?" His heart began to beat very fast when he realized that he would be the host now, not the person who kept watch on the outside verandah. He calmed down, somehow found the courage to go around, open the door of the car and ask, with a mixture of fear and cruelty,

"Aren't you getting down?"

He saw her troubled face for a second in the glow of the car light as she opened the door. He felt unsteady as they walked over the dead leaves piled in the courtyard.

"Careful, there's a step here." He held out his hand. The blood rushed to his face when he caught her soft hand in his trembling fingers. He let go of her hand in the verandah. The door took longer than usual to open. He switched on the lights and said, with the air of a host, "Come in, don't you want to see?"

He showed her the kitchen and the corridor. Then he opened the door of the bedroom. "This is the only room I use."

She began to go through the books in the wall cupboard with the broken door. For the sake of saying something, he asked, "When are you going to demolish this place?"

She ignored his question. "I lost a lot of my books, but I still have quite a number."

"I'd like to see them."

"When are you leaving?"

"I've not decided. Tomorrow, or the day after."

He stood quietly like a sentry guarding the women's quarters while she looked around the room. Suddenly, she said in English, "I can read your thoughts."

He pretended not to have any thoughts at all.

"Don't judge me, don't think I am spoilt and spiteful. The thing is, I am worried. It's been a very bad day for me!"

He held her hand to show her the way through the dark courtyard. At the gate, he suddenly lost control and began to speak in a language incomprehensible to himself.

This was a dream in which a princess had graced a shepherd's hut. I am a nobody. But I used to stand at the window and look out for you.

She tried to withdraw her hands, but he held them tight.

"I worship you!" He had often marvelled at how easily words came to him when he needed them.

He told her, as she got into the car, "I'm not leaving."

"Um?"

"I want to go on seeing you. Until now, I had nothing to dream about. Now I can wait for the princess to come again to the shepherd's dwelling."

The car roared away. Minutes later, he realized that he was standing alone at the gate.

When he lay down, he became aware that a haunting fragrance clung to his fingertips. The night blossomed around him like a flower through the memory of that fragrance and filled the world like a black lotus. He laid his head on one of its petals, listened to the music of the waves and slept.

6

He asked the driver to turn into the small one-roomed travellers' bungalow on the outskirts of the town. Anxious to establish the fact that he had been there many times with the Mudalali, the driver said,

"There's a big tourist home on the other side, it's more convenient."

He pretended he had not heard. The building was enveloped in darkness. It did not look as if anyone had stayed there recently, for the courtyard was covered with dead leaves.

The driver had to honk two or three times before the watchman shuffled out of the darkness. He waited till the watchman put on the light and opened the front door before he got down from the jeep.

The rough tiled floor was chipped and the cane on the chairs torn so badly that they could not be used. The mirror was foggy. The old Coorg watchman wore a tattered coat and a cloth around his head. He opened the cupboard, took out a sheet and spread it over the worn mattress. Then he picked up the earthen water pot, opened the bathroom door with difficulty and went out.

He stretched his legs out on the table and lit a cigarette. The driver came in.

"The tourist home is more comfortable. No one usually stays here alone." He smiled meaningfully, to emphasise "alone."

Sethu did not attempt to hide his displeasure. People had begun to talk to him now with great respect. Menon had been the first, then the employees when he went to the yard or the mill or the accounting department. This driver was the only one who had not fallen in line. Sethu had noticed it all the way here. Even when he answered the fellow in monosyllables, he had tried to be familiar. It had annoyed Sethu very much when he had picked up Sethu's matches from the seat to light his beedi. And here he was now, hovering arrogantly around the room.

He watched the curls of smoke from his cigarette freeze in the cold air and said, without turning his face, "Driver, take my case out of the car." He enjoyed seeing the man's face darken at his authoritative tone. Would he answer back? Go on, if you dare.

The man brought the box in and banged it on the table. Sethu thought contemptuously, wait and see, you're all just beginning to know how it will be!

There had been a lot of changes in the office, the mill and the yard of late. Was it after the Mudalali had started to send him for auctions, or before? Menon's sharp eyes saw everything. He certainly knew that Sethu often saw the Mudalali's wife at home. The first time he had felt a breath of scandal, he had been proud of himself. He longed for the moment when the news would reach the Mudalali's ears with a mixture of fear and delight.

When Menon rushed into his house one day, Sethu was prepared for the worst.

"The Mudalali is not well. He's in hospital."

The hospital yard was filled with cars. The Mudalali had fallen down in the bathroom at night. The servants had hurried up hearing his wife scream and found him unconscious. Someone said, "It's a stroke. He's paralysed." When he returned home a month later, one side of his body had become useless.

The watchman came in after filling the vessels in the bathroom with water and asked in broken Malayalam what Sethu would like to eat. He called out to the driver, "Take the watchman into town." He told the old man to get him something light, an omelette with bread perhaps, and gave the driver five rupees.

He got up and opened the window when they left. Wisps of mist floated over the treetops like memories. It felt much colder. He pulled down the sleeves of his shirt and lit another cigarette.

When they got back, he asked the watchman to give the driver something to sleep on.

"Yes, Mudalali."

He saw the driver look enviously at the second cot in the room.

A car drew up outside just as he was about to fall asleep under the old, smelly blanket the watchman had brought him.

There were voices on the verandah and then a knock. He got up and opened the door.

"Hullo!"

Karunakaran from Ollur, Muhammad Sait from Kochi and a third man whom Karunakaran introduced. "Iyengar, one of the biggest exporters in Madras."

"How is Srinivasan?"

"He's better." Sethu thought of the scene he had witnessed when he went to take leave of the Mudalali. He had been struggling to make his way to the bathroom using only his left hand and leg and holding on to a rope for support. He had driven away the servant who came to help,

"Get out, you son of a dog."

Illness had aggravated the cruelty in the Mudalali's eyes and the sharpness of his tongue. He spent his days on a mattress in a corner of the living room, holding pigeons close to him, as the ayurvedic physician had advised. In the evenings, he moved into the bedroom with the help of the servants.

"Why did you choose this place?"

"It's very quiet."

Karunakaran's eyes were bloodshot and his breath smelled of whisky.

While they drove along, they remarked to each other on the beauty of the Coorg women with their pallus pinned across their breasts. He joined their discussions on the feats they had performed at the recent auctions and said to himself, I belong with these people now, who deal in transactions that run into lakhs of rupees.

They dropped him back after midnight. He had only one thought in his mind, that if he held back from bidding at the auction next day, Iyengar would give him five thousand rupees.

Five thousand rupees!

At ten next morning, Karunakaran came up to him in front of the depot.

"You haven't forgotten what we told you last night, have you?"

"I don't forget so easily."

They shared out the money in the tourist home. The Sait said, "This is not over, we can't finish without Iyengar's bottle as well."

Sethu got up, intending to leave at once, but they persuaded him to stay and hinted at the possibilities the night offered. He managed to extricate himself. The envelope with the five thousand rupees lay inside his vest, next to his skin.

Roaring down the hill, he left. The jeep was not fast enough. He longed to get back to the city. He had begun to love the minutes he spent at the window of his house, looking at the gate through the slit in the curtains. When the car door closed, the doors of his heart would open, and then the moments would fall gently like petals from a faded flower to the beat of her high-heeled shoes on the cement steps. Lying in her arms, enveloped in scent and colour, he would feel the strength of a rakshasa flowing through his veins.

He had become very fond of the little house on the outskirts of the town. There were pale green curtains now at the windows, flowered drapes at the door, and blue-bordered sheets on the bed. The window screens caressed the room into a cool, soft darkness.

There was a record player which he could operate from the bed.

"I am going to give you something. A companion for you." She stood in her yellow satin petticoat, showing him how to operate it. A worker arrived from the yard and he went out to talk to him. The man remarked,

"I saw the Mudalali's car outside."

"Yes, I brought it." He glowered at the man, as if to ask, do you need more explanations, and the man left quickly.

He listened to her like an obedient student as she described pop singers.

"Pat Boone sings about a fool's paradise; Tony Brent, who sang "Dark Moon" was Indian."

"My pet, don't be so formal, call me by my name."

"I can't. It feels strange."

"You must. Call me, you girl. I like it."

He laughed.

"My pet. Aren't you my darling boy."

The silken strands of music wove a magical world around them. Until at last he was left with the scent of her hair on the pillow and the crumpled sheets. He would feel a pleasant ache when he was alone and begin to wait for the moment when he would hear her footsteps again on the cement path.

It was the third day after he got back from Coorg. A Sunday. He got up thinking, she's sure to come today. He came back from work by noon. The servant boy had cleaned the house, filled water in the bathrooms, put his food in the tiffin carrier and coffee in a flask.

He said, "You can go now. Come back at eight." The Mudalali had trained the boy to obey without asking questions.

He waited at the window, looking out at the gate, and saw someone who looked like the accountant, Pachukutty. He realized with a start that it was Parameswara Ettan.

Parameswara Ettan blew his nose noisily and came in. Sethu tried to smile.

"You've just arrived?"

"I came yesterday. She's not well, she's been admitted in hospital." "She" was Edathi Amma.

"What's wrong with her?"

"She's been ill for a couple of months now. She vomits all the time. She might need an operation."

Sethu pushed a chair towards him. Parameswara Ettan undid the buttons on his coarse bush-shirt and blew on his chest.

"Have you had lunch?"

"Yes. How do you manage your food here?"

"There's a boy who gets me food from the hotel."

He asked a lot of unnecessary questions about Edathi Amma's illness. Did she have fever? Or a stomach ache? He did not want to give Parameswara Ettan a chance to talk. Was the hospital comfortable? She was in a general ward now. She could have someone stay with her only in a special ward. Parameswara Ettan began to talk about the rates for special wards. He said,

"Don't worry, I'll arrange all that."

He sat down to eat but found he had no appetite. He felt troubled. Parameswara Ettan would soon ask why he never went nome though he lived only sixty miles away. He made a pretence of eating, stacked the dishes and came out. Parameswara Ettan was looking through an old newspaper.

"Didn't Achan write to you?"

"I wrote yesterday. And sent money." He always wrote the same words on the money order. Letter follows. But he never wrote. As soon as he began to make money, he had started to send money orders, as regularly as one paid instalments to a merchant.

"Amma expected you every Sunday. I waited for you as well, two or three Sundays."

"I wanted to come, but the proprietor fell ill. I've been very busy. So many responsibilities, even on Sundays."

He became aware that he was talking disjointedly and tried to hide his confusion by lighting a cigarette. As he blew out the smoke he realized this was the first time he had ever sat down in front of Parameswara Ettan, and that he had even dared to smoke.

He moved the packet of cigarettes towards Parameswara Ettan who took no notice if it.

"It's a bad time for us. Amma is not well either. She's always in bed."

"Can't you take her to a doctor?"

"We took her to Moosa. And Doctor Lassar came home once or twice." Parameswara Ettan took off his glasses and wiped them. He took out a cheap brand of cigarette from his pocket, broke one in half and lighted it. Sethu felt a pang of pity. His brother had suddenly grown old over the last few years. The hair above his ears was grey. Disgusting scabs had formed on the patches on his head where his hair had dropped.

He became conscious of the silence and asked, "Which ward is Edathi Amma in?"

"Sixteen. It's upstairs, at the end of the corridor."

Sethu was tense. The car might come at any moment now. There was a meeting of the Mental Hospital Committee at two and she had said she would drop in on the way back.

"Where did you stay last night, Ettan?"

"I took a room in a hotel near the hospital. I thought it would be difficult to find your place at night."

If Parameswara Ettan did not leave now, he would miss seeing her. He went in, changed, came out and said, "I have to meet a buyer at the warehouse."

His brother got up.

"You can rest here, I'll get back quickly."

Parameswara Ettan answered as he had hoped he would. "No, no, I'll leave now."

"I'll come to the hospital as soon as I'm free." He locked the door. At the crossroads, he said, "Go straight on, you'll get a number nine bus. It will drop you right in front of the hospital."

He crept furtively back to the house like a thief. As he opened the door, he heard her car brake outside the gate.

7

The unpleasant odour of the hospital reminded him of unhealed wounds.

His sister-in-law lay on an iron cot with a red blanket upto her waist. Her face looked pale. Her tired eyes lit up when she saw him. He had expected her to find fault with him, but she seemed more hurt than angry. "I've been waiting since yesterday."

"It was only when Parameswara Ettan came that I knew." He examined the chart at the foot of the bed with the air of an expert. "We'll have you moved to a special ward. It's more convenient, I can come and see you whenever I am free. Don't worry, we'll arrange everything."

"I get news of you. So good fortune has come your way, then."

He smiled, "Oh, well."

"I don't need your money. But can't you write once in a while?"

He kept quiet. It seemed so long ago, the time when he had roamed over the hillside to find her little raw mangoes and jnaval fruit.

She asked him to sit down at the foot of the bed. "I want to stay with you for a day after I'm all right. I have so much to tell you."

"You'll feel better soon. You must stay with me for a few days before you return."

"It's the thought of the children that worries me."

Visitors were crowded around the beds and the ward had grown very noisy.

"It's nearly a month and a half since I went to your house. Not since Amma fell ill," she said.

She began to talk of the village and he suddenly felt distanced from the clamour in the ward. Edathi Amma told him about the thief who went to steal and fell into the well. Her eyes narrowed when she laughed.

"Did you know Madhava Ammama stays at home now?"

"No."

"He's bought Yousuf's provision shop. They say it's doing well."

"I heard that."

"You know that the Vadakkethu property has been divided?"

He had not known. Nor had he known about Madhava Ammama's shop. Yet he said, "Someone mentioned it to me recently."

"The little one, Karthu, is married. Her husband is in a workshop in Salem or Tanjore or somewhere like that. He's from Ummathoor."

And Sumitra? He fought down the desire to ask about Sumitra.

Sumitra and Devu had each taken their share, said Edathi Amma and separated. Sumitra lived by herself in a house she had built on the hill. Devu was at Vadakkethu. Madhava Ammama visited her sometimes, met the children and gave Devu some money.

Sethu found it easy to visualize the family quarrel that took place on a Sivarathri day as Edathi Amma began to describe it.

Madhava Ammama had opened a tea stall on the day the villagers celebrated Sivarathri. It was a profitable venture. Unni Namboodiri was appointed cook. Madhava Ammama slapped Unni Namboodiri in front of everyone because the idli batter had not been ground finely enough. Devu and the children were in the shop at the time. Devu intervened and Madhava Ammama hit her as well. That night, everyone heard Devu's screams from Vadakkethu. Madhava Ammama had walked out of the house.

He did not go back although Amma had tried her best to persuade him. Kandankulangara Menon had spoken to him on Devu's behalf, after which he went sometimes in the daytime, to see the children.

"Sumitra is ill as well. She has hysteria."

People said it was because she had built her house near the shrine of a Brahmarakshasu. One day, after a bath in the river, she had run across the fields, dripping wet, screaming. That had been the beginning. When they had caught her finally, at the edge of the field, she had been unconscious.

"Who does she stay with?"

"Whom does she have?"

Parameswara Ettan arrived with milk, bread and oranges, and scolded Edathi Amma, "Can't you hold your tongue even when you're ill?"

The bell rang and visitors had to leave. Parameswara Ettan said he would go out with him.

"Why don't you give up the hotel room and come and stay with me?"

"It's only two-and-a-half rupees and it's right next door. I'll stay there." Ettan invited him to his room in the little hotel.

"Come in. You're not in a hurry, are you?"

"No, no."

Ettan took off his shirt and sat on the bed. He had grown even more haggard than Achan.

"How much leave do you have?"

"Two weeks. If I extend it, it will be on loss of pay."

Ettan seemed about to say something. He lit another cigarette, in an attempt to hide his uneasiness.

"I've been wanting to write to you, but what's the use. You never reply."

Sethu felt himself grow smaller. He could offer no justification. He swallowed and sat quietly.

"What have you decided about the Pushpoth girl?"

"I'll think about it later."

"No one disapproves. If someone said something unpleasant earlier, don't take it seriously."

"We'll see."

"When?"

He avoided a direct answer and talked instead about how busy he was. He was going to start a business and needed capital. His mind was full of plans.

Ettan's continued to look at him expressionlessly.

"I'll come home soon."

"Mm." Ettan did not sound as if he believed him.

He got up and held out the hundred rupee note he had kept ready.

"Here, keep this with you. It's better to shift her to the special ward tomorrow."

"No, that's all right, I have enough for the moment."

He was not sure how to persuade Ettan to take the money.
"Really, I don't need it."

He folded the note and put it back in his pocket.

Walking through the crowded streets, he thought of Sumitra,
alone in her hut by the Brahmarakshasu shrine. The noise and
crowd around him faded and he saw the jnaval trees and hills of
a lost world. He thought of the little boy with the torn shorts
tucked into his waist thread, combing the hillside for a fallen
jnaval fruit that was whole. He remembered how thrilled he had
been when he finally found one and gifted it to Edathi Amma
and watched a tint of violet spread over her pretty white teeth.

As he grew tired and his pace flagged, thousands of city sounds
encircled him again, screaming.

8

The river had run dry. He walked over its parched bed, leaving
the lost years behind and climbed onto the road.

New stone steps had been built at the bathing ghat. The
thatched shed beyond the river had become a small tiled mosque.

The young sixteen-year-olds who passed by looked at him
admiringly.

There was a high school now near the village. In the old days,
children stopped going to school after the fifth class and helped
in the fields or in the shops. He was sure everyone sent their
children to high school now.

He felt contemptuous and a little sad, looking at the thinly
pencilled moustaches behind the beedi smoke and the turned up
collars. He imagined these village princes setting out with their
certificates in search of a livelihood.

It seemed so long ago now, the time when the city had lain
before him like a great secret, with its thousands of closed doors
that would open by magic. He had waited, sweating and gasping,
in front of its many arched gateways, watching other people go
in and out with resentment and envy.

The first thing that caught his eye as he walked down the road
was the ugly statue on the new tiled house by the river. Whose

house had it been? The mapilla fishmonger's. Next to his hut
there had been a double banyan that spread its shade over the
road all day. It had been cut down. Bullocks freed temporarily
from their yoke used to lie in its shade, chewing cud, their bells
tinkling softly.

The path over the fields leading to the Kandankulangara house
which had been broad enough to allow a bullock cart to pass was
much narrower now; bits had been cut off on either side.

He did not read the new board by the roadside. The harvested
fields lay shrivelled and dry, waiting for the Medam rains.

His heart began to beat faster when he reached the Vadakkethu
gate. There was no one outside. Would someone catch sight of
him through the gap in the areca nut palms?

The stone steps at the entrance to his house were chipped. A
coconut palm had pushed its way through the corner of the
blackened wall, overgrown with moss, and hung over the fields.
The worm-eaten gateposts shook when he touched them. The
house reminded him of a hunched up old woman with a shaven
head basking in the sun with her eyes closed. He quickly ran up
the steps. He had to bend his head so that it did not hit the rafters
in the verandah.

A dark, emaciated girl came to the door and peered out.

Padmu! The little snot-nosed child whom he used to carry on
his hip through the areca nut grove, with Cheriamma's shouts
pursuing them!

"Come on, girl, where's Cheriamma?"

Her voice trembled with happiness. "Amme! It's Sethu Ettan."

Crows and chickens pecked at the reddish worms in the heap
of dung near the wall. He stood with his hand touching the rafter
and remembered how he used to reach out to it with his thumb
every week to measure his height.

Cheriamma came out dragging her feet, wiping the spittle
running out of her mouth with the back of her hand.

"Look who's here now. Do you remember us at all, child? It's
been so long."

She leaned against the door and wept. He hurried to help the
porter take his box down from his head.

Age had not changed Cheriamma very much. There were more
red patches around her lips and she had grown greyer and thinner.
There were red scars on her wrinkled feet as well.

"We've been waiting for you so many years, not just one or two." Her words were drowned again in tears. He went in. The whole house, the verandah, the outer and inner rooms looked much smaller than the images he had treasured of them in his mind.

Through her tears, Cheriamma lamented, "I don't have all that long to live now."

Padmu stood at the door with a pathetic smile. He said to her, with the authority of a family member, "Ask someone to take that box upstairs." He noticed that she had changed into a clean mundu. He gave her two rupees to give the porter. She said to her mother softly as she went out,

"Sh, keep all that crying for later. We have visitors."

Cheriamma calmed down. "Get him a grass mat, child," she said.

He came out to the verandah once he was sure that she had stopped crying. The easy chair usually placed there for Achan was missing. The lime used to repair the worm-eaten patches on the wooden seat had begun to peel off.

Padmu said hesitantly, "The screws of the easy chair have come out, it's not safe to sit on it."

The visitors had entered the courtyard. Narayanan Nair. Appu Nair. He did not make out Sankunni Nair immediately, since his protruding teeth had been extracted.

They greeted him with smiles, and spoke in voices full of respect.

"Ah, so you still remember the way home."

"What's the news, Narayanan Nair?"

Someone had seen Sethu from the road and made a guess, they said. Narayanan Nair had come to ascertain whether it really was Sethu.

"Do sit down. Bring a mat."

"No, no, I don't need a mat."

They sat on the chipped floor. Sethu leaned against the pillar and Cheriamma warned him, "Your mundu will get dirty."

Sethu did not take the mat which Padmu brought him.

"Why didn't you write that you were coming? Achan was here yesterday. He didn't tell us you would be here."

"I was free suddenly."

"Did you come by train or by car?"

"By car to the other side of the river."

"We need a bridge over our river. People like you go to so many places, meet so many highly placed persons, why don't you try to get it done?"

He pretended to be interested in what they had to say about the hot weather and the disease that had attacked the areca nut palms.

Sankunni said, "I walked with your father up to the road. He's not as healthy as he used to be."

Sethu started to talk about the city, the price of rice, the profit in the timber trade. When he ran out of subjects, Cheriamma hinted, in an effort to get him to herself,

"Why don't you have a wash and change? You've made a long trip."

The visitors asked whether he would be staying a few days.

"I haven't decided."

"Why don't you come along with us and meet everyone?"

"Later."

After they left, an old man hobbled in with a stick. Padmu said,

"It's Chinnan Menon."

Cheriamma sounded irritated, but he detected a note of pride as well, "You've hardly set foot in the house and the whole village seems to know!" She called out to Padmu to bring a mat. Kandankulangara Menon had to be treated with respect, after all. Menon hoisted himself up the steps with difficulty and asked,

"So, did you make me out?" Sethu smiled and invited him to sit down. Menon fanned himself with his mundu and said, "I have asthma. I consulted Dr Gopala Menon and he prescribed all kinds of medicines. But I can hardly sleep during the full moon period."

He asked Cheriamma for a drink of hot water. When he stopped gasping, he asked Sethu, "What are you doing now?"

"I have a small business."

"Timber?"

"Um."

"Your own, Sethu?" Sethu grunted.

"I've been asking your father to write to you. When I heard you were here, I thought I'd come myself."

Cheriamma was right. How quickly the news had spread that he was home!

"I'm not sure whether you've seen my youngest son. I didn't educate him. He failed his ninth, he's no good at studies. He's been idling at home for three years now, you must find him a job somewhere."

"A job these days. . . ."

Menon did not allow him to finish. "It doesn't matter what it is or where. You are," he paused for a moment. "You can manage it now. I couldn't possibly ask other people."

"Let me think about it."

"I'm the only one left in the tarawad. You must have heard that we had a partition in the family."

"Yes, I heard."

"I have to go across the river this evening, so I thought I'd come and see you at once. When can I send him?"

"Let me find out. I'll write to you."

Menon left. Cheriamma brought Sethu tea in a bell-metal glass. "He drinks all the time. That's why he fell out with his brothers."

The tea smelt of fresh goat's milk. He put the glass down. Cheriamma asked, "Do you want more sugar? Drink it up quickly before someone else comes."

He gulped down most of it, gave her the glass and lit a cigarette.

"We don't need your money." Cheriamma's voice trembled. "This is your place and you should remember we're all here for you. Do you realize how many years it has been? Not just one or two, child. Nine years! I've kept count."

Nine years.

He got up, afraid that she would start talking about the events of those nine years.

He went to his old room above the front verandah. Memories from the past slumbered in the faint light that crept hesitatingly through the rounded window bars. Were the verses and addresses he had scribbled on the wall still there? He would have to light the lamp to find out. The familiar musty odour of bell-metal stained with verdigris still clung to the room. He hung his shirt and vest on the foot of the bed, took out a towel from his bag and lay down on the wooden ledge.

Did the room look darker than before? Or was it because he was so tired that he could not see the smooth ochre coloured floor clearly?

He heard Cheriamma give Padmu instructions. Then she went to the eastern verandah to make excuses for him to someone waiting there.

"He's lying down. He had to leave the car on the other side of the river and walk. Come again tomorrow. Look, Thami, the Cheria Thampuran won t go away in a hurry, you can see him. Come later."

Cheriamma came slowly up the stairs. "So many people to see you, cherumans, mapillas!" She laughed, showing her blackened gums. "They all want something from you, they've heard you're minting money."

She added, "You're looking healthy enough."

She began to talk about her ailments. By evening, her feet hurt so badly she could not walk. She'd thought it might be rheumatism and tried massaging them with oil. Her digestion was not good, food nauseated her.

He listened, making a sound of assent now and then. Cheriamma fell silent and gazed out of the window for a long time, inhaling snuff and rubbing the end of her flat nose. Then she suddenly asked,

"When Parameswaran's telegram came, you were not there, were you?"

"No," he answered slowly turning his face to the wall.

He looked at her again and he saw her wipe her eyes. "We waited till the morning train arrived before cremating her, thinking you would come."

That cool May night. That day had started with a blazing sun.

He had woken up at nine in the hotel room with a heavy head. The sun had already become hot. The thought that they would give the verdict that day took shape in his foggy mind. The night before, he had blotted out the thought in drink before he fell heavily asleep.

It was the hotel where he had once worked as a part-time clerk. There were waiters who still remembered.

"Who is in number fourteen?"

"Sethu Mudalali."

He picked up the cup of coffee with unsteady hands, took a gulp and called Reception. "A large whisky."

The court would assemble at eleven. All his new found friends would come by ten to give him moral support.

Would she have slept? He wondered whether to call her and the telephone rang.

"How are you?" Her voice always soothed his taut nerves.

"I am all right." He said, to comfort her, "Don't worry about anything."

"Are you worried?"

He laughed lifelessly.

He had guessed that the registered letter contained the order for his dismissal when he signed for it. He had already vacated the house in expectation. He had read the letter with a sense of disgust and then telephoned her.

"I have a piece of good news. I'm no longer your husband's salaried employee."

She had warned him as soon as her brother-in-law had been sent for from Bombay. He and the lawyer had spent a whole day at her husband's bedside, conferring in low voices.

He was not perturbed when they served a charge on the grounds that he had embezzled large sums of money from the business. He woke up his lawyer at the dead of night and requested him to file a counter case, after calculating the amounts due to him for having removed certain files from the office and adjusted the figures. They owed him a lakh of rupees and part of the profits.

When they approached him for a settlement, he said, "He's the Mudalali, isn't he? Let him fight his case and win."

"The Mudalali will withdraw the case. You know the condition he's in. We're not sure whose fault it is. In the name of humanity."

He laughed aloud and they were shocked.

"Why are you laughing?"

"Nothing."

In the name of humanity?

"What are we to do?"

"Whatever you want. You can even decide that I am not human."

One night, he asked Lalitha, "Do you have the courage?"

"For what?"

"For whatever happens."

"I came here because I had courage. I thought I would not come but I could not stay away."

"File a suit then, if you have courage."

"For what?"

"Divorce."

Her face suddenly grew pale. He got up when the silence became unbearable and went to the bathroom to change. She was seated at the dressing table combing her hair when he came out. He looked at her reflection in the mirror for an instant and then withdrew his eyes.

She walked out to the dark lane where her trustworthy driver had parked the car. Her footsteps faltered now and then.

She called him unexpectedly that night. "I am ready."

"What?"

"I am ready."

Next day, she had listened with an expressionless face while the criminal lawyer explained what "extreme mental cruelty" and "incompatibility" meant.

Eleven o'clock.

He thought his nerves would break, they were so taut. The telephone rang. The lawyer's rough voice said, "It's going to take till one o'clock. Don't worry."

The sun blazed outside. The fumes of the duty free whisky that the peon of the merchants' Club had smuggled in coursed through his stomach. The lawyer called again just as he was slipping into unconsciousness.

"Congratulations! We've won."

He burst into laughter. Was it he himself he had to congratulate? He had told himself many times that this was the moment he had been waiting for his whole life.

The lawyer, who had a reputation for being able to change the face of truth, was offering him congratulations!

"You're congratulating me?"

He was suddenly aware that he had not achieved anything. Who had won, then?

The telephone rang again and he heard her tired voice.

"Are you happy?"

Happiness, pleasure—it made him laugh.

She insisted that they leave at once, she wanted to escape from everyone for a few days.

Parameswara Ettan's telegram must have come that evening. They had already checked into the well-known hotel near the garden on the river.

Standing on the private balcony of their third floor suite, she talked about the children. He had booked a trunk call to his office. When it came through, the clerk said to him,

"There's a telegram for you."

"From where?"

The young man seemed hesitant to reply. He said angrily,

"Open it and read it out."

"It's from your house, Mudalali. Mother . . . mother expired."

He put the phone down, moved aside the curtain dividing the living area from the bedroom and took a cigarette from the table. She came in and asked,

"What happened?"

"Nothing." He did not look at her face. He stood in the balcony, longing to weep, but his heart had hardened like rock.

"Your tea will grow cold," she called out.

He watched the crowds moving amongst the squares and circles of the garden in the artificial moonlight of the lamps. The news stood just outside his mind like a traveller in search of shelter— Amma was dead!

He went in and saw a look of reproach on her face. She had put on a new perfume and was rubbing Max Factor cream on her wrinkled eyelids.

He lit another cigarette, sat down and stretched out his legs on the low stool. She repeated, "Your tea is cold."

Was she finding fault with him?

"Pour it into the sink."

Had he sounded rude? She seemed more nervous than surprised. He noticed her lips trembling. What is it? What happened? Her eyes were full of unasked questions.

Nothing. I'm all right.

He lay on his half of the wide double bed, breathing in her perfume and asked himself, where was the thrill he used to feel when he heard her footsteps on the stone steps?

The mattress felt cold and so did her flesh. He closed his eyes and felt them smart with tears. He could still not cry then. Once, he thought he sobbed. He controlled himself and heard her soft voice,

"What is it, darling?"

Nothing. Nothing is wrong with me.

Her warm fingers ran gently over his chest and he drew away.

"Tell me, what is it?"

"Nothing."

Nothing. The dark night was nothing and the long path he had travelled was nothing. The delight he had experienced during those moments of waiting and the scent of the pillow, all was nothing. You are nothing, the facts and figures you gave me are nothing. This expensive hotel room and the symbol of the lion on the windscreen of the car are nothing. You will not understand. Nothing, nothing.

"Tell me, please."

"It's nothing."

The honeymoon that had not yet begun ended that cold night, on a pillow wet with tears.

The wasp that had been circling the parrot's cage doubtfully went back into its hive.

Cheriamma said,

"God was good to her in that she did not become a burden to anyone. All of us pray for that. All I want you to do, child, is to find a husband for this girl of mine. You know I think of you as my son. That's all I want from you. Once that is done, I'll have no worries left."

He sat very quiet.

"What is it, Sethu?"

"Nothing."

9

Padmu lighted the wick on the front steps at dusk. It glimmered faintly, like some half-forgotten grief, in the waning evening light. A child, probably from Vadakkethu, intoned its prayers mechanically. An old film song drifted in from the direction of the rosewood forest in the south. There must be a wedding in progress, he thought. The child at Vadakkethu stopped chanting.

He walked up and down the yard, Cheriamma said, "We can heat some water if you want a bath, and you can bathe by the well after dark."

She complained about the cheruman, Thami, who had still not made a screened shed near the well though she had told him to do so many times.

"I just need a wash."

The illam compound was enveloped in darkness. At first sight, the shabby house seemed deserted, then he saw a chimney lamp move behind the blackened bars of the kitchen.

The path to the illam was overgrown with plants and weeds. His heart turned over when a black form moved near the broken fence. Someone came towards him. He made him out when he drew close—Unni Namboodiri.

Unni Namboodiri had grown quite grey and looked like a man in his sixties. He wore a dirty towel that barely reached his knees.

"What news, Unni Namboodiri?"

"I just heard that you were here."

"Come and sit down."

Unni Namboodiri sat on the verandah near the stone steps. The wick had gone out.

Padmu brought a lamp. Sethu saw Unni Namboodiri's face clearly in its gleam and was suddenly afraid. The prickly stubble on his chin was completely grey, his teeth were worn and blackened and his straggly hair was as rough as coconut fibre. Anyone who met him on a lonely country road was sure to run away.

Unni Namboodiri darted quick looks at him from time to time and then lowered his eyes.

"Do you still go for temple festivals, Unni Namboodiri?"

"No."

He waited for Unni Namboodiri to talk, to burst as usual into loud laughter. But he was very quiet.

"How many children do you have Unni Namboodiri?"

"Three." He added after a moment, "They're all girls. I lost the only boy I had." A festival was celebrated in his wife's family temple after an interval of twelve years. Unni Namboodiri had sat right on top of one of the walls, with the child on his lap and his grip had suddenly loosened.

"I watched him fall. As he fell." Cheriamma was at the door. She said softly, "Amme, Mahamaye!"

An uneasy silence settled on them again.

Cheriamma asked, "Did you sell the mango tree which gives those delicious little mangoes, Unni Namboodiri?"

"Yes. They've given us fifteen and owe us ten more."

He guessed that Unni Namboodiri must have come to him for help and decided to give him ten rupees when he left. Unni

Namboodiri moved right up to him. He smelled of the earth, of
betel leaves and sweat.

"When are you leaving?" he asked.

"I've not decided."

"Then." Unni Namboodiri hesitated and Sethu said, "Tell me,
come on."

"If I come with you Sethumadhavan, can you get me a job
somewhere?"

"Get you a job, Unni Namboodiri?"

"Yes."

Sethu smiled. "Who will look after the illam?"

Unni Namboodiri's laugh was not the foolish laugh of old. He
seemed to be trying to hide the trembling of his voice.

"What is there to look after now? Govindan does not give us a
single grain of paddy. And after we lost the areca nuts . . . it's all
a mess."

Sethu wondered what to say. Unni Namboodiri said, "I don't
mind cooking or serving."

He saw Unni Namboodiri's eyes glisten in the dark and took a
quick step backwards.

"All right, Unni Namboodiri, we'll see what we can do."

Unni Namboodiri's black form dissolved into the darkness.

"They demolished everything, even the wooden storerooms,
to sell the wood. His wife looks more miserable than a cherumi
woman," Cheriamma said.

Cheriamma insisted he have a wash. "Will you eat now?"

"I'm not in a hurry."

"Madhavan comes very late. He says trade is best at dusk."

But Madhava Ammama came earlier than usual. He took off
his creaking slippers and sat down, the keys at his waist clinking.
He had put on weight. He wore a mill made T-shirt with a collar
and had a towel with a red border over his shoulder. He lit his
beedi with a lighter. Sethu noticed that one of his front teeth was
missing.

"Why didn't you bring the children?" he asked.

The children? *His* children? They were waiting for another
decree from the court. She must be wondering now how they
should address him when they came home. He fumbled for a
reply.

"I came away in a hurry. Just decided suddenly."

"I come there occasionally to buy provisions. But I don't know your place and since I always come back the same evening, I never have time to go looking for it."

Madhava Ammama took off his vest, asked for a towel and made his way towards the well.

"It's a terrible season. There's not a drop of water in the river."

He overheard Padmu ask Cheriamma softly whether to fry the pappadams whole or in bits. Cheriamma asked her to make an extra curry, a liquid coconut chutney and went into the kitchen with her.

This time yesterday, he had been at K. A. Menon's housewarming party. While listening to Menon talk in heavily slurred accents about the bombing in Rangoon he had been glancing at the sofa by the radio from time to time, trying to warn her silently.

That evening, when she had groped for the car keys on the table and thrown them into his hands, her eyes had been full of appeal. So he had asked, "Coming?"

"Do you want me to?"

She talked too much when her speech began to slur. There was a time when they used to talk endlessly. In the end, they would ask each other,

"What did we talk about?"

Nothing!

My God! So much time had gone by, and now?

Now, words had become brittle showpieces in a glass case, to be used only on special occasions.

The unpleasant memory of the first cabaret show conducted in the newly opened hotel in the city still lingered in his mind.

She said, "I'll come if you don't mind. Or I can tell Mrs Menon that I have a headache. Headaches are a blessing in disguise now, thank God!" The last few years had taught him to hide emotion behind a smile.

"Get ready."

On the way, she told him about the Menons. He was very wealthy and she was his second wife.

The house was beyond the city limits. The cold of the sea wind and the roar of the waves pierced his ears. The driveway was full of cars. She looked longingly at one of them and asked,

"It's an imported Morris Oxford. Whose is it?"

"I don't know."

She must have calculated its price in her mind.

Introductions and polite phrases were exchanged.

Mrs Menon was everywhere, a glass of gin in her hand. She could have been mistaken for Menon's daughter. The daughter, a sixteen-year-old, brought him a tin of cigarettes.

A sports car screeched to a stop outside and someone got out. Sethu glanced at his wife. Pleasure had ironed out the wrinkles on her face.

The tall young man who got out of the car had bushy eyebrows and reddish lips and wore a copper bangle on his hand. As if to emphasize his height, he bent his head as he came in through the door, forcing everyone's attention onto himself.

Menon introduced him. He was an engineer, newly appointed in a Marwari firm. Indrajit.

He went around, meeting everyone, and said, "Indrajit, yes. But I have to disappoint you. I am not Ravana's son." He sat down between Sethu and a doctor and lifted his glass. "Cheers!" Confidence overflowed from his words, his looks, his stance. Sethu felt jealous.

Glasses emptied and filled. Music flowed from the stereo players. The laughter grew louder. He kept an eye on his wife, even while listening to the man sitting next to him talk. Careful, careful.

She pretended not to see the warning in his eyes. Was the half-empty glass in her hand her second or third? On the pretext of getting himself a box of matches, he went up to her and murmured, "Careful."

She did not raise her head.

Mrs Menon knew how to make a party lively. "Circulate," she commanded. Everyone had to change places.

The Sindhi proprietor of the flour mill and Menon invited Sethu to go out with them for a breath of fresh air. Menon insisted that they take their glasses into the garden.

Menon animatedly described the swimming pool he was going to make. The indistinct murmur of the sea could be heard behind them, like the reverberation from a distant temple festival.

Someone whistled, "One, two, three, I love you," from the terrace.

Every time he reminded himself uneasily that it was getting late and tried to leave, Menon would tell him how young the night still was.

He finally escaped with Mirchandani's help. In the dining hall the middle-aged insurance broker was running his fingers over Mrs Menon's palm, reading it.

"Where is she?"

"Oh, don't be a pest. Leave her free." Her words were slurred. She could not hold her head up properly and it kept sliding on to the palmist's shoulder. Disgusted, Sethu went into the house. People were huddled in small groups.

"Did you see my wife?"

"Worried?"

Someone laughed. He stayed with them a couple of minutes, to prove he was not anxious, and slipped away.

He found her on the terrace. The hand with the copper bangle was wound around her shoulder.

He watched her coldly as she staggered down the spiral staircase, expecting her to trip and fall. If she lost her grip on the aluminum railing, she would collapse in a heap at the foot of the twenty-seven steps and a red stain would spread slowly over the ground.

He was startled when the car door slammed. Had he shut it himself?

He pretended not to hear her sobs.

They passed the fishermen's huts and the lighthouse and turned into the city. The frightened street lamps seemed to be fleeing behind them. He made a turn and came up against a high wall. He pressed his foot on the accelarator and began to laugh. The endless waves of his laughter merged with the screech of metal and tyres.

He heard fear in the silence beside him.

An isolated lamp-post that could not escape him toppled over and he hooted with laughter.

"You're mad."

"Yes, all of us are mad, this car and the lamp-post as well. Yes." He laughed again.

And so I reach your gate. The day always ends here. I go through the garden you fashioned so artistically, open the door and enter your bedroom. I stand by your cold mattress with all the futile anger of an impotent man, full of regret for the lost opportunity, the moment when the skidding tyres wailed and broken metal screeched.

There were no questions when the black and yellow taxi arrived at the gate in the morning. When the servant placed the suitcase he had packed in a hurry on the seat, he had waited fearfully to be asked. But no, he did not have to tell her where he was going.

Madhava Ammama came into the verandah, smearing vibhuti over his forehead. "Krishna, Guruvayoorappa, protect us!" He asked, "Why are you sitting in the dark?"

"Just like that."

He got up. Cheriamma called out, "Come and eat. I laid the leaves long ago."

Padmu followed them with the lamp.

Cheriamma said, "I could not get good fish. The cheruman boy hunted all over and brought a handful of veloori."

"I'll arrange with the fishermen tomorrow, if you are staying."

He did not answer.

He enjoyed the drumstick leaves cooked with dal and Padmu refilled his deep plate again and again. Although he did not want a second helping of rice, Cheriamma insisted. "Just a handful, with buttermilk."

After dinner, he walked in the yard. Padmu spread Madhava Ammama's mattress on the verandah. Cheriamma said, "Your mattress is spread upstairs, Sethu. Tell me when you're going to sleep and I'll send a lamp."

"A little later."

"Aren't you going to Achan's place?"

"Yes, I must."

"Achan isn't well at all. Why don't you go and see him sometimes?" She called out to Padmu, "Eat something, girl, and go to bed. I don't eat at night. I have terrible problems with my acidity."

Cheriamma sat on the floor and stretched out her legs. Madhava Ammama had begun to snore.

"I suppose you know that Pushpoth Thangamani is in Bombay."

He turned his face away, afraid that she would see it, even in the dark. He could hear his own heartbeats.

"Destiny decides for each of us. I heard she came home to have her second baby."

He walked unsteadily to the wall and stared into the banana grove, where darkness and the wind played with the leaves. He hoped Cheriamma would not say anything more. She sighed.

"Bring her and the children here some time. I want to see her."

"I will." His throat was parched and he spoke with difficulty.

"I'll go to bed. Give me a lamp."

"Take the hurricane lantern. I'll light another one inside."

He went up, lowered the wick and lay down. Cheriamma brought water in a brass jar, left it on the ledge and waited, obviously to say something to him. He pretended he was sleepy.

Once he was alone, he put the lamp out.

It looked as if it might rain. He longed to hear the sound of raindrops on the banana leaves. But it did not rain. A jackal howled somewhere on the hillside.

A faint breeze blew through the little window. He lay in the dark with his eyes closed, hoping to feel calmer. Maybe he would sleep tonight without a tranquillizer. He decided not to think about nights when sleeping pills erased memories, or about the painful days when saws seemed to run through him.

It was years since he had been to the temple. He thought he would go in the morning. He had not prayed since he was a child. What would he pray for when he went to the temple?

There was nothing to pray for. He knew what he wanted, a second chance. "Please give me another chance."

He would always stand outside the closed doors of a temple, praying for boons that would never be granted.

Always.

One more chance!

He felt as if heavy rain clouds were weighing down his heart in the merciless Medam heat.

He turned over and opened his eyes. Moonlight fell through the little window. He sat up, full of gladness. The world was bathed in moonlight as far as he could see, like a marvel, a dream. The same moonlight that had woken him up years ago.

He sat up, leaned on the window sill and looked out. Thousands of white mandaram flowers seemed to have blossomed in the sky. The white moonlight gleamed through the undone tresses of the areca nut palms like a dream. A terrifying beauty flowed through the empty courtyard. Silver tendrils played around the shadows in the banana grove.

He felt sad that he could not see the moonlight raining over the dry sand of the river bed from here. Darkness hid the pala tree on the way to the illam. He thought of how the creepers moving in the breeze resembled the form of a rakshasi with tangled hair.

Amma's southern field was just above the spot he was looking at. Had the coconut sapling he had planted on the heap of earth there grown?

He remembered the stories he had heard as a child, and was afraid. The Gandharvan at the foot of the pala tree, Karineeli from Meleparambu and the Brahmarakhshasu from the illam would be setting out now, to walk in the moonlight.

Everytime he drifted into sleep, he woke up with a start.

One of the bottles in the little box in his suitcase contained tranquillizers, but he was reluctant to get up and search for it.

He chanted, "Arjunan, Phalgunan, Parthan, Vijayan." Famous names, and then "Kireeti." He chanted louder and louder, until he was comforted by the sound of his own voice.

The sound of a creaking door woke him up. He rubbed his eyes and opened them, to find it was day.

He went softly down the stairs. No one was up yet. Madhava Ammama had covered himself with his mundu and was still fast asleep.

He went up the hill by the path on the west. There were so many changes. Beds had been dug and prepared for tapioca in the place where the jnaval grove used to be.

On the other side of the parched river, slivers of light spattered the eastern sky like drops of blood.

The little semicircular cave where the goats used to take shelter in the rain had been here. Now that the hillside had been levelled and the path widened, it had disappeared.

The teak tree shorn of leaves that used to be by the bamboo thicket had been cut down. Wet leaves were heaped around its ant-eaten stump.

He saw the low mud walls and the thatched roof just beyond the palms. He felt quite calm as he entered the cowdung-smeared yard. When he saw the closed door, he suddenly wanted to call out her name.

He heard footsteps behind him and turned. Startled, he realised it was Sumitra.

She had just had a bath and had wrapped a wet, ochre coloured mundu around her. Water dripped from the ends of her
thick, matted hair. The bones above her sunken cheeks jutted
out. Her eyes opened wide when she saw him. When he looked
away, she said,

"It is Pooyam today, I went to the river at dawn for a bath."

He was silent.

"Sit down."

She opened the door and went in. He continued to stand there,
drawing his fingers along the platform outside the house.

She came out and asked, without a trace of emotion, "Why
don't you sit down?"

Had she not made him out?

Her bluish lips seemed to be muttering something silently. The
wide vibhuti stripes on her forehead showed clearly as the
moisture dried. Drops of water still trickled from the tips of the
tangles that stuck out through her untidily knotted hair. A pale
glow flickered in her eyes above dark patches of shadow, faint as
that of a wick lit at dusk.

"Sumitre."

For an instant, her lips stopped moving, then began their
indistinct mutterings again.

"Do you live here alone?"

"God is with me."

Was she mocking him? He looked at her thin, chapped wrists
and the bones jutting out beneath her neck.

"I heard that you were ill."

"It's a lie."

"Sumitre!"

For a second, her eyes looked vulnerable, in a face as pale as
thumba flowers that had been trampled on.

The words that crowded to his lips froze and remained unspoken.

"Do you hate me?"

Sumitra laughed. An echo of the laughter he had heard years
ago ran swiftly through his mind.

"I loved you."

Sumitra laughed agian.

"Love?" He lowered his eyes and heard her say, "Sethu has
loved only one person, ever. And that is Sethu himself."

When he looked at her again, she smiled and asked, "Isn't that so?"

He did not answer.

Sumitra sat down near the wall and started to pray as if he was not there.

He cleared his throat. "If there is something I can do."

"Narayana! Narayana! Narayana!" Her voice grew louder.

He stood there quietly for a few minutes and then walked away, his head bent.

The morning sky was flooded with pale colours. The east looked as if it was spattered with blood.

On the farther shore, wagons with heavy loads went up the steel railroad bridge. The screech of the wheels tore into his ears above the roar of the railway track and the odour of wet logs.

10

Wisps of bluish mist floated over the dew-wet sand. His long shadow tried to keep pace with him as he walked along the deserted banks of the river in the gentle morning sunshine.

His tired footsteps lagged as he looked into the dazzling spires of light high above the trees and remembered how he had once wanted to write poems about the sunrise. About the morning sunlight blossoming like flowers through the crevices in old temple walls, and fingers of light prising open the eyes of invisible lotuses.

How did they go, those two lines he had scrawled in pencil on the wall of his old room? He could not remember. His mind was as empty as the parched river.

His feet kept sinking into the endless stretch of sand and each time he pulled them out, he thought helplessly that he could not remember.

The cheruman carrying his suitcase caught up with him.

In the distance, the steel bridge and the railroad track shivered. The river, his river, dreaming of floods even as it grew dry, lay behind him like a lifeless body drained of blood and movement.

Glossary

adiyan	:	term used by a person from a lower caste to designate himself/herself while talking to someone from a higher caste
ameen	:	an employee of the Civil Court
anna prasanam	:	a ceremony conducted when a child is fed rice for the first time
anterjanam	:	a namboodiri woman
Brahmarakshasu	:	the spirit of a Brahmin who died a premature or gruesome death
chandu	:	a coloured liquid used to mark the forehead
cheruman	:	one of the lower castes {masc.}
cherumi	:	one of the lower castes {fem.}
Chettiar	:	a merchant community
Chettichi	:	fem. gender of Chettiar
chunam	:	lime paste
deepam	:	a lamp
embrandiri	:	a Brahmin, usually a pujari
gulikan	:	an evil spirit that has to be propitiated
Hidumban	:	a rakshasa; a demon
homam	:	a ritual performed before a sacred fire
illam	:	the residence of a namboodiri
jenmi	:	landowner
kanji	:	rice served with the water in which it is cooked
karanavar	:	the head or senior most member of a joint family
karyasthan	:	manager
kasavu	:	gold thread, usually woven into a border

kavadi	:	bow-shaped wooden structure decorated with peacock feathers and flowers, carried on the shoulder as an offering by pilgrims going to Subramania temples
kindi	:	metal mug of bell metal, silver or copper, with a spout; used to pour water
konam	:	a narrow piece of cloth used to cover the genitals
koothambalam	:	a hall set apart in the temple for performances
kooja	:	a pot to hold drinking water
koothu	:	a dance-drama performed in temples
kovilakam	:	the residence of a princely family
kuvalam	:	a tree the leaves and flowers of which are sacred to Shiva
Mahamaya	:	one of the names of the Devi
mudalali	:	owner, proprietor
naivedyam	:	food offered to a deity
nalukettu	:	a sunken courtyard with four wooden pillars flanking it
nazhi	:	a measure, about one-third of a litre
niramala	:	an offering made in a temple in which the shrine is decorated with flowers
panakam	:	a drink made with water, jaggery and cardamom
para	:	a measure for paddy or rice, about thirteen litres
pathayam	:	a wooden structure to store grain; it can also refer to the room itself where the grains are stored
pottu	:	a mark made on the forehead
pradakshinam	:	ritual circumambulation of the temple
pulaya	:	one of the lower castes
rowka	:	a blouse, the ends of the which are knotted above the waist

sambandham	:	a contractual marriage relationship
sastrams	:	the scriptures
tarawad	:	a joint family
Thampuran	:	form of address for someone of a higher caste
thekkini	:	a room on the southern side of the house
thirtham	:	sacred water
tirumeni	:	form of address used for a namboodiri
Variar	:	a community that has duties and rights in the temple
Vishu	:	the Malayali New Year, in mid-April
yakshi	:	a female spirit that can change its form at will and exercise an evil influence
yali	:	a mythical lion-like animal; sculptures of the yali are often seen in the temples
yejaman	:	owner, master

List Of Malayalam Months
With Approximate Equivalents in the Gregorian Calender

Chingam	:	August-September
Kanni	:	September-October
Thulam	:	October-November
Vrischikam	:	November-December
Dhanu	:	December-January
Makaram	:	January-February
Kumbham	:	February-March
Meenam	:	March-April
Medam	:	April-May
Edavam	:	May-June
Mithunam	:	June-July
Karkitakam	:	July-August